NIG

ED GORMAN

Ed Gorman became a full-time writer after twenty years in advertising, and is acknowledged as being one of the world's leading writers of dark suspense. He is the founder and editor of *Mystery Scene* and lives in Cedar Rapids, Iowa with his wife, novelist Carol Graham. Amongst his other novels are *Cage of Night*, *Blood Red Moon*, *Hawk Moon* and *Harlot's Moon*.

Praise For Ed Gorman

"I rate Gorman as highly as Crumley, Ellroy and James Lee Burke."
–Scotland On Sunday

"Gorman has a way of getting into his characters, and they have a way of getting into you"
– Robert Bloch, author of *Psycho*

"Gorman pulls things off with sleek bravura, reclaiming the field from the legions of cardboard cutout serial killers"
– Time Out

Ed Gorman

NIGHT KILLS

CT Publishing

First published in Great Britain by CT Publishing, 1998.
This edition 1998 CT Publishing.
Copyright © Ed Gorman 1990

A CIP catalogue record for this book is
available from the British Library.

ISBN 1-9020020-3-2

9 8 7 6 5 4 3 2

Book design and typography by Crow Media Design.
Printed and bound in Great Britain by Caledonian
International Book Manufacturing, Bishopbriggs, Glasgow.

I would like to thank Chris Cox and Iris Bass of Ballantine for their patience; Sue and Dennis Runyon for helping revise the material on spina bifida; Bill of The Bridge in Minneapolis for teaching me about the teenage underground; friends in various ad agencies who answered innumerable rush questions; the people at the Chamber of Commerce who updated me on the beautiful city of Minneapolis, where I spent my early years; Peter Wagtskjold for reading the galleys for geography; and the Twin Cities homicide detective who convinced me that planting false evidence really can work. Despite all the help, mistakes may still have been made, and they are mine alone. – EG

Dedicated in fondness and friendship to Gerda and Dean
Koontz

NIGHT KILLS

EMMA WAS KILLED ON A TUESDAY, which meant it was Mr Pinkham day. Actually she sort of liked Mr Pinkham, or at least she felt sorry for him. Sometimes pity was a stronger pull for Emma than affection. Anyway, Mr Pinkham. He was fifty-nine, wore custom-tailored dark suits that helped disguise his girth, smelled of cigarettes and hair spray, and boy, did he tip. On her last birthday he'd given her two hundred dollars in cash in a baby-blue Hallmark envelope that also contained a sentimental card. Mr Pinkham was in banking and was obviously rich. In nearly eleven months of seeing him, she'd detected only one small kink. He liked her to daub herself between the legs with strawberry flavouring before he got down to business. Given some of the men she'd known, this was not a real kink at all.

One other thing about Mr Pinkham: His wife was dying. Cervical cancer. Once, after he was finished and dressed and pouring himself a drink, he started telling Emma about the process of chemotherapy his wife was undergoing, and then he started crying so hard, he had to go into the bathroom and throw up. When he came out, he was still crying. She helped him over to the bed and held him and rocked him and kissed him tenderly on the cheek and forehead over and over again. Then Emma started crying. She wasn't even sure why. It was just that sometimes everything seemed so sad.

That Tuesday she was to meet him for shopping at Saks Fifth Avenue in the Gaviidae Common, the Twin Cities' only real snotty shopping mall. You felt special just walking around the five levels – Burberrys, Pendleton, the San Francisco Music Box Company, and Anne Klein, they were all there – you didn't even have to buy anything. You just felt special.

It was nearing closing time. Mr Pinkham had phoned to say that he'd had a long day at the bank and an even worse day at the hospital. His wife was slipping, slipping. Whenever his wife got very bad, Mr Pinkham became impotent. Both he and Emma knew this from experience. On such days he always met her at a mall. Buying her things seemed to make him feel better for some reason. Then they'd usually have dinner – how Mr Pinkham loved to pour A-1 sauce on his steak; drown it to the point that Emma would laugh and laugh – and then he'd walk her to her car, pay her, and

9

*tip her, just as if they'd spent time in bed, and then kiss her chastely
on the nose. Always on the nose, with his dry little mouth. Emma
invariably found this sweet and squeezed his hand goodbye in response.
Then Mr Pinkham walked to his huge new Chrysler and got inside
and tooted goodbye.*

*A call came for her at Anne Klein, where she was looking at silk
blouses with stand-up collars and three-button cuffs, wondering if
they were right for her. When she heard herself paged, she asked the
salesperson where she might take the call. The woman smiled and
directed her to the office. She was the same salesperson who had five
minutes ago told Emma how beautiful she was – so long and graceful
a neck, so perfect yet exotic a face. Emma had always found women
better at giving compliments than men. They just knew how to do it
better.*

*The call was from Mr Pinkham. He was terribly sorry, but the
doctor was now saying that Mrs Pinkham might not last the night.
Emma could tell Mr Pinkham was struggling not to cry. For the first
time ever she said "I love you" to Mr Pinkham. She didn't even worry
if he'd misinterpret it. She just said, "I love you." She imagined he
needed to hear that very badly. Then he did start crying, just a little,
and said, "I love you, too, Emma." Then he hung up.*

*In the parking lot Emma stood by her new Mustang convertible
inhaling the chill autumn air. She could smell snow coming. Poor
Mr Pinkham. She wished he could enjoy the night.*

*In the car she turned up KJJO. She needed to hear good strong rock
and roll. It was sort of like taking vitamins.*

*In twenty minutes she was on the Crosstown headed home. When
she came to her exit, she glanced by instinct in the rear-view mirror,
and for the first time she saw him, the man who'd been hiding on the
floor in back.*

He said, "Just keep driving, bitch, just like you're headed home."

*By ten o'clock they were driving county roads. Gravel dust glowed
silver in their wake.*

*At a farm that had obviously been deserted, the outbuildings
leaning so pitifully they seemed about to collapse, he had her pull in.*

She got out, just as he told her to. She kept quiet, just as he told her to. She took off her clothes, just as he told her to.

He felt her breasts — she had very nice breasts — and then he slid his hand between her legs. He complained how dry she was there. "You fucking bitch." He backhanded her hard across the mouth.

She started crying. She thought of when she'd been a little girl on the farm near a small town named Coon Rapids. She thought of her high school graduation night, the only time she'd ever really gotten drunk in her whole life, and of giving up the struggle to keep her purity. She thought of moving to Minneapolis. Of working in the law office. She was now only twenty-eight yet it seemed she'd done so much in her young life and it whirled by her, voices and images and even smells. Memory.

He stabbed her first in the abdomen, ripping the knife through her stomach, and then he started stabbing her in the chest and face. She held up her hands to hold him off but that only gave his knife new targets. He cut and slashed and hacked at her fingers until several of them were just bloody stubs. Before she died, she had time to stare down at several pieces of her fingers in the dust.

Finally he stabbed her in the forehead. By this time she was on the ground, and he was straddling her. He left the butcher knife sticking out of her forehead as he unzipped his trousers and started putting himself into her.

Afterward he lay next to her in the moonlight. They might have been lovers. His whole chest heaved. He was sweaty, sticky, exhausted. Blood-covered. The stench of her was terrible. He closed his eyes, felt the breeze dry his sweat. In the distance cows stirred and mooed. Then pigs. Dead corn stalks rattled in the wind. Skeleton bones.

Fucking bitch.

From the trunk he took the tarpaulin. He spread it out and wrapped her up in it tight. It was awkward carrying her back to the car. He sort of staggered. At least she wasn't leaking. The whole idea of the tarpaulin was that there wouldn't be any blood.

In the car he turned up the radio good and loud. God, did he need a drink. He was careful to drive the speed limit, but still, on those rutted county roads he could hear her bounce and bang.

God, did he need a drink.

11

1

THE WAY BROLAN FIGURED IT, probably not more than three or four couples would get a divorce because of the party tonight. For an advertising shindig that wasn't so bad.

The place was the Hyatt Regency in Nicollet Mall in downtown Minneapolis, the time was 8:37 p.m., and the occasion was the Brolan-Foster Agency's winning the Down Home Bakery account, which had annual billings of slightly more than ten million dollars. In the Twin Cities it was one of three accounts agency presidents would hand over their teenage daughters to win.

Dinner for sixty had been in The Willows, with its mirrored pillars and ceilings, with its seemingly endless amounts of smorgasbord, pâtés, seafood and vegetable marinades, mousses and salads. The agency people took up about a third of the place, and it was easy to spot them. They were the ones giving drunken champagne toasts every five minutes and then breaking into applause. Some of the restaurant's other guests found this amusing. Some wanted to go over and punch in a few faces. Hovering waiters asked again and again if there could be, uh, just a little more quiet. Chuck you, Farley, and the horse you rode in on.

Finally the party repaired to a bar down the street. Shouts and laughter like gunfire erupted on Seventh Street as the agency folks wandered down the deep canyons made by the fifty-one-storey IDS Centre and several department stores, including Dayton's. One couple, whose respective husband and wife had been unable to be at the party, stood in the centre of the street alternately kissing and then pointing up at one of the tall buildings where Brolan-Foster had its agency on the ninth and tenth floors. The chill night only made all this insanity even more fetching and precarious – soon enough it would be bitter Minnesota winter; soon enough they would be home and sober with their respective mates. But for now it was time to laugh and shout and hit on whomever you could get away with hitting on. Before the predicted snow came the following day.

The five bartenders behind the bar looked as wary as cops at a particularly unruly demonstration. In less than five minutes the place had filled up, the jukebox thundered rock and roll, and people usually so staid they looked like Bible college graduates were out there shaking their asses as if they were trying to get rid of them.

Brolan paced. He was a pacer. Maybe that was why, at forty-five, he was reasonably trim. Pacing. He'd paced his way through nine different jobs in twenty-three years in advertising, paced his way through a divorce, and paced his way through three earnest but hopeless affairs. He tried hard not to think about Kathleen Logan. Jealousy never did anybody any good, least of all somebody as naturally suspicious and pessimistic as Brolan. So, even in his dinner jacket, his startling white hair and gaslight-blue eyes complementing the black outfit well enough that he should be able to pick up somebody that night, he paced.

In fact, he hated parties, and he hated groups of drunks. One or two drunks at a time was all right, but groups of drunks were oppressive. All that hand-shaking, back-patting, laughing in your ear. All that repeating of the same thing over and over and over. All those sudden embarrassing moments of overmuch sentiment. ("I couldn't ash for a b'er boss'n you, Frank, I really mean that, no shit.") Pacing was partly a way of avoiding all this stuff's being inflicted on him. It was harder to hit a moving target.

The time was 9:57 p.m., and nearly everybody had wandered in by then – account executives, art directors, media buyers, copywriters, television production people, and the accounting department.

He was at the bar having a straight club soda when his partner, Stu, came over. Earlier this evening, Stu had gone somewhere.

"This is just incredible, isn't it?" Stu said. He had the slightly unkempt, chunky look of a college lineman, his blonde hair still worn in something resembling a Beatles' cut, his wine-red dinner jacket giving him the air of a high school heart throb at his first prom. Despite a certain hard-ass quality, there was a peculiar vulnerability about Foster that most people sensed, and many

13

ED GORMAN

people enjoyed. Maybe that was how you could account for his
otherwise inexplicable success in the agency business over the
past few years. Quite on his own Foster had been able to snag
several of the Twin Cities' largest accounts. As the creative side
of the partnership, Brolan knew that the agency could compete
with anybody. They had three particularly good writer-artist
teams. But even so, Brolan was spellbound by the way Foster
had been able to go out right after they'd opened up shop for
themselves and start landing the biggies.

Foster rattled his glass. "You as hungover as I am?"

"Worse, probably."

Foster laughed. "It was like college days last night."

At 3:23 the previous afternoon, Brolan and Foster had been
informed by telephone that the Down Home account was theirs.
Down Home was especially nice to win for two reasons. First
because it more than tripled agency billings and took them from
the status of a small shop to one of the majors (as a major
agency, they'd be more impressive when they pitched major
clients). And second because they'd stolen the account from
Richard Cummings, their former boss, and a man of whom it
had been said, "He gives psychosis a bad name." Until that
afternoon, Cummings had been head of a twenty-million-dollar
shop. Until then.

"You remember that woman?" Foster asked.

"From last night?"

"Right."

"Uh-huh. Sort of, anyway."

"What the hell was it all about?"

"One of us must have said something."

"You remember saying anything nasty?"

"Huh-uh."

"Neither do I. Boy, that was spooky," Foster said. "Throwing
that drink in your face."

"No shit."

The previous night they'd gone out celebrating by themselves.
Though Foster's wife, Dana, had wanted to go along, Foster

14

convinced her this was kind of a 'guy' thing and that the next night, at a dinner party the agency was hurling together, she'd have her fun.

Both Brolan and Foster had grown up in Minneapolis, Brolan going to Washburn High and Foster to Southwest, and both graduating from the University of Minnesota, so they knew a lot of places to hit.

Around midnight they ended up in one of those little hotel piano bars where salesmen always try to put the expense account hustle on divorced secretaries who are just starting to look matronly. They'd been standing at the bar quietly having one or two final drinks for the evening, talking about all the plans they had for the agency, when a beautiful woman in a simple white blouse and floor-length dark skirt bumped against Brolan, spilling his drink all over the arm of his sport coat.

Being drunk, and having something of a temper anyway, Brolan started to swear, not at the lady particularly, just swear in general at whatever dopey god permitted such little irritating accidents to happen.

The woman said, "That's not the sort of language a gentleman should use in front of a lady."

Brolan, angry with her contemptuous tone – had she ever thought of apologising for dumping the drink? – started to tell her that despite her beauty he was not necessarily going to act like a gentleman.

Which was when she threw her drink in his face.

It was one of those terrible moments when everything seems to freeze, when everything seems to become hushed, when everything about the knowable universe becomes irrational and spooky. One moment you're having a quiet drink with your best friend and partner, and the next you're in some insane kind of confrontation with a great-looking woman who appears to have been sired by the same man who gave the world Richard Speck.

Irrationally Brolan had swung his arm out, not to strike her, just to claim some space for himself that he didn't want her to invade. The bartender, having misinterpreted the gesture, jumped over the bar and got Brolan in a hammerlock. "We don't

15

hit broads in this place, ya got me, pal?" the beefy guy had
shouted into Brolan's face.

Brolan spluttered that he'd had no intention of hitting this
"broad," but it did no good. Other eyes were on him now,
watching, disapproving. Some drunk asshole trying to cream a
broad. Hate guys like that.

The woman was gone. Vanished.

"Let's go, Frank," Foster had said gently.

"Lucky I didn't call the freakin' cops," the bartender said. He
was still mad. To Foster he said, "Get your pal outta here right
now."

As they stood talking about what had happened the night before,
Foster said, "I kept waking up all night and thinking about it. It
was really crazy."

"Tell me about it." Brolan shuddered. He had always worried
that he drank too much. At least that's what his ex-wife had told
him. Things had been so out of control with that woman in the
bar. He kept seeing and hearing fragments of the incident. Total
loss of control. Scary shit. No doubt about it.

"Hey," Foster said.

"What?"

"Look at your hand."

Brolan looked down at his hand. Twitching. Lordy.

"It's past, my friend. Last night. The woman and all that.
Past."

"Yeah. I know that, but my nervous system doesn't seem to
have gotten the message."

"God, Frank," Foster said, putting a heavy arm on his
partner's shoulder. "We deserve to have a good time. Am I
right?"

"You're right. When you're right, you're right."

"For six years we bust our asses, and people laugh at us – those
little pissants, they'll never amount to anything – and finally we
make it big. And, in the meantime, we finally get even with our old
boss." He hoisted his glass, spilling rum-and-Coke all over his
wide hand. "To the two most wonderful guys in the world!"

"Us," Brolan said, hoisting his own glass.

"You're goddamn right, us," Foster said, shouting over the din of disco music and the sweet seductive lies of adultery. "You're goddamn right."

By midnight the place resembled a high school prom. The men had all ripped away their bow ties and cummerbunds, the women had dashed all their corsages and no longer worried about their hair, and most of them danced in their stocking feet, having kicked off their shoes an hour before. It wasn't just the young people dancing, either. The grey-hairs from the accounting department were out there, too. The mood was melancholy but in a nice way, couples holding each other tight, dancing to slow music there in the darkness, lit only by the lights behind the bar. Every once in a while somebody would jump up on a chair and shout out another toast to the Brolan-Foster Agency, but mostly there was just the slow dancing. If anybody remembered, or cared, that the next day was a workday, nobody let on.

Kathleen Logan showed up at twenty minutes to midnight. She wore a white sheath that emphasised both her height and the perfect curves of her body. She threw back her long mane of ash-blonde hair as she stood on the edge of the dance floor looking as if she were trying to figure out whom to attack. When she saw Brolan, she smirked. He was dancing with a plump but very nice secretary named Joyce Conover. Kathleen's smirk said she was amused by his choice of dance partners.

Abruptly the music became rock again. Catcalls went up, but a few of the more energetic couples pleaded for just one or two fast songs. One of the couples fancied itself quite the dance duo. They loved to show off. They jumped out on to the floor, holding hands, and proceeded to do some serious showing off. The other couples were good enough sports to stand around and clap for them. It was sort of like a dance number from a 1956 Bill Haley rock 'n' roll movie.

Brolan was back at the bar with Foster when Kathleen came over. It was late, and he was getting drunk, and he didn't want Kathleen to be as beautiful as she was. God, she was beautiful.

17

He'd always sensed that she'd destroy him in some profound and irreparable way.

She first addressed Foster. "You look nice in a dinner jacket." What should have been a compliment sounded more perfunctory than sincere. Foster was something of a chauvinist. He didn't unduly care for aggressive or successful women. But because of modern business mores he had no choice but to accept them. Kathleen had long sensed "Foster's displeasure," as she called it whenever Brolan and she were alone. Foster and Kathleen were famous for not getting along.

Foster flushed slightly, even drunk as he was, obviously sensing Kathleen's ironic tone. Ordinarily Foster would be out on the dance floor with his wife, but she was home with the flu. She'd already called three times to tell him how much she missed being at the party.

"Thank you, Kathleen. You know how much respect I have for your sincerity," Foster said. He grinned at Brolan.

But Brolan was watching Kathleen and thinking back on their affair. He should have known better than to try an office romance. They'd hired her after a look at her unimpressive resumé – two junior account executive jobs in minor Chicago agencies – and one hour in her thrall. She surprised both of them by being (a) intelligent, (b) organised, and (c) inventive where working with clients was concerned. Her first job was keeping happy, strictly in the business sense, of course, a man who manufactured watering systems for livestock confinement (this was the Midwest, after all). In six months she showed the man how to develop his product to work for other species, forge a new distribution deal, and triple his business. Subsequently he tripled his billings with the agency. She asked, and reasonably enough, for a promotion to full account executive. Brolan-Foster gladly gave it to her, along with her own office and a parking space with her name on it in the ramp adjacent to their building. It was around this time that Brolan first slept with her. From that point on he had feared her as he had never feared any other woman. He couldn't even tell you why exactly. Not exactly.

"I'm sorry I'm late," Kathleen said, her blue eyes smiling. But of course she wasn't sorry, Brolan thought. She was always late, and she never offered any explanations. He assumed there was another man somewhere. Brolan was getting less and less good at handling the whole thing.

The music slow once more, she stretched out her hands and moved toward the bar. "Would you like to dance?"

Foster nodded to Brolan and walked away.

Instinctively, and hating himself for it, Brolan started to push away from the bar and into Kathleen's arms.

On the floor they held each other at a respectable distance, not wanting gossip to start. Even in the shadows her blue eyes were startling in their clarity and inscrutable beauty. All you could ever know for sure about Kathleen was that something was going on with her, something you would never find out about. It wasn't only lust he felt for her; there was real esteem and respect, too. She'd come from a difficult childhood, one of both poverty and violence, and had through sheer willpower bettered her lot in the world. On those long snowy weekends when their affair had first started, he'd gotten to know a very different Kathleen – a sweet, gentle, wry spirit with whom he felt real kinship. He couldn't recall ever being happier, feeling more loved or needed or protected. How pure his love for her felt. And then it changed. She began showing up late for dates; taking mysterious weekend trips; answering her phone secretively in the other room. He wanted her to be the Kathleen she'd once been, back there at the tender outset. But he sensed that those had been the golden days, and that only darkness lay ahead.

"Foster's sure in a good mood," she said sarcastically.

"He thinks you hate him."

She laughed. "He's right. I do."

They danced a while longer. He was surprised that he felt even worse with her than he'd felt without her. He was afraid he was going to go through it all again – how afraid he was, how lonely he was – reduce himself to an undignified whiner and complainer. In a way he preferred his old reputation with women – volatile and decisive, willing to leave when things went badly.

19

At this moment he was the sort of man he despised, the self-absorbed romantic. Spare me, O Lord.

"Would you like to come over tonight?" she said.

"I'd better not."

"Really? Why not?"

He tried a smile. "I want to spare us both the soap opera." She smiled back.

"Gee, Brolan, do you get into soap operas? I'd hardly noticed."

"Right."

"Maybe things'll work out for us," she said.

"And if they don't –"

She shrugged her lovely shoulders. "If they don't, we can always be good friends."

"Ah, friendship," he said.

"It's better than being enemies."

"Not always," he said. "Sometimes it hurts more to be a friend than an enemy."

"You take it all too seriously."

"Yeah, I guess I do, don't I?"

"You're being sarcastic, aren't you?"

"Yes."

"I think we learn from each relationship. Each one makes us better."

"You and Oprah."

"You're getting serious again."

"Heaven forbid."

So, they danced. They didn't talk. There was nothing to say.

Brolan looked around. People were starting to pick up all the dinner jackets and cummerbunds and high heels they'd tossed so carelessly into the shadows. Lights were coming on. Nothing was more depressing than bars at closing time. You got a hard, clean look at the ravages of liquor and age and loneliness. He knew he would look like shit, an ageing man trying to stay young. But she would look beautiful. She always did. Even at dawn, in need of a toothbrush and a hairbrush and a shower, she somehow managed still to look beautiful.

"Could I ask you a question?" he said.

"The other-man question?"

His cheeks grew hot. He felt like a fumbling teenager. "Yeah, the other-man question."

"I've tried to be polite."

"In other words, none of my business."

"In other words, none of your fucking business." And with that she jerked herself from his arms and walked quickly across the dance floor and into the shadows.

But before he could go after her, Foster was there and slapping him on the back. All the house lights were up. You could see the cracks and the water stains in the decor. You could see the age and the alcohol on faces. Everybody looked blown out now and long past the joy of winning the account. There was even a certain sadness, and Brolan felt it especially.

"You're driving, my friend."

"What?" Brolan said, forcing himself to look away from Kathleen, who was turning toward the front of the place, hurrying.

Foster dangled the keys to his Jag in front of Brolan's face. "Walk a line, my friend."

"Oh, shit."

"C'mon. This is serious business."

They went through this every time they drank. Who should be driving. Brolan tended to hold his liquor a little better, so usually he drove. He walked a straight line across the dance floor. He had no problem. Earlier he had felt he was getting drunk. By this time he felt sober in an empty, almost cold way.

He took the keys from Foster, and they started to the door.

The back pats and cheers were considerably slower and more reserved now. "You guys did a great job," somebody from the art department said to Brolan and Foster. Foster drunkenly issued his standard public relations line. "We couldn't have done it without everybody in the agency pitching in."

But Brolan was having a hard time talking at all. He felt he wanted to cry or smash something, or both.

21

2

BACK IN THE FIFTIES trips to downtown Minneapolis always meant a movie at the RKO Orpheum on Hennepin or the Radio City Theatre on South Ninth. Afterward you hung around the Rexall Jacobsen Drug Company trying to catch the attention of pretty Swedish girls who couldn't have cared less about your stupid grinning and flirting, and then checked out the latest copies of *Mad* and *Amazing Stories* (with those neat Valigurksy covers) or – if you were feeling especially brave – a magazine with pretty girls in it. In those days the tallest downtown building was the Foshay Tower, and the biggest events those involving Senator Hubert Humphrey and his rallies for such causes as old-age benefits and civil rights. Of course in those days the remnants of Minnesota's old Communist party still existed, though its members tended to be hard-headed Norwegians instead of soft-bellied Russians.

Brolan recalled all this as they made their way down Seventh Street to the parking garage. Foster was drunker than he'd thought, stumbling and weaving along, twice bumping into Brolan. In the graffiti-covered elevator taking them to the tenth story of the parking garage, Foster even cupped his mouth as if he were going to vomit.

"We did it, pally," Foster said when he said anything at all. "We did it. We picked up goddamn Down Home."

"Not we, my friend. You. I'm just along for the ride."

"You're the best copywriter round."

Brolan grinned and clapped him on the shoulder. Foster had always been a brother to him, maybe to substitute for the brother he really had. Steve was a physician in Chicago, not only successful but a mass-going Catholic with a Betty Crocker wife and three *Leave It to Beaver* kids. The time Brolan's eighteen-year-old son, Rick, had been arrested for public intoxication at a Vikings game, Steve had called under the guise of commiserating. But actually Steve had wanted to remind his older brother what a mess he'd made of his personal life and say it was no wonder his eldest was carrying on in the same tradition.

In what he later had to admit was guilt, Brolan had exploded, telling his preening, perfect brother exactly what he thought of him and his Barbie doll family. Then he'd smashed the receiver down so hard, it pulled the wall phone from its moorings.

But with Foster it was different. Foster thought Brolan was crazy, too, but unlike Steve, he had a real affection for Brolan, even for Brolan's excesses. In fact, at a business retreat once, Foster had admitted that he sort of lived vicariously through Brolan. At least sometimes. All those babes.

So, it was easy for Brolan to like Foster. To feel protective of him, grateful for everything. To be always thanking him for the way he held the agency together and made sure they always made payroll (when you had thirty-nine employees, payroll was your cross and payday your Good Friday) and for the fact that each year they showed a better and better profit.

He was thinking all these fond things of his good pal Foster when the shorter man said, "Oh, shit," turned to the corner of the elevator, and let go with a stream of yellowish chunky barf.

"You okay?" brother Brolan said, trying to avoid exactly looking at the mess.

Foster nodded yes and gave him the thumbs-up sign and then started barfing again.

Brolan would sure hate to be the next guy who got on the elevator.

The parking garage smelled of the day's fading heat and car oil. Only a few vehicles sat in the shadows on the slanting floor. The cars, even Brolan's new 300-E Mercedes, looked like tired beasts dozing. The garage's low ceiling always made Brolan nervous. He suffered from mild claustrophobia. He could imagine the roof's caving in and his being buried alive, suffering for hours, gasping and crying out for each breath, pinned in the darkness and dust waiting for death itself.

They went past Foster's copper-coloured Jag. Foster didn't even look at it. Between his excess weight and the slanting floor, he was out of breath. "Son of a bitch," he said. "This is like mountain climbing." Then he added, "I'm so goddamned fat."

Brolan said what he always said, what Foster wanted him

always to say. "You're not fat. You just need to lose a few pounds."

It was sort of like telling Brolan that his hair was really brown beneath all that white stuff.

"Sure, pally, sure," Foster said.

As they reached the car, Brolan thought he heard the exit door nearest them squawk shut. For a long, irrational moment there in the deep shadows of the garage, the smell of exhaust harsh in his nostrils, he had the sense that somebody had been watching him as he'd made his way with Foster up the ramp.

Then he thought he heard distant footsteps running down the concrete stairs behind the metal exit door.

But who would have been watching him, and why? He realised suddenly how isolated they were up here; how deep the shadows were; how far away the city seemed, even though they were in its belly.

He might have mentioned all this to Foster but what was the use of talking to somebody as drunk as Foster was?

He walked over to the Mercedes, the passenger side. First get Foster all squared away, all buckled up, then take care of himself.

"Can't find the old hole?" Foster laughed. "That's what I said to Suzie Simmons once. I can't find the hole, Suzie."

Brolan waggled the key in Foster's face to show that everything was all right.

Foster started to make another joke.

"Shut up," Brolan said quietly. "Please."

"What's wrong?"

But how could Brolan explain it? This sense of dread, of something wildly wrong in an otherwise familiar universe, some terrible sense that matters had gotten horribly out of hand?

"C'mon," he said, very sober now. "C'mon and get in the car."

A few minutes later they were wheeling out of the garage. On the steering wheel, Brolan's hands were trembling.

3

GREG WAGNER WOKE UP TO David Letterman's smirking at him. Actually Letterman was smirking at a young actress who'd just told him of her mystical experiences, but the camera had pushed in tight on the gap-toothed TV host, and so he gave the appearance of smirking directly at Greg. Of course by now, age thirty-two, Greg was used to people smirking at him. He was four feet nine, and spent a lot of time in his electric wheelchair. He'd been born with spina bifida. While the hump on his back had been diminished by surgery, he was still unable to feel anything in the lower part of his body. He could not always control his bowel or bladder functions. This made winning the hearts of beautiful women more than a little difficult.

He had fallen asleep in front of the TV. His first thought on waking was: She's dead.

He wasn't sure why he thought this, but he knew that it was more than a simple pessimistic thought. He knew – was somehow absolutely certain – that God, or something, had granted him the power to know her fate.

And he knew – despite the past twenty-four hours of hoping against hope – that she was dead.

Emma.

Dead.

He moved away from the TV set into the kitchen. The duplex had been built specially for him. He could wheel or walk anywhere inside it handily, quickly.

In the soft blue kitchen – "It's such a peaceful colour," the matronly decorator had clucked – he took a can of Diet Coke from the refrigerator and drank half of it down in three quick gulps. God, was he thirsty.

Taking more of the Coke, he looked around the kitchen. Actually he agreed with the gushy woman who'd decorated both sides of the duplex. This soft blue was a peaceful colour. The custom-built oak cabinets and antique drop leaf table, two ladder-back chairs, and Oriental rug also contributed to the sense of harmony and civility. Like the living room, with its

ED GORMAN

beamed ceilings, deep leather furniture and built-in bookcases, the kitchen was a place where he could shut himself away. Inside this duplex he was the master. It was the world that was odd, not he.

Knowing he shouldn't – he hadn't been doing his exercises a lot lately – he went over to the refrigerator again. This time he got out a slice of balogna, folded it in half, and started munching on it. The fat content was probably something like 99.9%. Wonderful.

He went back to the living room, surprised that he'd been hungry in the first place. Because he knew she was dead. Knew it.

A reddish glow from the fireplace flickered across the painting of Linda Darnell that hung to the right of the fireplace itself. Darnell was a beautiful actress from the forties, his favourite era. He collected fanatically all sorts of movie memorabilia, from pin-back movie star buttons with the likenesses of Greta Garbo and Joan Crawford on them (both from the early 1930s and worth a great deal of money) to original lobby cards that depicted such stars as Hedy Lamarr, Abbott and Costello, and Carmen Miranda. This was another means of escape, and how he loved it, entombing himself within the confines of the Technicolor fantasies of the forties – Ty Power as Zorro, Clark Gable as Rhett, and Alexis Smith as anybody. He thought Alexis Smith was the most beautiful woman he'd ever seen. He played *Stallion Road*, her 1947 picture with Ronald Reagan, at least once a week on the VCR.

Only when he thought of his one and only trip to Las Vegas a few years before did he become depressed when confronted with all his movie memorabilia. In Vegas he'd met many of the people he'd corresponded with over the years, and while on paper they'd sounded like nice, normal people, they'd turned out to be sad oddballs. Just as desperate for love and acceptance as he was. He should have felt right at home – they seemed to be far more accepting of him with his curved back and wheelchair than he was of them – but he'd left after the first day, flown back home, and

26

sat in his living room and cried. For the first time, he despised all his silly movie things – the Bette Davis doll, the Ruby Keeler ice cream cup lid, the painted plaster of Paris Rudolph Valentino-Vilma Banky *Son of the Sheik* bed lamp and incense burner – the pathetic little icons that gave him his pathetic little pleasures. Later, on that first night back from Vegas, he'd taken the black hard-wood walking cane he'd someday hoped to use (before the doctor said that that particular operation would not be successful) and smashed half of what he'd owned.

Remembering that terrible night, he went over to the phone, lifted the receiver, and dialled Emma's number. Almost instantly the phone began ringing on the other side of the duplex, where Emma lived.

Correction: had lived.

The phone rang and rang, sounding lonely, mournful.

He had never deceived himself about Emma. She was no mental giant. But she was a beauty, and she was possibly the kindest, most tender person he'd ever known. Being a prostitute had not coarsened her in any way. She still retained that curious farm-girl innocence and the sweet, soft laugh, and when his own nights grew too long and treacherous – there'd been a few suicide attempts in the past, and she knew about them – she helped him from his chair and sat with him on the couch, her sweet white arm around him, and they watched TV, just as if they were real lovers; and one night, she let her breasts slip through the sheer fabric of her dressing gown, and he'd held them and kissed them and revelled in the acceptance and love they represented.

He listened to the phone ring a few more times.

Dead.

Setting the receiver back, he went over to the radio to see if there was any news of a body being discovered anywhere.

Sobbing overtook him, his slight body and enlarged head trembling, shaking with grief so violent, it hurt his back.

Emma.

Dead.

4

IN ST. LOUIS PARK new money drove Mercedes sedans and Jaguars and the occasional Ferrari. Old money still tended to drive Cadillacs and Lincolns. Brolan had lived here for the past six months, after getting a very good deal from an acquaintance of his whose agency was going down. The man was moving to the West Coast, too many people here mad at him. Chapter 11 tends to ruin friendships.

The house was a board-and-stucco English Tudor accented with a brick facade and a tall chimney. The front door was enclosed by a brick archway and opened on a vaulted and skylighted entry hall. The vaulted living room, stone hearth fireplace, and three bedrooms were way too much for a divorced man, but given the tax advantages the place gave Brolan, he couldn't afford to live anywhere else.

As he guided his car into the right stall of the two-car garage, the door having just lifted automatically, he glanced around the neighbourhood. No signs of life. His neighbours weren't the partying kind, especially not on a weeknight. With the window down, he shivered slightly. During the past half hour, he had felt the weather shift. Autumn was coming to an abrupt halt in the Twin Cities. This happened most years. Tuesday it was in the seventies; Wednesday it was in the twenties.

Then he thought about the parking garage, the sudden sense of dread he'd felt. And still felt. There was no explaining it... It was something he simply sensed.

"Wish my garage looked this good," Foster said.

"Huh?" Brolan said.

"Your garage."

"What about it?"

"It's so neat and orderly."

"Oh. Yeah. Right."

Foster stared at his partner, trying to look sober. "You're acting weird."

"Just tired is all."

"You sure?"

Brolan nodded. "Let's go inside and get something to eat."

"Like the old days."

Brolan smiled. "Yes, like the old days." And for one of those rare moments, he felt sentimental about his ex-wife. She'd always been their babysitter; Brolan and Foster would stagger back to Brolan's, and she'd fix them a midnight breakfast and they'd sit up till dawn drinking coffee and sobering up and making plans for the agency they were going to start someday.

"That sounds good," Foster said, and then promptly banged his head against the roof of the car as he tried to get out.

The moment Brolan opened the kitchen door and walked inside, he knew for sure something was wrong. This time he had a reason for his paranoia.

Flakes and flecks of dried autumn leaves were scattered across the landing floor. He flipped on the light leading to the basement.

He could see the leaves on each step of the staircase.

Somebody had been in here and recently. This was the cleaning woman's afternoon. She would have worked the place into a spotless condition. Certainly she wouldn't have tracked in leaves without cleaning them up.

"What's the hold up, ole buddy?" Foster said behind him.

Brolan continued to stare down the steps.

His sense of dread was almost overwhelming now. Something waited for him in the basement. Something…

"Why don't you go over and sit down?" Brolan said to Foster, trying to sound calm.

"By myself?"

"Sure. I just want to check out a couple of things, and then I'll make us some breakfast. How's that sound?"

Foster shrugged. "Great, I guess." He looked around the kitchen. It had been designed for a real cook. A butcher-block island with a huge iron rack held a battery of pots, plans, and utensils; while such perks as a new dishwasher, two big pink sinks, and enough fine china to make a duchess jealous filled the rest of the space. All this stuff had been left here by the guy who'd fled after taking Chapter 11. He'd told Brolan that in LA only wimps cooked.

Foster tottered over to the kitchen table, pulled out a chair with some difficulty, and then, with even greater difficulty, sat down.

Foster looked over at Brolan and waggled his fingers in a kind of Oliver Hardy gesture. Then he promptly put his head down on the table and went to sleep, like a schoolboy who could no longer endure the physics lesson.

Maybe it was better that Foster was out, Brolan thought.

Brolan walked over to the drawers built into the cabinet. He looked at several butcher knives before selecting one with a stout wooden handle.

He turned and went back to the steps leading to the basement.

Shaking his head, feeling sluggish from the alcohol he'd had earlier in the evening, he descended the steps.

On his way down, he had an almost comic sense of himself and what he must look like at this moment. An advertising exec all dressed up from a party carrying a butcher knife in his right hand. Must be a melodramatic sight.

When he reached the bottom of the stairs, he felt again that he was being watched. But by whom?

The basement was strictly standard issue, a part of the house none of the previous occupants had really done anything with. There was a large room – invariably referred to as the 'rec room' – that held a lumpy J.C. Penney couch that had been new about the time the Beatles were first appearing on Ed Sullivan; there was a Motorola black-and-white TV console, a small bookcase filled with *Reader's Digest* condensed books, a poster of a psychedelic rock group circa 1970, and a stack of record albums that ran to the Partridge Family and 1910 Fruit Gum Company. Presumably, kids had lived in this house once.

The other parts of the basement consisted of a laundry room with matching white Kenmore washer and drier, a huge sink, and an entire shelf filled with empty and never-used preserve jars that were now covered with dust.

After checking out both the rec room and the laundry room,

Brolan realised there was only one place left.

He tightened his grip on the knife.

The final room was the furnace room. A large green Lennox squatted there. Brolan peeked his head in, flipped on the light, and looked around. The furnace looked familiar. Nothing funny there.

And then he saw the freezer.

Tucked into the corner of the furnace room was a long, white chest freezer which one of the previous occupants had left filled with everything from boxes of Libby's broccoli to Birds Eye peas.

Except now the contents of the freezer were no longer inside the freezer – now they were piled neatly on the floor all around the freezer.

Something else was inside the long, white chest now.

Brolan knew for sure because down the white side of the freezer ran red, red blood.

The furnace made a popping noise kicking in. Brolan jumped and gasped, terrified. His heart pounded.

He looked once more at the contents of the freezer placed all over the floor, everything from a huge turkey to a fish with its head still on.

Then he looked back at the red blood dripping down the white side of the freezer.

He took three steps over to the white chest and pulled open the lid.

The odd thing was how comfortably she seemed to fit inside there, almost as if this were a coffin and not a freezer at all. She was completely nude and only now beginning to show signs of the freezing process, ice forming on her arms and face. But he could tell she hadn't been in here long because of the smells. The blood. The faeces. The bodily fluids and juices. These still smelled oppressively fresh.

And of course he recognised her. No doubt whatsoever who she was.

He remembered their confrontation last night, and her throwing the drink in his face.

31

ED GORMAN

And tonight she ended up here. Dead. In his freezer.

Again Brolan was struck by the comic aspect of all this. Who the hell would empty a freezer and put a corpse into it? Who the hell hated him enough to do this?

He found himself staring at her again. One of the wounds had been across her wrist, and it was this wound from which the blood had been dripping, apparently after being banged on the edge of the freezer.

He wanted her to talk. He wanted her beautiful eyes to open, and he wanted her to talk, and then he wanted her to listen. He wanted to say this was all some terrible mistake and he was sorry and wouldn't she please put her clothes on and go home.

Please.

Upstairs he made a double-strength pot of coffee, eight eggs in a big electric skillet, six pieces of toast and then – as an afterthought – six strips of bacon. He tried not to notice how badly his hands were shaking.

After getting the food on, he went to work on Foster. He shoved his hands under Foster's arms and half dragged the man into the nearby half bath where he threw cold water on his face, squirted some toothpaste in his mouth, and then filled his hand with a cup of coffee. He forced Foster to drink the coffee before they left the bathroom.

Back in the kitchen, Brolan shoved the food at Foster and said, "Eat."

"Jesus Christ," Foster said, more sober now but cranky as hell. "What's going on, anyway?"

"Just eat. Then I'll tell you."

"Aren't you going to eat?"

Brolan looked at his food. "Uh, no."

"Why not?"

"Not hungry."

"How come?"

"Foster. Please eat. Please. And drink lots more coffee. I need you to be sober."

"You look like shit."

32

"Thanks."

"That's not a gratuitous insult. I mean you really look like shit. What happened, anyway? Did I pass out and miss something important?"

"Eat. Please."

So Foster shrugged and ate. He popped his over-easy eggs so that the yellow ran free, and then he started dunking his toast in the yolk. The bacon he ate ravenously and with his fingers. He finished everything on his plate within minutes. Then he raised his eyes and stared at Brolan's plate. "You're really not going to eat?"

"No."

"You mind if I eat it, then?"

"Be my guest."

Foster took the edges of Brolan's plate and pulled it over to him. He shrugged then and dug in.

Halfway through his pig-out, Foster raised his eyes again. "You still look like shit."

"Thanks again."

"Something's really wrong, isn't it?"

"You going to give me a clue?"

Brolan sighed. He had to tell Foster sometime. May as well be now. "When you're finished there, I want you to go down to the basement."

"For what?"

"To look around."

"And what will I find?"

"A woman."

"Is she naked?"

"As a matter of fact, she is."

For the first time, Foster stopped eating. He even pushed the plate away. "All right. what the hell's going on? There's a nude woman in your basement, and you don't look very happy about it. Ordinarily you'd be very happy indeed. So I can infer from that that there's something wrong with this woman. Right?"

"Right."

33

"This is when I wish I still smoked." Foster sighed and looked straight at his partner. "She's dead, isn't she?"

"Yes."

"Jesus Christ. You're not kidding me now, are you?"

"I wish I were."

"Jesus Christ."

"She's the woman from the other night."

"The other night?"

"The one I had the run-in with."

"The one who spilled the drink on you?"

"Yes."

"Jesus Christ. How did she get into your basement?"

"I don't know. But I wish you'd go down there and check things out. Then why don't you come back up here and we'll talk."

"You mind if I pee first?"

"Fine with me."

So Foster peed first and then he went down to the basement.

Brolan sat at the table drinking coffee. None of this made sense. None of it.

In ten minutes Foster came back up. He sat down at the table across from Brolan and said, "I've got to ask you something."

"What?"

"You didn't kill her, did you?"

"Are you crazy?"

"I had to ask. I had to know."

"Well, now you know."

"So you call the cops?" Foster said.

"You're forgetting Linda Rollins."

"Linda Rollins? The woman you used to live with?"

"Right."

"What about her?"

"Remember the charges she filed against me when I tried to move out. Domestic abuse?"

"But you didn't do anything to her."

34

"Right. But I'm not sure either the police or that judge believed me. I always had the sneaking suspicion that they really thought I did slap her around on occasion."

"But she dropped the charges."

"But only after two months. And she made it look as if she were doing me a favour instead of admitting that she'd made the charges up."

Foster said, "I don't see where this is going, old buddy." Brolan sighed and shook his head. "I call the police and tell them there's a woman in my basement. Then they find out that this woman and I had a run-in in a bar the other night. And then they find out about the charges Linda Rollins put on me and –"

Foster said, "Goddamn, I see what you're driving at. But if you don't call the cops, what the hell'll you do?"

"At least try to find out who the woman was. Try to find out who could have brought her over here."

Brolan stared down at his right hand lying on the kitchen table. It was beyond trembling now. It was shaking violently.

"You're not doing so good, are you?" Foster said gently.

"No, no I'm not."

"Maybe you'd better call the police." His tone remained soft. "Maybe it'd be easier that way, Frank."

"I just want to find out who she was. I just want this to make a little sense before I go to the police."

"And meanwhile leave her downstairs?"

Brolan looked over at him. "She'll be pretty well preserved there, anyway."

Foster said, "Frank, are you absolutely sure you don't want to call the police?"

Brolan sighed. "That's the only thing I am sure of right now, my friend. The only thing."

5

Wednesday Morning

IT WAS THE USUAL DESPERATE STUFF. Rumour had it that a large client of Brolan-Foster's had been seen lunching with the president of a rival agency. A two-inch videotape that was supposed to air on Cleveland television that night (this was a political year, and Brolan-Foster had taken on two candidate accounts) had somehow gotten lost in transit, and everybody (including the hysterical man working on the client's side) was frantic. A perpetually dissatisfied employee in the art department was trying to get several lost souls to band together and demand even more comprehensive health benefits (Brolan-Foster now paid the best in the Twin Cities). A key copywriter had fallen off the wagon again and this time – to avoid firing – was promising to join AA. Brolan looked at a pencil layout for the agency's third largest client (a retail chain) and felt acid start working its way up his stomach, oesophagus, and throat (a pen-and-ink drawing that was supposed to look fashionably little-girlish just looked amateurish instead). And the accounting department had left the latest balance sheet on his desk in a large manila envelope marked FYI. This had been a particularly good quarter.

Brolan kept his door closed through all this, of course. He'd gotten at most an hour's troubled sleep last night, finding himself three times descending the basement steps to peer into the freezer. To make sure she was still there. (What the hell did he expect? That she was going to get up and run away?) At seven o'clock he'd said hello to Mr Coffee, draining off two cups before the machine even stopped burbling, and then had a quick one-mile run on the treadmill machine he kept in one of the extra bedrooms he didn't know what else to do with. He used an electric razor instead of a safety razor to shave because he was afraid he'd mutilate himself. And he put on several slaps of after-shave because he knew that he was already sweating all over his freshly showered skin. He permitted himself only one more look at the dead woman. Opening the freezer lid, he looked down with tired, sober eyes at the blue-white flesh, at the gouges and slashes and cuts on her slender, gorgeous body. He wondered again what kind of man and what kind of frenzy could have led to this. An image of Richard Cummings, his former boss and a card-carrying sociopath, came to mind. Cummings with his layered, carefully-moussed dark hair; Cummings with his chiselled handsome face and dead blue eyes; Cummings with fists the size of a professional heavyweight's. Cummings could have done something like this. For sure.

From his office he answered Foster's third phone call.

"How's it going, pally?"

"Better than I would have expected, I guess."

"I wish I could get out of my lunch plans."

"You've got to see Fenwick. No doubt about it."

"What're you going to do?"

"For lunch?"

"Yeah."

"Dunno yet." Pause. "Have you seen Kathleen yet this morning?"

Foster paused, too. Foster and his wife, Dana, were always trying to line Brolan up with somebody. Somebody who was – in Dana's inelegant phrase – marriage material. To the Fosters, Kathleen Logan did not qualify. They saw her as the femme fatale of Twin Cities advertising. At thirty-five, ambitious in an almost chilling way, she'd already caused two legendary marital splits on her way to her vice presidency at Brolan-Foster.

Foster said, "Can I be honest, pally?"

"Okay."

"With all the troubles you've got right now, do you really need to be worrying about Kathleen?"

"Isn't that sort of my business?"

"You getting pissed?"

"Yeah. Sort of."

Foster sighed. "It's your life, pally." Irritation sounded clearly in his carefully selected words. Then he softened his tone. "Hang in there."

Brolan's tone changed, too. "I appreciate everything, Foster.

I really do."

"I know, pally. I know."

Around eleven-thirty there was a knock on his door. He looked up from the storyboards he had on his desk. The boards depicted a new blue snowblower sucking up all the snow on an entire block and changing a winter scene to deep summer. It was a great visual idea if the right special effects man could be found on the West Coast.

"Yes?"

"It's Kathleen."

"Oh."

It was strange, he thought. Here he was, ass-deep in the worst trouble of his life – a dead woman in a freezer in his basement, for God's sake – yet he still brooded over his love life. In St. Cloud prison you didn't have a love life. Or not the kind Brolan preferred, anyway.

She came in. That morning she wore a dark blue suede shirtdress with matching belt, white nylons, and pumps that matched the tint of the dress. Her ash-blonde hair was glossily arranged in a pageboy, her gorgeous blue eyes showed no hint of sleep lines, and her eminently kissable mouth was neatly stained the colour of blood. When she parted her lips to smile, he looked at teeth so white, they would have made a dentist weep with joy. She said, "You seem to have left about ten notes on my desk."

"I wanted to talk to you."

"You know how Shirley loves drama." Shirley was Kathleen's tirelessly gossipy secretary. "Maybe you don't care about your reputation among the employees, but I do." She stared straight at him. "I really tried to be nice last night."

"I just want you to be honest, Kathleen."

Closing the door behind her, she came a little farther into his office.

She said, "You look pretty bad."

"Thank you."

"I meant that in a friendly way."

He sighed. "I know you did. I'm sorry for my mood."

She came over and leaned down and kissed him. He couldn't tell at that rushing moment which made him dizzier – the intoxicating aroma of her perfume or the touch of her soft lips on his.

"I'm not trying to be a bitch about this," she said. "I really do need some space to think."

"You have any plans for lunch?"

"That's why I got in late this morning. I'm working out Kilgore's next ad budget with him personally. We met for breakfast. He wants me to meet him for lunch, too."

She turned and faced him, once again, as if to say: Go ahead, Brolan, accuse me of sleeping with my clients. I dare you. He thought of well-tanned, fleshy, white-haired Harry Kilgore. He looked like a TV minister. Actually he owned a chain of eighty computer stores. He'd been one of the few people to survive the computer boom and bust of the mid-eighties. Many ad agencies had overextended credit to computer hotshots and had been forced out of business when the hotshots took bankruptcy. But not Kilgore. Kilgore became a millionaire many times over.

Brolan did wonder if she was sleeping with him, of course.

"I need to get back to my office," she said. "I'm only here for a few minutes."

He stood up and walked over and took her by the elbows and drew her to him. He started to say something – something that would partly be rage and partly be the tenderness he felt for her despite everything – yet when his mouth opened, no words came out.

She leaned over and kissed him on the mouth again. He felt an exhilaration he could scarcely contain. He wanted to grab her and make love to her right there in the office. He wanted to shake her till she came to her senses and agreed that they should plan a life together.

But he said nothing; nothing.

"Kilgore says to say hello," she said as she walked back to the door. She gave him a cute little wave. And was gone; gone.

6

TWO YEARS BEFORE, for Christmas, he'd bought them both computers complete with modems. He used his for all sorts of purposes, but mostly she used hers to write her 'novel.' Actually it was more of a diary than anything else. All about how a young girl came from a Minnesota farm town and worked for a time at a law office and then met some rich young men and then changed her life considerably by becoming a special kind of prostitute. She never worked the streets; she never worked the bars. Taxi drivers couldn't tell you anything about her, and horny salesman in town for a convention would never set eyes on her. But she was a prostitute nonetheless.

There was a man Greg Wagner hated a great deal, and it was the man who made all of Emma's appointments for her. He specialised in rich men, and to his credit, he was careful never to allow anybody very kinky to be with Emma. About the worst it ever got – according to Emma's computer diary – was a man who wanted to wear Emma's silk underwear while they were doing it. In her diary Emma noted that the whole incident had struck her as being one-half funny and one-half sad, one of those confounding things in life that you can't quite figure out. There were a lot of things in her diary about the men she was with. In her sweet way Emma had liked most of them. Particularly Mr Pinkham. Emma always included Mrs Pinkham in her nightly prayers, though she sensed from Mr Pinkham's drab mood that chances for Mrs Pinkham's survival were pretty slim.

Greg Wagner always read her diary. This required no great skill on his part. Because both computers had modems, he could simply link up and read away. Emma not only knew about this but encouraged it as well. One of the reasons she'd wanted a computer (she'd wanted to pay for it, but Greg insisted it was a gift) was so that she could learn to write. She was a great fan of horror fiction, and someday she wanted to write a novel that would "scare the willies" out of everybody. She especially liked strong female protagonists, the way they could be both tender and tough when need be. This was how she saw herself, she'd often confided to Greg. In truth, of course, she wasn't tough at all. She let her pimp, Kellogg, run her life completely.

Three times Greg had offered to loan her the money to start life anew (life had been both malicious and charitable to Greg; true, he'd been born with spina bifida, but he'd also inherited about 3.2 million in real estate). And she'd almost made it, once especially. But Kellogg was a charmer – not only handsome but cunning and pleasing in the way of many sociopaths. And so, again she would fall back – "Just a few more appointments, Greg, I promise, and then I'll quit for sure." But she never did. She wrote at her novel every day – she'd read an old John Steinbeck interview wherein Steinbeck recommended three pages a day for those "serious about writing," and so, virtually without fail, she did three pages a day in the saga of her life.

And once a week or so Greg, finished buying new movie icons and viewing shipments of videotapes (he'd recently finished a run of serials set in the jungle, *Jungle Jim* and *Nyoka the Jungle Girl* being especially good), would tap into her computer and read what she'd written. Then he'd write her a page or two of criticism. Gentle, constructive criticism as to how she might improve this sentence or better begin that paragraph. How appreciative she was – soft, moist, grateful kisses on his cheeks and forehead, as if she were trying to prove to him that she found him perfectly acceptable the way he was...

In fact women did find Greg quite handsome, whatever the rest of the world might think about him. He was, of course, desperately and painfully in love with her. This was an affliction suffered by many men, men with spina bifida included – invariably falling in love with perfectly formed women who could be theirs only in fantasy. There was a ludicrous side to this – in none of the various versions did the Hunchback of Notre Dame ever win the woman – but there was also a tragic side. Greg had seen other men in wheelchairs like his become suicidal over the fact that they could never possess the beautiful woman they'd fallen in love with. During his therapy sessions with Dr Stephenson Greg had learned that he was attracted to gorgeous normal women so he could punish himself. ("Couldn't it be that

41

I just like good-looking women?" Greg had said laughingly to the doctor.) But this was before he'd met Emma, before he'd rented her the other side of his duplex, before he'd fallen so helplessly in love with her. After that it was to hell with Dr Stephenson's maxims. It was better to love somebody unobtainable than to love nobody at all. For all the grief there was a commensurate joy – having her stop over a few times a day, always calling before she went out in the evening, many times getting home early and sitting up with him and watching some old movie with Alice Faye or John Hodiak. Yes, it was better to love somebody unobtainable than to love nobody at all. This was Greg's deepest truth.

In the morning Greg had sweet rolls for breakfast. Two of them and with large wipes of butter. The doctors at the therapy centre were already grousing about his weight. You've got to exercise more, Greg. But that morning he was so tired, he needed a sugar high to get going. In addition to a caffeine high, that is. He also had a Diet Pepsi and two cups of coffee.

He was ready.

Sometime during the night – half-awake, listening for her familiar footsteps next door but realising, too, that she was gone from him forever – sometime during the night he'd suddenly recalled something she'd said to him about a very strange thing that Kellogg had wanted her to do. She'd pleaded with Kellogg that she didn't want to do it, but he'd said it was important, and that she'd damned well better do it.

But Greg couldn't remember what it was.

Something…

His only real hope was the computer. Perhaps she'd written about this, and he could tap into it.

After being properly charged by all the sweets, he rolled into his book-lined den. Indian summer had spoiled him. He was used to a flood of warm sunlight splashing across the hardwood floor. But not that day. Grey sky and chill temperature boded snow.

He moved over to the computer, turned on the power, and

proceeded, over the next forty-five minutes, to tap into her diary.

It was almost shamefully easy, the way he found what he was looking for so quickly.

Around three-thirty that afternoon, after a lunch of sliced-ham sandwiches and a piece of pumpkin pie, and a good crime movie called *The Falcon Goes to Hollywood*, he phoned the guy.

He did it right, too. He put a handkerchief over the receiver, and he lowered his voice.

And he scared the hell out of the guy.

That was the one thing Greg could tell for sure. How scared the guy was.

Then, when he was finished, he lay back in his wheelchair and closed his eyes and thought of Emma, her face and her soft skin and the gentle way she'd always treated him. He knew he'd never see her again.

In the afternoon Brolan looked at girls. Ordinarily this was the favourite part of his job. And why wouldn't it be? You sit in a fashionably appointed screening room and look at videotapes of women of every description looking their best. The object was to find a new Stolda's ice cream TV pitchwoman, the former one having landed a part in a cable-system sitcom. You look at films of women, videotapes of women, glossies of women – and sometimes the local talent agencies even send women over live. Today, however, they were all on tape.

Sometime after lunch he had started smoking again. At first it had been a few puffs on a mooched cigarette. Soon enough he'd asked one of the couriers to go get him a pack of cigarettes. His plans were to put in a reasonably full day – be no more or no less cheery than he ever was – and then to start backtracking the dead woman by going to the bar where he'd met her. Maybe the bartender there could at least give him a name and therefore a starting point.

"She's gorgeous," Tim Culhane, the production manager said.

Brolan's attention returned to the screen. "She is gorgeous. Too gorgeous."

43

ED GORMAN

"You want frumpy?"

"Not frumpy. Just somebody who won't put other women off."

Actually the woman on the screen reminded him in some dark way of Kathleen. Desire and anger worked through him as he recognised the similarity between the women. He still couldn't believe that even when he was so deeply in trouble, Kathleen could have this effect on him.

"Why don't we look at the next one?" Brolan said.

Brolan sat at the front of the sloping screening room. There were twenty movie theatre seats. In front of the large movie screen was a forty-five-inch video screen. This was what they'd been using the past hour.

The next one up was cute and perky. Brolan did not usually like cute-and-perky, but since it was the polar opposite of Kathleen, cute-and-perky looked great.

"How about her?" Brolan said.

"Her?" Culhane sounded surprised. Tall, muscular, thanks to weight training and running, Culhane still wore his blonde hair shoulder-length – but it was sculpted hair, Hollywood hair, and bore no kinship to the sixties or flower power or any of that. He was handsome in a somewhat overly dramatic way, always posing, and given to the sort of loose-fitting, expensive sports clothes you found on the West Coast. Brolan and Culhane had never gotten along, but the past six months had been especially bad. Brolan, who was solely in charge of promoting creative people, had passed Culhane over in favour of someone else for an executive job. Culhane was neither a forgiving nor understanding man. "She looks like the girl next door."

"She's cute."

"Last time I checked, you hated cute."

Brolan sighed. "All right. Next one, then."

The next one was redheaded and had the sort of reckless beauty that always got to Brolan. The most beautiful woman he'd ever seen in films was the young Rita Hayworth, and anybody who remotely resembled her was welcome to come into Brolan's life at any time.

44

"God," Tim said. "She's great." He looked at the sheet that identified where each actress was from. "Chicago."

"Much acting experience?"

Culhane read silently for a few moments. "Actually quite a bit of stage work. Lot of dinner theatre but some small-theatre stuff, too. *Peer Gynt* and *Hedda Gabler.*"

Brolan nodded. He could see her as Hedda, one of his favourite creations. The remote beauty, the inscrutable motives. Not until then did he realise that Kathleen reminded him of Hedda, too.

"Can you see her in a nice suburban dress, with a nice suburban manner, hawking ice cream?"

"Absolutely," Culhane said.

"Good. Then let's get her in here for an audition sometime soon."

Moments after Tim flipped the switch on the VCR, the screen went dead. The screening room, which had a ceiling covered with acoustic tile, was quiet in an almost eerie way. That was why the door's creaking open at the rear of the room made such an unearthly noise, like fate announcing itself.

Culhane looked up and said, "Oh, hi, Kathleen."

Hearing her name, Brolan felt as if he were back in seventh grade. When the other boys knew you 'liked' a certain girl, but you were afraid to show them that you did. Brolan stared straight ahead, as if he found the empty screen fascinating.

Culhane, obviously sensing the mood, took the videotape from the VCR, put it back in its box, and said, "Well, I'd better be going. Think we made a good choice." He nodded goodbye.

"Thanks, Tim," Brolan said. He had still not turned around.

The closer she came, the more erotic her perfume got. He felt tense, angry, yet desperate to see her.

She walked down the sloping aisle until she was two rows of seats past him. She looked so trim, her calves perfect, her ankles a dream. She turned around and faced him.

"Kilgore has added thirty percent to his next year's advertising budget," she said.

"Great."

45

"That's pretty big news, isn't it?"

Kathleen always liked to be complimented.

"It's very big news," he said. "Good work." He had to remember that he was her boss as well as her lover. Or at least one of her lovers.

She said, "That isn't really why I came in here."

"No?"

"No. I wanted to say that I'm sorry about this morning."

"Oh." He cleared his throat, not knowing exactly what words to shape.

"I'm still in love with you," she said.

Seventh grade again. Or at least not adulthood. He felt embarrassed and happy beyond imagining and terrified, all at the same time. Maybe especially terrified because falling in love with Kathleen was scary stuff.

"I love you, too," he said.

"Maybe we can get through this."

"I hope so."

She had come no closer to him. Nor he to her. "I'm really trying to work through some things. I – I'd like a little more time."

How could he say no, after she'd come to him with such an air of reconciliation?

"All right," he said.

She smiled. "Do I have to give you a dollar to come over here and kiss me?"

She didn't even have to give him fifty cents.

Half an hour later Brolan was in his office finishing up the last-minute duties of the day – looking at a stern letter from the Screen Actors Guild about the impending actors' strike; calling a client and doing a little hand-holding, the man concerned that his bills were running too high (in fact, per-hour profitability on this particular account had been sinking steadily) when the intercom buzzed.

"Yes?" he said.

"Line three."

"Any idea who it is?"

"Sorry. He wouldn't give a name."

Brolan thought a moment. "All right. Three?"

"Right."

She clicked off.

Brolan picked up the phone. "Hello?"

"You don't know who I am."

"All right."

"But I know who you are."

"I see."

"And more significantly, Mr Brolan, I know what you've done."

Brolan felt acid beginning to eat up his stomach and run up to his chest. Boiling.

"I really should hang up," Brolan said.

"But you won't."

"What makes you so sure?"

The male voice – muffled somehow – said, "Because you want to hear what I'm going to say next."

"And what will that be?"

"That you killed Emma."

"I don't know any Emma."

"Of course you do, Mr Brolan. We're both grown-ups here. We shouldn't try childish games."

"Who is this?"

He reached in his desk drawer for some antacid tablets.

"I want you to meet me tonight, Mr Brolan."

"Where?"

"At the end of this conversation, I'll give you the address."

"What if I don't show up?"

"Then I go to the police. Would you like that, Mr Brolan?"

Brolan's throat was starting to constrict. "I'll have to think this over."

"Nine o'clock, Mr Brolan."

And then the man gave him the address.

"Did you write that down, Mr Brolan?"

It was the turn of the other man to pause. "We pay for our sins, don't we Mr Brolan?"

47

With that he hung up.
Brolan had two more antacid tablets.

7

AFTER WORK Brolan went home. The first thing he checked
was the freezer. The woman was still there, blue-tinted and
almost embryonic in the way she was hunched over. In the
kitchen he had a cheese sandwich and a handful of potato chips
and a Pepsi. High school repast. He tried watching the local
news, but after it was clear that there would be no mention of a
missing woman, he went upstairs, changed into jeans, a blue
sweatshirt, and a pair of Nikes. Restless, he decided to kill the
remaining two hours before his appointment by driving around.
He did that sometimes when nothing else made any emotional
sense – just drove, one with wind and darkness, ego and identity
vanished. He was probably never more relaxed than at these
times.

The address he'd been given turned out to be near North Oaks,
a relatively recent development that sat on the edge of the
suburbs. By nine, snow flurries had started flecking his
windshield, and the wind was so hard, it rocked his car. As he
drove through a small business district with a strip mall and
some other stores on the other side of the street, he thought of
Christmas time, the way people bent into the furious wind,
hurrying on their way home to warmth and shelter. How
innocent his life of even twenty-four-hours before seemed now.
No dead women in freezers.
He had no trouble finding the address. It was an impressive
duplex designed to resemble town houses. No lights shone on
either side. He rolled to the kerb and shut off the engine. Wind
continued to rock the car. He had another forbidden cigarette,
and as he sat there smoking it, he sensed eyes on him. Knowing
eyes, watching.

Taking only a few drags before flicking the cigarette into the darkness, Brolan got out of the car and started up the walk. Actually few lights shone in the entire prosperous middle-class neighbourhood. He wondered if everybody there was elderly.

At the door he raised an ornate brass knocker twice and let it fall. It sounded metallic in the chilly silence.

No response.

This time he used his knuckles.

Still nothing.

The impression of eyes watching him remained. He wondered for the thousandth time since the phone call who the caller was and how he knew about the dead woman and why he thought Brolan had killed her.

His hand fell to the knob and turned it. He pushed inward and felt the door start to open.

This didn't make much sense. Who left their front doors unlocked this way? Images from a thousand TV cop shows came to him. He'd walk inside and find the man who'd called him sprawled dead on the floor. The killer had left the door open on his way out.

Frightened but curious, he pushed his way inside.

Darkness, a shadowy gloom illuminated only by ghostly streetlight through gauzy curtains. The shape of fashionable furniture dark against the greater darkness. He inched inward, keeping the door behind him ajar in case he needed to run. The floor was hardwood. Even walking on tiptoe he made a certain amount of noise.

Once his eyes began adjusting to the gloom, he could see more clearly. The living room looked like a popular-culture display in a museum. The walls carried several framed blow-ups of movie stars, from Gary Cooper to Marilyn Monroe. An enormous TV screen sat between two sections of built-in bookcases that were filled with VHS tapes, everything neatly filed and apparently alphabetised. He got close enough to read some of the titles on the books in the other cases. They ran from titles as serious as Andrew Sarris's surveys of American film to books about Saturday matinee serials.

He was just about to explore the other parts of the duplex when he heard a thrumming against the hardwood. At first he didn't recognise the sound. But within moments his mind registered: wheelchair.

And so it was: a wheelchair bearing a small, somewhat twisted man rolled into sight, there in the ghostly light from the street. The man wore a dark turtleneck and what appeared to be jeans. His hair was combed back in a trendy way.

Brolan would have felt pity for such a man except the man was making it very difficult for him to do so.

The man was pointing a .45 at Brolan's chest.

"You're Mr Brolan?"

"I've got to tell you. Guns scare the hell out of me. I wish you'd put that thing down."

"In due time, Mr Brolan. I have some questions first." A kind of unreality came over Brolan. He was standing in a darkened room with a crippled man in a wheelchair. The man held a gun on him. Back home Brolan had found a dead woman in a freezer chest. Images burned and faded; all this was like a fever dream he prayed would end soon.

"I want to talk about Emma," the man said.

"I don't know any Emma."

"She was hired to walk about and bump you in a certain bar the other night."

"Hired? What the hell are you talking about?"

"Hired," the man said. Then he added, "Why did you kill her?"

Carefully Brolan put a hand to his head. Despite the chilly night and despite the fact that the duplex was not exactly warm, Brolan's head was wet with sweat. As were his back and his shorts. "Do me a favour."

"And what would that be?"

"Don't say that anymore. That I killed her, I mean. I don't know who you are, and I don't know who she was, but I didn't kill her."

"But she did bump into you the night before last?"

"Yes."

"And then what happened?"

Brolan shrugged, his eyes focused on the .45 in the man's hand. Wind rattled windows; sleet sprayed like tossed sand against the glass. "We had words. I was pretty drunk. I don't remember. But it wasn't anything serious." He smiled at the craziness of all this. "It certainly wasn't something you'd kill somebody for."

"You're not telling me everything, are you, Mr Brolan?"

Brolan said, "Who was she?"

For a time the man didn't speak. In the shadows Brolan could see that the man's gaze wandered away for a time. Brolan decided this was the best chance he'd have to slap the gun away.

He lunged.

The man raised the .45 and pushed it right against Brolan's forehead.

Brolan's sweat turned chill; he felt as if he had a terrible case of the flu.

He withdrew from the man. The man kept the gun pointed level at Brolan's heart.

"She was the woman I loved," the man said. "Do you find that funny? That a man like me would love a woman like her?"

"Why would I find that funny?"

"Pathetic, then? Perhaps you find it pathetic, Mr Brolan."

"You loved her. That isn't hard to understand."

"Then you can understand why I want to kill the man who killed her."

Brolan paused. "You still think I did it?"

"Yes."

"But why? What motive would I have?"

"That's what I want you to tell me, Mr Brolan." As the man spoke, Brolan let his eyes roam the dark room. He saw a leather recliner to his right that he could dive behind if he were quick enough and lucky enough.

The more the man spoke, the more aggrieved he sounded. For the first time Brolan began actually to believe that the man might well kill him.

Brolan said, "We could help each other."

"And how would that be, Mr Brolan?"

"We could help each other find out who really did it."

"What is it you're not telling me, Mr Brolan? You're like a little child. I can hear guilt in your voice, but I need you to be more specific."

Brolan dove then.

Without any grace, without any apprehension of injuring himself, he pitched his body to the right, aiming directly for the side of the chair that would shield him from any bullets.

He lay there, panting, sodden with his sweat, waiting.

No sound but the wind and the heaving of his lungs.

The man said, "You were too quick for me, Mr Brolan. It's the advantage of having a body capable of action."

Brolan said nothing.

The man laughed. It was a short, harsh sound. It almost seemed to pain him. He tossed something heavy to the floor. "It wasn't a real gun, Mr Brolan. I bought it at a Republic Studio auction. Have you ever heard of Lash La Rue?"

Getting up from the floor, Brolan said, "You little son of a bitch. You were holding Lash La Rue's gun on me?"

8

HE LIKED THE DANGER. Oh, to be sure; he liked the sweet young sex, too, but it was the danger itself that was the real thrill. He'd once bought a girl here who said she was thirteen, but he suspected she was even younger. Happily.

The place was Loring Park, not so far from the Guthrie Theatre. Despite the best intentions of the city council and various outraged civic groups, parts of Loring Park remained a meat market for a very special kind of shopper.

Take tonight. If you knew where to look, finding the kids willing to sell themselves for dope or food or yankee cash was easy enough. You drove to a certain section of the park, and there they were.

Now, in the way of his headlights, they looked more than

delectable. (Girls only. In his twenties, worried that he might be gay, he'd tried it once with a guy. It had neither excited him nor even shamed him especially. It just bored him. No; for him it was girls only). There were about a dozen girls ranging from the ages of perhaps fourteen to maybe sixteen or seventeen. Fat ones, skinny ones, white ones, black ones, clean-looking ones, dirty-looking ones. The boys, if you were interested, ran along the same lines. His own preference was usually the same – a short, thin girl with largish breasts. He even had a special preference in nipples. He liked smaller ones that came taut and erect quickly under his thumb. And one more thing: He liked innocent faces. In an era of breast-fuckers, mouth-fuckers, butt-fuckers, and God-knew-what-else, he considered himself still a romantic. He fucked faces. Sad little-girl faces especially.

He saw her in the arc of his headlights as he went up a small incline. She stood this side of a copse of trees. He knew immediately she was the one. Not too scruffy, not Girl Scout clean. A wan, pretty face and a body that looked ripe beneath a blouse, denim jacket, and jeans. She had long blonde hair blowing now in the steady wind. She made no concessions to him – no whore smile, no whore jiggle of ass or touching of breasts or pussy. Had some self-respect. He liked that.

He pulled up alongside her. He always did the same thing. Opened the passenger window and pushed his face out in a big grin. Then he waved the crisp new fifty-dollar bill in her general direction.

"Is that really a fifty?" she asked. Judging by her voice, he'd put her somewhere around fifteen. A little more knowing than a real kid. Been around some but not too much. That was another thing he liked about her.

"It sure is."

"And it's for me?"

"If we get along."

"I think I've seen you before."

"Oh?"

"Uh-huh."

"Aren't you cold out there?"

She smiled. It was a halting smile and all the lovelier for its hesitancy. He tried not to notice how much dental work she needed. "Yeah, I guess so."

"Why don't you get in, then?"

"I got to tell you."

"Got to tell me what?"

"There's some stuff I won't do."

"I'm a pretty normal guy."

She grinned again. This time there was just a hint of irony in it. That part he didn't like so much. "If you say so," she said, "but I'm serious."

"About the stuff you won't do?"

"Right."

"Well, you tell me what those things are, and I promise I won't ask you."

"And I get the fifty?"

"And you get the fifty."

She got inside. She smelled of cold night air and cigarettes and just faintly of sweat.

She shut the door.

"What's your name?" he said.

She looked at him oddly. "Are you a cop?"

He laughed. "Hardly."

"Then why do you want to know?"

"Maybe I'm just being polite."

She shrugged and looked out the window at the park that was quickly fading from view. "Denise."

"That's a pretty name."

"I don't want you to put it up my behind, all right?"

He smiled at her little-girl crudeness. She was a find, was Denise. "All right," he said.

"And no rough stuff."

"You don't have to worry about that."

"One guy really beat the shit out of me once. I had to go to the free clinic."

"Anything else?"

"Huh-uh. As long as you wear a condom, I mean."

He smiled again. "I'm well supplied."

She looked out at Hennepin Avenue. On this part of the strip all the houses and businesses looked as if they could qualify for urban renewal.

"Mind if I ask where you're from?"

"You sure ask a lot of questions."

Her sweet little pussy would more than make up for her sour attitude, he thought. "Has it ever crossed your mind that maybe I like you, and I'm interested in you?"

"Yeah. Right." They drove some more. She said, "St. Louis."

"Beg pardon?" His mind had been drifting.

"I'm from St. Louis."

"Oh. That's a nice city. The Gateway Arch and all."

"Well, I'm not actually from the city."

"From a small town not too far from there."

"Farm girl?"

"Yeah. There somethin' wrong with that?"

He smiled. "No; just asking." He drove a while longer, and then he said, "You don't like it, do you?"

"Like what?"

"You know. Having sex for money."

"Seems like I don't have a lotta choice."

"Can I be honest?"

She stared out the window, shrugged.

"That kind of turns me on," he said.

"What does?"

"That you don't like it."

"I'm happy for you."

"You should take that as a compliment. It just means you've got some dignity; some self-respect."

"Yeah, I've got a lot of self-respect all right." He took her hand. At first she resisted; nothing obvious, simply held back.

He took her hand and placed it on his crotch.

"Feels good," he said.

"Right."

He smiled again. "You really don't like it, do you?"

"Would you like it, mister? Somebody always pawing at you?"

He started thinking very seriously about where it was going to happen. Where exactly he was going to kill her.

She said, "I'm sorry I'm so down tonight. It's my mother's birthday."

"That should make you happy."

"She's dead."

"Oh. I'm sorry."

"So, it kind of bums me out. She was only forty-one." Then she said, "So, I still get it, right?"

"Get it?"

"The fifty?"

"If you're a good little girl." She looked out the window again. It was time. They were nearly out in the country. He needed a dark road.

He was getting excited.

9

ONCE THEY GOT THE LIGHTS ON and started talking, both men calmed down. Greg Wagner even rolled his wheelchair out into the kitchen and got them a couple of Diet Pepsis. As Brolan sipped his, he decided that there wasn't much alternative to telling Wagner the truth. So, he told him all of it. Her throwing the drink in his face the night before the murder. Finding the body in the freezer.

"She's in the freezer?" Wagner said.

"Yes."

"How about turning her over to the authorities?"

"Right. And guess who they'd blame for killing her." Wagner stared at him.

"I guess you're right."

In any other circumstance Brolan would have been checking out this living room carefully. Especially the video library. Brolan enjoyed old movies. He'd read Norman Cousins's book about recovering from cancer, how once a day you had to treat yourself to pure enjoyment. For Brolan that meant putting his home phone on answering service and getting a big bowl of popcorn and a couple of ice-cold soft drinks and watching some old westerns. He liked particularly the Allan "Rocky" Lane pictures of his boyhood, even though Rocky had ended up rather ingloriously doing the voice-over for *Mr Ed*.

Brolan found himself smiling a lot. He always did this around people with handicaps. He felt sorry for the guy and wanted to be sure the guy knew it. At this point he was not able to see anything but the man's spina bifida. But all the movie icons in this orderly, beautifully appointed room told him a great deal about Wagner's soul.

"I just don't like thinking of her in a freezer," Wagner said.

"I don't, either. But I don't have much choice. Not until I find out who killed her."

"You may have killed her, Mr Brolan."

Brolan stared at him. "Do you really believe that?"

"I'm not sure yet." He paused. "Do you have any ideas?"

"One very good one."

"Who would that be?"

"A former boss of mine named Richard Cummings."

"Why would he kill Emma?"

"So he could blame me. He hates me."

"Why?"

"I took one of his biggest accounts. We both own ad agencies."

"For that he'd kill a woman?"

"You don't know Cummings."

As he spoke, Brolan watched as Wagner straightened himself in the chair. The pain inherent in the movement was obvious on Wagner's face. When he was straightened out, Wagner said, returning Brolan's blunt stare, "Why don't we get it over with, Mr Brolan?"

"Get what over with?"

"Your questions about my condition."

Brolan felt his throat constrict. "Why would I ask questions like that?"

"Because right now a part of you thinks I'm a freak, and the other part of you is wondering why I talk so normally. For a freak that is."

"No, I –"

"I was born this way. Spina bifida."

Brolan sighed. He could imagine the struggle life had been for this man. "I'm sorry."

"So am I. Maybe if I'd had a body like yours, Emma would have fallen in love with me."

Brolan laughed sourly. "I haven't done so well with women, believe me."

Wagner offered him a grin. "You've probably done a little better than I have." He pulled himself up slightly in his chair. "There's no cure at present and very likely won't be one in my lifetime. I've gone against great odds just by living this long. I'm thirty-two, in case you're interested." He smiled again politely. "I'm sorry if I'm making you uncomfortable."

"Well –" Brolan said.

"If I irritate you, go ahead and get irritated. If you feeling like patting me on the shoulder, don't be afraid to touch. What I have isn't contagious, Mr Brolan. And if you make an innocent slip of the tongue and say something you think might hurt my feeling – it probably won't. Not if it's innocent. I remember a next-door neighbour I had once. She was always saying why didn't I 'run over' and have a piece of cake. And then apologising profusely because, of course, I can't run over. Not literally, anyway."

"You're a hell of lot braver than I'd be. I'd be complaining all the time."

"No, you wouldn't, Mr Brolan. Because if that was your attitude, you would have died in your teens. If not before."

Brolan nodded.

Wagner sat up and raised his glass again. Brolan could hear the carbonation fizzing. "Shouldn't drink this stuff. Really eats out your stomach."

Brolan patted his own stomach. He drank too many carbonated beverages himself. "You said I could ask you a question."

"Yes."

"Why the hell'd you get me over here, anyway?"

"I'm going to believe you, Mr Brolan. That you didn't kill Emma. And therefore I'm going to use you as my surrogate." Wagner nodded to a charcoal portrait of Charlie Chan. "I watch a lot of detective movies, especially the ones with very elaborate puzzles. Charlie Chan, for one. Have you ever seen the Hildegarde Withers pictures?"

"Afraid not."

"They're very good."

Brolan grinned. "Believe me, there's nothing I'd rather be doing right now than watching a movie."

Wagner hoisted the glass to his mouth. Ice rattled. As the fake gun had, the glass looked almost too big for his small hands. But he handled it dextrously. After setting the glass back down on the end table, he said, "You're the most likely suspect."

"I wish I could disagree with you."

"Somebody hired Emma to walk into that bar the other night and start some trouble with you."

"You're sure of that?"

"It's on her computer." He then explained how he was able to hack into her system.

"But she didn't give the name of the person who hired her?"

"Afraid not, Mr Brolan."

Brolan stared at him. "You seem to have known her pretty well."

"As I said, I was in love with her."

"I see."

"And she was kind to me, too. Kind in a way that was never patronising. She accepted me, Mr Brolan, for what I am and for my limitations. I can't tell you how good that feels."

Brolan nodded.

Wagner picked up his glass again. He stared straight at Brolan. "You really didn't kill her, did you?"

"No."

"It was very unlike her to do what she did the other night.

Walk into the bar and bump into you that way. Obviously she needed the money; obviously somebody hired her."

"If I knew who hired her, I might know who killed her."

"I agree, Mr Brolan. And so I have a deal to propose."

"A deal?"

"Yes." He sipped his Pepsi and set the glass down again. He rolled his wheelchair farther into the living room, closer to Brolan. "I'm a very smart man, Mr Brolan."

"I don't have any doubt about that."

"And I know a great deal about Emma."

"I know that, too."

"But what I don't have is a body that enables me to pursue her killer."

Brolan found himself drawn deeply into this conversation. "Go on."

"You could be my body, Mr Brolan. You could go all the places I'd go, ask all the questions I'd ask, chase down all the people I'd chase down. Then you'd be off the hook, and I'd have her killer. How does that sound?"

"Very reasonable."

"You'd be willing. to do it? Work together on this?" Brolan laughed unhappily.

"I don't have much time. I need to come up with answers fast. You can help me."

"But there's just one promise I need from you."

"Oh?"

"When you catch the killer – male or female, it doesn't matter – you turn the killer over to me."

"For what reason?"

"My own reasons, Mr Brolan."

"I'm not sure I like the sound of that."

"I need your promise, Mr Brolan."

Did Brolan have any choice? "All right. You've got it."

"Good. Now we can get to work."

Brolan was confused. "Work?"

Wagner rolled his chair over to the computer. When he turned it on, it made an electronic whining noise for an instant; then an orange flare exploded in the centre of the screen.

"Why don't you come over and join me, Mr Brolan? I'll need your help. We're going to make computer profiles of all the suspects we have on hand."

Brolan smiled. That was the first good idea he'd heard since finding a dead woman in his freezer the previous night.

Wagner said, "Why don't you go get us a couple more Diet Pepsis, Mr Brolan?"

10

THEY WERE DRIVING ROUTE 494, out by the airport, when he took an exit abruptly, hitting first an access road and then a gravel road.

"Where we going?" the girl asked.

"Nowhere in particular."

"I'm kinda hungry."

"How about afterward we go to a Perkins'?"

"Can you get pancakes this late?"

"Far as I know."

"I love their pancakes," she said. It was the first time she'd sounded enthusiastic about anything.

She fiddled with the stations. Trying to get the very best rocker. He wondered about her taste. So far she'd tuned past Bruce Springsteen, Michael Jackson, and Elton John. Whom did she like anyway? Then a soul group came on – a pretty good soul group actually, though he had no idea who they were – and she settled back and closed her eyes and gave herself over to the music. He saw her slight body sway in rhythm to the radio. He felt his erection stiffen. Definitely an erotic little trick. Definitely.

In ten minutes they were driving past a new housing development. It was one of those projects that looked as if it had been hurled up over the past twenty-four hours – boxy designs and low-pitched roofs and asymmetrical front facades. Its lights seemed obstinate against the rolling prairie night. Then

61

it was gone, a dim fluttering light on the horizon behind, and they were once again in headlight darkness, dust rolling up and coating the car a rough silver.

It was probably going to be much like the other night. He had the same knife, same tarpaulin. Only this time Brolan wasn't going to get a chance to do anything with the body. Fucking Brolan. Smart-ass. Or thought he was, anyway.

He pulled off the road onto a hard mud path where tractors were driven through a gate in the surrounding fence.

"I thought I was going to do you while you were driving."

"Changed my mind," he said.

She looked around. An owl sang lonely on the night. "I don't like it out here. Creepy."

"I think it's pleasant. No hassles."

"You going to let me see your condom?"

"Sure." He reached in his rear pocket and took out his wallet. Three Trojans in red cellophane crackled as he took them out. He waggled them at her. "See?"

"Okay," she said. She shrugged. "You want to – uh, do it or what?"

"Why don't we just kind of hold each other first?"

"Sure. I like it when people hold me. Sometimes I even have daydreams about it. People just holding me, I mean. Sort of like my mother used to."

"I'll bet she was a nice woman."

"She was real nice." Denise sounded as if she were going to cry.

He reached across the car and brought her to him.

She kissed incredibly well, her little tongue moving quickly inside his mouth. He took her right hand and guided it to his erection. She took it with a hard, professional grip, beginning to stroke him immediately through the material of his trousers. He began gently bucking against her. It was as if she'd grabbed his joy stick and was literally steering his body around the car.

It was difficult to concentrate on what came next. While they were still kissing, while the thought of orgasm began to have overwhelming appeal to him, he brought his hands up from behind her back and fixed them quickly on her throat.

She knew at once what was happening. She tried to say something, to call out, perhaps.

But his hands were tight on her throat – he could feel the muscle and bone of it – and he knew that only after he had killed her would the sex be truly satisfactory.

She startled him by getting one of her small hands up free and raking her fingernails across his throat.

This time it was he who cried out. Little bitch.

He heard the door open behind him – he hadn't thought to lock the doors, a very bad mistake – her taking advantage of the moment when she'd stunned him with her nails.

Then she got her knee and foot into the action, finding enough purchase in the car to start kicking him as he continued to strangle her.

He paused long enough to slap her very hard across the mouth, to reassert his domination, but she continued to kick, and her kicks were starting to hurt – on the shin and two or three times in the stomach.

Then she was free.

Screaming.

Falling backwards out of the car.

Panic blinded him for a moment. And paralysis.

He looked down and saw her hit the dirt path they'd pulled onto. But before he could move to do anything, she was scrambling to her feet and running down the road in the direction they'd just come.

Little bitch.

Jerking the car into reverse, whipping around so he would have a straight shot at her, he started down the road.

She looked as if she were crazy. She ran with her arms flailing and her voice so shrill, she was probably giving herself a sore throat.

He knew then what he'd have to do. He aimed the car to the left-hand shoulder of the road, directly at the point she was running. Even a glancing blow from the car would stop her. Maybe not kill her. But stop her. And he could finish the job himself. Hell, at this point, given all that she had done, he wanted to.

She was smart, the little bitch.

Just as his hood ornament matched up with her spine, she surprised him by pitching herself straight down in the gully running beside the road. She vanished.

He had to fight with the brakes to keep the car from going down into the gully, one of those slow, fishtailing, stomach-turning halts that you're not sure will work till the very last second.

In the splash of his headlights, he saw her scrabbling up the dusty gully on the other side. When she reached the top, she grabbed on to some rusty barbed wire, crying out as her hands were cut, then hurling herself through the strands of wire. She landed with a dead thump he could hear all the way from where he was. But then she was on her feet and running across a cornfield.

He whipped the car as close to the edge of the gully as possible, killed lights and engine, and took off, running.

Down the gully, up the gully, through the barbed wire (not cutting himself as she had), and then into the cornfield proper. With the stalks all dead and lying on the ground, he had no trouble seeing her. His first impression was that she was running to nowhere in particular. Just running to escape him.

But as he bore on – chest heaving, heart pounding, a million vile words for the little bitch filling his mind – he finally saw what she obviously saw.

The twinkling lights of a farmhouse on the low, dark horizon.

Only then did he begin to notice the wind and the rain that was fast becoming sleet.

Only then did he begin to notice that she was outdistancing him very badly.

Only then did he begin to notice that he would never catch her.

Bitch.

Fucking bitch.

Exhausted, he fell to his knees in the dead cornfield, stalks crackling beneath him like snapping plastic.

Sleet washed his face; wind took the sweat from his scalp. He took off the wig and the beard then, right there in the cornfield.

She would report a man with dark hair and a Vandyke beard. She would also report a car that within the hour would be returned to the rental agency.

Nothing to go on.

Absolutely nothing.

Then he felt in his back pocket for the wallet he'd planned to plant near the murder scene (just far enough away that it looked accidental). It was gone.

And then, there in the cornfield, he started laughing. There was panic in the laugh and frenzy, but there was also ironic satisfaction.

The little bitch had taken Brolan's wallet.

11

IN ALL, BROLAN AND WAGNER spent five hours working through the files on Emma's machine. What emerged there – for Brolan, at any rate – was a portrait of a very lovely but very naive farm girl who had soft, private dreams of being some sort of princess. Her writing was filled with references to the great Disney animated movies, *Snow White* and *Cinderella* and *The Lady and the Tramp*. She rented these for home video and watched them again and again. These movies – and the old copies of *Photoplay* and *Modern Screen* from the thirties that Wagner had loaned her – seemed to be her principal reality. About the men she went out with she had little to say. This or that man might be "nice," this or that man might be "nervous," this or that man might be "rude," but beyond that they had neither faces nor souls. They were just what she did for a living and nothing more. A few times she talked about the possibility of getting a venereal disease or even perhaps AIDS but she confided to her diary that she knew that "God just wouldn't let that happen."

Most of the names were there, most of the meeting places. It was a mosaic of the Twin Cities – occupations ranging from department-store head to doctor to policeman. Meeting places that included the Walker Art Centre, the Civic Centre, and the St. Paul Cathedral. Mention of bitter winter, soft spring, fiery summer. A compliment here for a certain after-shave, a compliment there for a well-cut suit. There was a man named Mr Pinkham for whom she developed a great affection. He was mentioned at some length at least thirty times.

Around four o'clock in the morning, Wagner having fixed them eggs and toast, they came to a file marked Advertising. Brolan's eyes did a cartoon-pop. Advertising? What the hell could that be all about?

"You're getting excited," Wagner said.

"Damn right I am."

"I'm hurrying as fast as I can."

"I know, I know," Brolan said, leaning over Wagner so he could read the screen.

The first two pages were prose. She talked about how glitzy she expected the advertising world to be. But for all its surface glitter, she'd found it a noisy, vain, empty world, people strutting around in dinner jackets at ceremonies where ad people constantly gave each other awards for their so-called creativity. John had set all this up. She said this three times. John had set this up.

Brolan said, "Who's John?"

Wagner paused. "Her – friend."

"Her pimp, you mean?"

Wagner said, "I was hoping we could be a little gentler, Brolan. She was a decent woman."

Brolan noticed two things: (a) that he was no longer "Mr" Brolan, and (b) that he'd hurt Wagner's feelings.

"I'm sorry," Brolan said.

Wagner looked up at him and smiled. "You try awfully hard to be an asshole, but you can't quite seem to make it, can you?"

Brolan laughed. "I guess that's a compliment."

So they went on. More adventures in advertising. One

executive had her get underneath his desk and do him while he was talking on the phone. Another executive had her do a striptease behind a huge blow-up of himself which had been used in an awards ceremony, asking her to kiss the blow-up and push herself against it. A third executive had asked her to let him beat her. She had refused.

It was somewhere in this sad melange of hired sex and kinky turns that the name Tim Culhane first appeared. When he saw it, Brolan's heart started pounding.

"Tim Culhane!" he said.

"You know him?"

"He's one of our art directors." He was the man Brolan had looked at videotapes with that afternoon.

"Let's see if there's anything else about him."

For the next twenty minutes they combed the files for any reference to Culhane. Brolan felt a giddy exhilaration born of exhaustion and desperation.

Culhane.

The man was always trying to prove his manliness. He swaggered around the offices. Whenever anybody gay appeared, he immediately started an undertow of innuendo. He gossiped with fat Shirley more than any other person – man or woman – in the shop.

Culhane.

My God, he was a wonderful suspect.

In all there were three more references to Culhane, each about the same. He had asked her if she would take his belt and work him over before they had sex. When she refused, Culhane got vaguely threatening. Then he'd calmed down and had sex with her. She noted that he never once kissed her or was tender in any way. He'd wanted anal intercourse, but when she'd refused, he settled for backdoor. It was as if he didn't want to look at her at all.

Brolan's mind was already racing ahead to his confrontation with Culhane the next day. Brolan thought again of how he'd given the executive post to Culhane's assistant. Culhane and his bitchy tongue were just too divisive to be in any position of real authority. He could easily imagine Culhane hating him enough to...

For a long stretch there was no more mention of Culhane or anybody familiar. Brolan decided to go to the bathroom and splash water on his face. Exciting as the news about Culhane had been, Brolan was getting groggy.

Like the kitchen, the bathroom had been cut to scale so that the four feet nine Wagner could reach things easily. In the mirror Brolan stared at himself. Once again a feeling of unreality came over him. Not even of nightmare. Just... an unlikely and harrowing turn of events. There were even comic aspects to it at certain times. A beautiful woman in a freezer. A man with a file full of scandal on various Twin Cities residents. A man (Brolan) so in love with a woman (Kathleen) that even in the midst of the worst crisis of his life he'd found time to plead and wheedle. At such terrible points in your life, you found out a lot of things about yourself. Brolan did not like very much of what he had found out these past forty hours or so.

When he came back to the computer, Wagner said, "Didn't you mention a man named Cummings?"

"Richard Cummings?"

"Yes. Richard Cummings."

"He's on there, too?"

"Right here." By then Wagner sounded as if he, too, was caught up in the whole process. He seemed happy that he'd been able to find another useful name for Brolan.

Brolan read the next four pages quickly. Cummings was just as kinky as he would have guessed – and just as violent. He'd twice slapped Emma and once, infuriated that she wouldn't do what he wanted her to, had dumped her off in the rain. Emma noted, with one of her rare flashes of anger, that her "friend," John Kellogg, forced her to continue seeing Cummings because Cummings was "so important" and could recommend both John and Emma to other important advertising people.

"How do I get hold of this John Kellogg?" Brolan asked.

Wagner smiled. "He lives over near Hennepin and Lake. He's under the impression – or at least he tries hard to give the impression – that he's an artiste and not a pimp all. He's a real piece of work, Brolan."

Brolan laughed. "I look forward to meeting him."

Brolan went over to the couch, and picked up his suit coat. He shrugged it on tiredly. He'd go home and catch a few hours sleep, then plod into the ad agency. He had a long day ahead of him. There was a good chance that one of the three men they'd talked about that night – Culhane or Cummings or Kellogg – had killed Emma and put her in the freezer.

"Anything you need?" Brolan said.

"No, thanks. I'm pretty self-sufficient."

"You make great scrambled eggs."

"You can thank the chicken for most of the work." The humour died in Wagner's eyes. "I want you to work closely with me on this. It's our deal, remember?"

"I won't forget."

"And when you catch the right one..." He let his voice trail off.

"I don't want you to do anything you'll regret," Brolan said.

Wagner just stared at him. "Let me know how things are going."

Brolan nodded and left.

12

Thursday Morning

WHILE ADVERTISING PEOPLE are no better or worse than any other group of professionals, they've developed a reputation, largely through the media, of being less than hardworking. God only knows how this got started. Walk into virtually any ad agency at any time of night or day, and you'll find demons at work, people obsessed and possessed by their jobs. Ask the art director who worked until three because a client changed his mind on a certain layout and wanted to see a new version by 9:00 a.m. the following morning. Ask the media buyer who's just been given an additional three hundred thousand to spend on TV, only to learn that the targeted states are Utah and Wyoming (not a lot of fun to buy, given their population, their demographics, and their scarcity of stations). Or ask the account executive who's just sat through a very mean-spirited client meeting, the client accusing the agency of being lazy, too expensive, and greedy (But other than that, you sort of like us, don't you? the account exec wants to say); and now said account exec must come up with a new presentation to mollify this puffing dragon, and he's got (he figures) maybe two days maximum to do so. Such execs have been known to sleep on their couches and exist on Domino's pizza for as long as forty-eight hours. So let's put that "lazy" canard to rest. While ad people may not be budding Mother Teresas – but then, look around and ask who is? – they certainly know how to work, and how to work hard.

Two meetings required Brolan's attention. One dealt with a thirty-second commercial one of the account executives was having trouble with. The client had thought it was too slow-moving. After the agency had re-edited it, the client felt it was too fast-moving. At the top of the meeting this morning the account executive, a plump, well-dressed man named Baines, said, "Why don't we get down on all fours and look at it from the client's point of view?" It was the oldest gag in advertising. It never failed to get a laugh.

So, Brolan had Baines show him both versions of the spot. The product was a local restaurant chain. In the first version the people in the spot all looked as if they were having a ten-course meal. The scenes went on too long for the message the tagline was trying to convey – "Fast food prices for real-food meals." True, "real food" implied the old tablecloth and the old personal service and the old well-balanced meal... but did it have to be presented so boringly? With Mantovani strings in the background? And with table candles that you wouldn't actually find in the place? Brolan could see exactly why the client would object to this version.

The second version looked like a fast food spot. No sense of sit-down, leisurely dining at all. So many scenes cut so quickly that the place looked like McDonald's with table candles. No atmosphere at all.

As with most things there was room for a happy medium. As he watched, Brolan made notes on a long yellow legal pad. When the lights came up in the screening room, he turned around and gave his quickly considered wisdom to Baines, noting that some scenes and techniques from number one could be merged with scenes and techniques from number two in order to get a better product.

"You agree with our esteemed client?" Baines was one of those guys who disliked clients on principle, forgetting, apparently, who the hell was paying his salary.

"I do."

"I kinda liked number one."

"Too funereal."

"Too what?"

"Too slow; too sombre. We want them to come to one of our restaurants and have good food. We don't plan to embalm them."

Baines shrugged. "I'll give your notes to the TV boys." Then he quickly changed to his favourite subject: the Vikings. "You catch them Sunday?"

"Afraid I didn't." Brolan was one of thirty-two people in the entire Twin Cities who did not follow the Vikings. Or the baseball team, either, for that matter. As more than one Viking fan had said, there was a special place in hell for people like Brolan. About that Brolan couldn't argue. There probably was. But it probably didn't have to do with the Vikings.

On waking that morning, Brolan's overriding thought had been to find out how it was that Tim Culhane had come to know Emma. And just how far Culhane would go to act out his obvious hatred of Brolan.

On the way back to the production department – thirty minutes before his next meeting – he stopped by Kathleen's office to see if she was in yet. Because she always kept her door closed whether she was there or not, it was difficult to tell.

Shirley, the secretary the account executives shared, sat Buddha-like behind her battleship of a desk. Before her, like treasure she was admiring, lay two pieces of pastry, a strawberry kolach and a long john. The latter was sugar-coated and had a huge white wiggle of frosting on its top. Just what Shirley, at maybe two hundred fifty pounds, needed.

As always, however, Shirley was a testament to what big-and-tall shops could do for their customers. She wore a dark suit of sensible cut (sensible, given her size), a turquoise blouse, and some attractive rhinestones here and there. Her fleshy face was made pretty with makeup. For a woman her size, she was actually damned attractive.

But only if you didn't know her. Shirley, alas, was the agency gossip. Oh, everybody gossiped, even those self-righteous people who said that they hated gossip on principle. Everybody carried stories of who was sleeping with whom, who might be gay, who had a drinking problem, whose clients were slipping away. It was nothing to be proud of, certainly, but it seemed ineluctably human – people, even those who were otherwise decent, even those who were otherwise caring and sensitive people, indulged in gossip.

But with Shirley it was different. There was a meanness, an excitement, a pleasure in her gossip. When she knew something about you, she smirked every time you passed by. And if you had offended her in some way – Shirley was easily offended – then stories about you mysteriously started making the rounds. The past spring an art director Shirley despised had lost ten pounds. Shirley said it was from AIDS. A few months later a media buyer Shirley loathed was said to be having her two children taken from her because of her wild life-style. The woman was forever tainted with the notion that she was a bad mother. And so on. People loved to hang around Shirley's desk and hear her viciously and cleverly work over people who weren't there. In her repellent way she could be quite funny. This gave her a curious power within the agency. Shirley was in some respects the agency's arbiter of taste and standards. You always wanted Shirley's approval; you always wanted to be on Shirley's good side. Because otherwise Shirley would cut you up behind your back. But that was the irony, Brolan had learned. No matter how much you kissed up to her, no matter how friendly she might seem on the surface, she would inevitably turn on you. Brolan always wondered why the people who sucked up to her couldn't see that. That when they were gone, it was they Shirley talked about. Brolan had wanted her fired several months before. Foster had convinced him that she did good work, got along with all the account executives, and was not really a liability. This was one of those instances when Brolan had deferred to his partner. Foster felt more strongly about keeping her than Brolan did about firing her.

As Brolan approached Kathleen's closed door, Shirley said, "Not in." She didn't look up from the paperwork she was doing at her desk. She liked to give the impression that, like nuns, she had eyes in the back of her head.

"I need to see her on the Falcon account."

Then Shirley looked up. Smirking. "The Falcon account. Yessir." Of course she knew all about Brolan and Kathleen.

"Has she called in?"

"No, but she told me she was having breakfast with Ken Gilman." The smirk again. Gilman was the hunky ad manager for one of the agency's manufacturing accounts. Gilman had made no secret at agency parties of pursuing Kathleen. With her eyes back on her work, Shirley clucked, "Third breakfast they've had in the past two weeks. They must really be working hard on that account."

Of course she wanted the satisfaction of seeing him hurt or angry. But he wouldn't give it to her. "Tell her I'd like to see her when she comes in'" he said, and walked slowly away from her office. He didn't want to give the impression he was running. At one point, though, he shook his head. He knew how frantic and

73

pitiful a figure Shirley would make him out to be to others in the agency. "Comes back here ten times a day. Always looking for her. Looks like a whipped puppy. I don't have the heart to tell him that she's screwing everything in pants." By this point he figured that being whispered about was just one of the costs he paid to pursue Kathleen. The other major tally was Foster's growing disgust with him. Foster genuinely saw Kathleen as a predator and saw his partner as jeopardising the agency by having a romance with her. In Foster's world men Brolan's age just didn't walk around lovesick. That sort of thing was done when you were in college, perhaps, but never after.

The second meeting concerned some disconcerting focus group tests. Raylan Chemicals, a major account of theirs, was about to market a new herbicide for agricultural use. Raylan was a respected name in the agricultural community, many farmers having used its products since the days when Herbert Hoover had promised to put a chicken in every pot. But Raydar 2 ("Hunts bugs down like radar") had been angrily criticised by six different groups of farmers in six different focus-group tests, one on the West Coast, one on the East Coast, the other four in the heartland. The objection was both simple and deadly: price. Several competitors had moved into the herbicide market lately and had been forcing prices down. Raylan was getting nervous. Profits had been sliding, and it was thought that profit potential for Raydar 2 would cheer stockholders.

The meeting was held in a small conference room. For most of the hour and a half – while two research-firm guys in Cricketeer suits and bow ties (no kidding) – slogged through page after page of statistics, Brolan stared out the window at the harsh grey day.

He tried to concentrate on the report and recommendations, but how could he?

The conference room opened on a hallway that led from the art department. Through the window to the right of the door, Brolan could see various art staffers bundled up and making their way to lunch. When he saw Tim Culhane pass by, he stirred in his seat. He wanted to run up to the man and throw him against the wall and ask him what he knew about the death of a prostitute named Emma.

Culhane, wearing a snap-brim fedora and a blast jacket, hurried past the glass and was gone. Brolan turned his attention back to the researchers and tried very hard to concentrate. He made it for four minutes, five maximum. Then he gave up entirely.

"Excuse me, Gil," he said to the agency account executive. "I've got to make a phone call. Why don't you take it from here?"

"Sure thing," Gil said, giving Brolan a tiny salute of goodbye.

Brolan thanked the research men and left.

He wished then he'd counted the people who'd left the art department. Back in the small cluster of offices – and the one big open-spaced production office – there were twelve employees. If all twelve of them had left – and it was now ten past twelve – he'd be safe in doing what he was about to do…

Culhane's office was in the rear, with its own door, a mark of privilege. Two director's chairs sat on either side of the door, spots for suppliers when they came to call. Brolan checked the open area. All the stools adjacent to the art boards were empty. A radio played an old Doors song. The place smelled of Sprayment and cigarette smoke.

Before he went into Culhane's office, he tried the two cubicles on either side. These didn't have doors. But they were empty, thank God.

Brolan went back to Culhane's office, looked around guiltily, and then opened the door and went inside.

A Dali and a 'blue period' Picasso were framed and hung on one wall. A variety of advertising awards filled another. Culhane's desk was messy with purchase orders and phone messages. Culhane was notorious for not returning his calls, even when they came from clients.

The place was carpeted and furnished sparingly. It gave the impression of being an order desk in a third-rate print shop. That was the way Culhane liked it, hippie defiance in the face of encroaching yuppiedom. In a way Brolan didn't blame him.

ED GORMAN

Two framed photographs stood on the desk. In one two
blonde little girls grinned at the camera. They were dressed for
winter. One was missing her two front teeth. The other looked
sad in a certain distant way. The other photograph showed a
thirtyish woman in a swimsuit. She was too fleshy for so small a
suit, and her hair was cut so short, it only emphasised her sagging
face. The same sadness in the little girl could be glimpsed in the
mother.

Brolan had no idea what he was looking for. Something.
Anything. He sat down in the swivel chair and started pulling
out desk drawers.

The drawers were as messy as the desktop. Paper clips and
half pieces of gum were thrown in with pencils and erasers and
dozens of pink, cheery phone messages. One drawer held maybe
twenty fast food coupons, everything from Hardee's to
Domino's.

Thinking he heard something, Brolan stopped. Frozen.
He felt like a small boy, sweaty and guilty and shaken.

A male voice called, "Tim? You back here? Tim?"

Brolan recognised the voice of a media buyer named
Meyers. Culhane and Meyers often had lunch together.

"Tim?" Meyers called again. His voice sounded
disappointed in the rolling silence of the big room.

Meyers came closer. His steps were big and flat, like a
clown's. He paused, maybe ten feet away, said, "Tim?" and
then waited a few seconds for an answer, then said, "Shit" to
himself and left.

Brolan went back to the drawers.

All the drawers but the bottom one were the same jumble
of business odds and ends.

The bottom one held very explicit girlie magazines and a
deck of playing cards that made Brolan sick in a very
judgmental way. He tried to believe that anything consenting
adults cared to do was their business, and basically he did
believe that. But he had never been able to quite accept
sadomasochism. The notion of pain equalling pleasure was
not something he could grasp. He always had the sense that

76

this was the sort of experience that could quickly get out of hand. Fun turned fatal.

The girlie magazines were harmless enough if you liked the type. The girls weren't pretty, and many of them were tattooed, and most of them were fat. All of them had their legs spread and showed you their wet pink sex. During the dreary days following his divorce, Brolan himself had bought magazines such as these. Not *Penthouse* and *Playboy*, which he still bought, but the down-and-dirties. At that time they'd held a curious appeal for him – their ambience seemed to be part danger and part sorrow. The women looked like the type who always turned up floating in a river somewhere. They bore no resemblance to Hefner's Playmates, with their radiant smiles and radiant bodies.

Done with the girlie magazines, he set the cards on top of the desk and proceeded to thumb through them. The men and women pictured wore leather get-ups that managed to make them look kinky and silly at the same time. Sometimes the girls held the whips; sometimes the guys held the whips. A few of the photos depicted people with fake blood smeared all over them.

All he could think of was Emma and what she'd looked like when he was setting her in the freezer. Her body cut up so many ways, so many times. He wondered if this was what all these people in the pictures wanted – either to be the killer or the killed.

Down near the bottom of the deck, he found the card that had the power to shock him. Even with a domino mask on, she was obviously Emma. She was being whipped by a fleshy man.

He put the cards in the pocket of his suit jacket, replaced the magazines, and then left the office.

In ten minutes he was inside his own office, the door closed, writing a letter to his partner, Foster.

I've decided, pally, that I need to stay home and get some work done.

I hope you understand.
I'll check in from time to time.

When he was finished with it, he took it down the hall to Foster's office. He folded it in half and set it on Foster's desk.

Then he was in the elevator and on his way to see his old enemy, Cummings.

He knew he was running out of time. He had to start searching. He just wished he knew what he was looking for.

13

HER SECOND NIGHT in the neighbourhood she'd seen two old drifters go at each other with switch-blades. In a way, scary as it was, it was funny, too. The guys were so old and so drunk on Ripple that they could scarcely get around. But they went at each other pretty good, there in a small circle of light supplied by a light bulb over a warehouse door. It seemed the two old farts had been sleeping in the same boxcar – there was a railroad siding maybe a hundred yards to the east – when one woke up, found he'd drunk nearly all his wine, and then decided to blame the missing wine on the other drifter.

In all the fight went ten minutes, and neither one of them laid a blade on the other. Not that they didn't try hard. Not that they didn't want to. They were both truly mendacious sons of bitches, hard-core types who'd probably spent a good number of years in the slammer, and who were dying out their days lost amid the urban homeless. In her six months since leaving St. Louis and wandering through the Mid-west with just her little for-hire body and her soft night prayers to keep her going, she'd met a lot of such people.

Denise thought of all this as she headed that morning for Papa's Place, a grungy restaurant near the sleeping room she crashed in when she had money from turning tricks. In her coat pocket rode the billfold.

She thought again of the guy who tried to strangle her the previous night. She still couldn't decide if the attempt had been real or if it had just been part of getting his kicks. Maybe at the very last second he would have let her go. Maybe.

Papa's was filled, as always, with working-class guys breaking all the rules about cholesterol by ordering three eggs, ham, and American fries. This was the meal Denise liked herself. Spend a few bucks on a breakfast like that, and you didn't have to worry about food the rest of the day.

In the back, in the booths, were the drifters and the hookers, female and male alike. Papa's was one of those very old places with a pressed-metal ceiling, two big wooden-paddle fans to move around the greasy, sluggish air, a wall-length of counter and stools, and a wall-length of booths. Against the back wall were pinball machines that looked kind of neat when they were all lit up at night. Next to them was a jukebox. The guy who ran the place was always arguing with the runaways. He claimed that his real "paying customers" liked country and western. The kids, of course, wanted Madonna and rap music and things like that. Apparently he didn't consider buying a Pepsi or two an hour proper qualification for being a "paying customer."

The kids were dressed for winter. The sexy clothes of summer had been replaced by heavy coats and pullover sweaters. There were ten of them scattered over three booths drinking, variously, pop and coffee. At the sight of Denise they waved and nodded but without much enthusiasm. Denise wasn't a particular favourite. She had a tough time talking about her feelings, and she distrusted almost on principle anybody who tried to get close to her. She'd been close only to her mother. But then her mother died. Denise had never forgiven her.

She went over to the last booth, where Polly sat. Denise hated the name Polly. It didn't fit the girl at all. A seventeen-year-old runaway from Ogden, Utah, Polly was, despite a few extra pounds, a classic beauty. Pretty as Denise was, she envied Polly her regal looks. But Polly was more than good-looking. She was the smartest runaway Denise knew.

ED GORMAN

Polly sat with Bobby, a handsome, dark-skinned boy, who was a favourite of men who cruised for boys. Bobby was seventeen and from a farm town up near the Canadian border. With his fashionable haircut and his cute, knowing face, Bobby gave the impression of being very sophisticated. But when he talked, you could tell he was a hick, with hick tastes. Bobby's big dream was to live in one of those condos near St. Louis Park and have a girlfriend. Bobby was always talking about girlfriends. He didn't want any of the kids to think he was gay just because he went with men.

"Hey, kiddo, how's it going?" Polly said. She always called Denise kiddo. For some weird reason Denise liked it. She guessed it was Polly's way of saying that she both accepted and liked Denise. Polly didn't call anybody else kiddo. Then, before Denise could say anything, Polly said, "You look kinda tired, kiddo."

"I am."

Bobby grinned. "Then throw yourself down here." He held his arm out as if he wanted Denise to slip right inside. She didn't mind playing around with Bobby – he was as nice as he was cute – but right then wasn't the time.

"Bobby, would you be mad if I asked to speak to Polly alone?"

"Whoa," Bobby said, grinning. "This must be serious stuff."

"It kinda is," Denise said.

Bobby shrugged. "They still playing hearts in that booth back there?"

Denise looked back in the booth. "Yeah. Why?"

"Then I'll go join them. Hearts are fun."

The kids played hearts all day sometimes, just waiting for the night and the stand they made on the streets or in Loring Park. Denise hadn't lived through a winter there yet, so she wasn't sure what happened when the snow started flying. Standing outside for long would probably get to be a drag real fast.

Bobby got up, kissed Denise on the cheek, and then slid into the booth behind them.

"You want some coffee?" Polly asked as Denise sat down.

"Huh-uh. Not right now, anyway."

Polly stared at her. "Wow, you really looked wasted." She narrowed her eyes and looked at the bruises along Denise's

80

cheek. "Some bad-ass tried to stomp you."

"Sort of, I guess."

"I won't go with those rough-stuff guys, kiddo. You got to watch yourself. Remember all the things I told you."

"I remember, Polly. I really do."

"Good." She smiled. She had a beautiful smile. She seemed so much older and more mature to Denise. Almost wise. "So, what's up?"

"I just want to ask you some questions."

"All right."

"I mean, they're not about me."

"Right."

"They're really not."

Polly smiled. "They're about a friend of yours."

"Well, let's just say they're not about me."

"If you say so."

Denise snuggled into the booth, trying to get comfortable. Not easy, when the booth was nothing more than painted pine board. The ass quickly got sore sitting on painted pine board.

"Say you were with this guy who tried to beat you up."

"Okay."

"But I mean real serious. Maybe he even tried to kill you."

"All right."

"And say that you managed to get away safely."

Polly nodded.

"And say that earlier you'd picked him clean, you know, taken his wallet and stuff. So, you knew where the guy lived and everything."

Polly frowned. "You're thinking of Chet, aren't you?"

Denise didn't say anything for a while then answered, "Yeah, I guess so."

Chet was a fifteen-year-old who'd gotten himself linked up with a doctor who was really into the rough stuff. The doctor enjoyed being beaten. Really severely. All the kids on the street thought this was hilarious. There was just something inherently funny about a doctor who wanted you to work him over (he particularly liked the sting of black

ED GORMAN

leather gloves). Then one day, when Chet was relating his latest experiences with this guy, one of the kids said, "You should tell this guy that if he don't start giving you a lot more money, you're going to start calling his family and his colleagues and shit like that, you know?" So, Chet took the suggestion and started shaking the guy down. How Chet's life changed. New clothes, access to the doc's convertible, lot of spending money. Even managed to work out a weekly deal with a not-too-bad-motel where he could stay. After a few months old Chet didn't even want to spend any time with the other kids. Considered himself too good for them. He no longer needed to turn tricks. He was shaking down the doctor. Then, after a while, Chet vanished. He didn't even cruise by anymore in the red convertible so the other kids would drool. He was just... gone. There was a lot of speculation. One story had Chet taking all his money and splitting for LA, where he was going to try to model. Another story had him taking off for Alaska, where he had a brother, and the brother had a wife and two kids and a big dog, and where Chet was going to forget everything he knew about the streets. A third theory – and the inevitable one – was that the doc got sick of paying Chet off and killed him in some fashion. A doc could do it good and maybe not even ever get caught. Anyway, Chet disappeared. People still talked about him. Whatever happened to him anyway? You really think the doc stiffed him?

Polly said, "It's pretty dangerous shit."

"I wouldn't ask for much."

"How much?"

"Couple hundred."

"This guy look rich?"

"He had a new car." She had dropped the pretense that she was talking about somebody else.

Polly sat there, with her gorgeous blue eyes and her somewhat imperious nose and her large, erotic mouth, and shook her head. "Kiddo, I don't think you want to get involved in something like this."

"I could buy some new winter clothes and stuff."

"I don't know, kiddo. What if he jumps on you again?"

"I'll take a knife." She tried to sound tough. "If he gets crazy again, I'll just pull the knife on him."

Polly laughed. "You don't see yourself right."

"Huh?"

"You think you're this real hard-assed street chick, but you're not, kiddo. You're just this lost little girl. I mean, I'm not tryin' to hurt your feelings, but it's the truth."

"I've managed to survive so far, haven't I?"

"Hey, don't get pissed, kiddo. I'm tryin' to be your friend. I'm tryin' to keep you out of trouble."

Denise shrugged. "I guess you're right. Sorry I got so uptight."

"It's all right." She reached across and patted Denise's hand. That was one thing Denise liked about Polly in particular. She wasn't afraid to act like your older sister or even mother. She smiled. "So, you gonna forget it, kiddo?"

"Yeah," Denise said. "Yeah, I am."

But of course she wasn't. As soon as she left there, she was going to look up on the city bus map the address she found in the guy's wallet. Then she was going to give him a surprise. One he'd never forget. One he'd be willing to pay for to forget.

After a time Bobby came back and asked if it was okay if he, like, you know, sat down. Bobby could be real shy sometimes, and that was part of why Denise found him so cute. So, he sat down and slid his arm around Denise and kind of flirted with her the rest of the time she was there. Denise liked Polly and Bobby so much; they were real friends. Maybe after she got the money from this guy, she'd do something real nice for them. Buy them sweaters or something.

In half an hour Bobby drifted away, and Polly announced that she had to meet somebody over by the Civic Centre. Denise assumed she meant a trick. Polly was very discreet, sometimes frustratingly so.

Denise sat there alone and finished her Pepsi. Before she left Papa's, she went in the back, near the toilets that always smelled like those scented skunks you hang off rear-view mirrors, and dug the wallet out of her coat. She flicked through several pieces of ID, some credit cards, and about sixty dollars in fives and tens, and found the home phone number listed on the this-wallet-belongs-to card. The phone rang five times, and then an answering machine came on and a male voice, sort of distorted by the machine, said, "This is Frank Brolan. I'm unable to talk to you at the moment. If you'd leave your name and number, I'll get back to you as soon as possible."

Standing there next to the sweet-smelling toilet, working men pushing against her as they made their way back up front, Denise smiled to herself, forgetting all the ominous stories Polly had told her about the boy named Chet. This was going to be easy and maybe even fun.

Real soon Denise was going to have herself some money.

14

NEAR THE UNIVERSITY of Minnesota was a small messenger service that would deliver virtually anything within the city limits. After leaving the agency, and taking along a plain white number-ten envelope, Brolan drove straight to the messenger service and asked if they had a mailing bag. The girl at the counter gave him one; Brolan went over to the customer counter and filled out the address he was sending it to. Then he took the playing card with Emma's photograph on it, circled her head in ink, and dropped the card back in the white number-ten. Then he put the number-ten inside the mailing bag he'd already addressed.

He took the bag back to the counter. The girl checked the address and said, "Three hours all right, sir?"

"Fine. How much will it be?"

"I hate to say it, but it'll be six dollars. There's a minimum, I'm afraid."

"I know." Usually this service delivered much heavier objects. In fact, the girl seemed puzzled – but didn't say anything – about Brolan's mailing something so light. He gave her six dollars and left.

John Kellogg was the name of Emma's pimp. Given his
address, you'd never guess his occupation, which was probably
why he was so successful at what he did. He had a condo not far
from the expensive Shorewood area. Everybody in the glass-
and-stone-and-wood six-plex seemed to drive a new Mercedes-
Benz. Seeing six of them arrayed together, Brolan had the sense
that he'd just entered a car lot.

Fog lapped at his face. Even this many hours from darkness,
the overcast sky set the day in a kind of limbo – not exactly day,
not exactly night. From one of the condos came the sound of
Dvořák, turned up as loud as a teenager would have a boombox.

Brolan went in the first door and checked the three mailboxes.
John Kellogg was in 108. Brolan went up the stairs. Dvořák's
music filled the hallways. He was surprised – even given the
good taste of the listener – that the neighbours didn't complain.
It was one thing condo owners and ghetto dwellers had in
common. Rude neighbours.

When he came to Kellogg's door, he knocked twice loudly.
No response. He listened to the music for a time. It had a
soothing effect on him. But soon enough images of a dead
woman in a freezer chest and images of prison came to him.
You're still the likely choice, pally, as Foster would say.

He knocked again, this time a lot more aggressively.

The guy who opened the door was probably around Brolan's
age. He was slender; his curly dark hair formed a widow's peak
on his forehead; his handsome features were outsize, lending
them a certain theatricality. He wore a blue V-neck sweater with
no shirt underneath, and a lot of astroturf hair spilled out of the
V. His jeans looked painted on. He wore no shoes. Behind him,
in a large room that was obviously intended as the living room,
stood an artist's easel with a canvas on it. Half-finished was a
watercolour of a bowl of fruit. The technique clearly stated that
this man considered himself a disciple of Renoir. The only
difference between the two men was that Renoir had had talent.
Even with his untutored eye, Brolan could see that this was not

a genius standing in the doorway.

"Yeah?" From the glance the man gave Brolan, it was obvious he was not exactly a big fan of Brolan's, either.

"You're John Kellogg?"

"Maybe."

Brolan had to smile. The man's surliness was almost childish. "I'm trying to locate a woman."

The man smirked. "Aren't we all?"

"Her name is Emma."

Something shifted in Kellogg's dark eyes. Not only recognition but some other emotion far more serious than merely recognising her name. Fear? Or was Brolan only finding what he wanted to find?

"Can't help you," the man said.

He started to close the door. Like a good encyclopaedia salesman, Brolan got his foot between door edge and jamb before the man could do anything more.

"I'd really appreciate five minutes of your time," Brolan said.

"You son of a bitch," the man said, glancing down at Brolan's foot.

Just then the Dvořák music swelled. Kellogg frowned and glanced, irritated, down the hall. Brolan used Kellogg's distraction to push his way in.

"Who the hell are you?" Kellogg said.

"You're Kellogg, right?"

"So what the hell if I am?"

"I want a straight answer." Brolan moved close enough to the man to rattle him a little.

Kellogg took a few steps backward. "Yeah, I'm Kellogg."

"Well, in that case, you can help me locate Emma." Brolan forced himself to calm down and looked around again. The room was covered with drop cloths on the floor and walls. The drop cloths had been wounded many times with paint splotches – red, yellow, green, blue. Over in the east corner stood a half-dozen more canvases. These were all finished, and each of them bore the influence of Renoir. Each was just as bad as the half-finished one on the easel.

"I don't know any Emma," Kellogg said.

"You should. You're her pimp."

"What the hell's that supposed to mean?"

"What the hell do you think it's supposed to mean, Mr Kellogg?"

"You're calling me a pimp?"

"Right."

"You bastard." But there was a singular lack of passion in Kellogg's name-calling, as if his honour wasn't quite worth the effort. He nodded his curly dark locks toward the canvas. "I'm a painter."

"I can see that."

You had to give Kellogg credit. At least he could pick up sarcasm. "And you must be an art critic?"

"Afraid not. I work in advertising."

Kellogg was passionate. His laugh was as scornful as Brolan had ever heard. "Advertising? I'm not the pimp. You are."

"Thank you." Brolan was used to being insulted about being an ad man. Almost everybody considered himself morally superior to ad people. Even pimps.

Kellogg looked admiringly at his canvas as he spoke. "So-called writers who write about cereal and so-called artists who design dog-food bags." When his head swung abruptly back to Brolan, his dark eyes were angry. "You're the pimp. Not me. And remember that."

From inside his coat pocket, Brolan took one of the pornographic playing cards. He handed it with a certain elegance to Kellogg, as if he were presenting some most impressive credentials.

Kellogg recognised what it was immediately. He looked as if he wanted to drop the thing on the floor. "What the hell's this thing?"

"Some people you know."

"I've never seen them before."

"Sure."

Kellogg handed the card back. "Exactly what the hell are you looking for anyway?"

"Emma."

"I've already told you. I don't know any Emma."

From somewhere inside the large condo, a telephone rang. "Shit," Kellogg said, shaking his head and glancing at his canvas. Obviously he thought he was quite good.

Without excusing himself, he trotted off in his bare feet to get the phone. Around the corner where Kellogg had disappeared, Brolan got a glimpse of a coral wall behind a beautiful marble fireplace, a settee, and an Oriental rug. Kellogg certainly hadn't gotten those things from his painting.

Brolan strolled over to where other canvases had been stacked against the wall. He couldn't resist the impulse to find out just how bad a painter John Kellogg really was. The first few canvases were just about what he'd expected. Fruit bowls and winter skating scenes done in the Renoir style. Then he came to a canvas that rattled him. Staring up at him, her lovely green eyes sorrowful, was Emma. Not even John Kellogg's lack of talent could ruin the beauty of her face. Like the other canvases stacked there, this one had a paper "sold" tag on the back. It was made out to a Charles Lane.

He had just stepped back to the canvas when Kellogg came back into the room.

"Probably the Louvre calling, wasn't it?" Brolan said.

"You're very funny."

"When's the last time you saw Emma? And don't tell me you don't know her."

Kellogg's scornful laugh sounded again. "I told that bitch not to freelance." He had picked up his brush; he set it down again. "You made the big mistake, didn't you, fella?"

"What big mistake?"

"You paid her for an evening or so, and then you fell in love with her."

"Is that something that happens often?"

Kellogg nodded. "Often enough. That's why Emma needed me."

Brolan took due note of Kellogg's past tense.

"Emma went on her own?"

"On the side. We had an argument."

"About what?"

"Why should I tell you?"

Brolan waved the playing card at him again. "Any idea who's behind these?"

"If I did, I wouldn't tell you." He picked up his paintbrush again. He turned around and began studying the canvas once more. Without looking at Brolan, he said, "You won't be able to pull it off."

"Pull what off?"

"'Taking her away from all this.' That's what you've got in mind, don't you? One of those corny redemptions you see in old movies. She's a beauty, I'll grant you that. But she's also a hooker through and through. She's one of the few women I know who actually enjoys this job."

"I'd like to find her. That's all I'm asking you."

"I haven't seen her for a couple days. Can't help you." Then he moved his brush to his palette and began the process of painting. "Now, why don't you flake off, fella?"

Brolan stared at the canvas. "You must have a special market."

"Huh?"

"Selling paintings to blind people."

"Funny stuff, asshole," Kellogg said.

Brolan left. He had concluded that he and John Kellogg were not in danger of becoming fast friends.

15

DAYLIGHT FADING COMPLETELY NOW, Brolan's next stop was a Perkins', where he had the hamburger platter, complete with french fries and lots of relish. Heart attack food. As he sat in a back booth watching couples of all ages come and go, he started thinking again of Kathleen. Strange, the people you sometimes fell in love with. People who seemed to mean you harm. Maybe that was the appeal. The risk. Yes. Risk. Suddenly, there in the glow of the soft lights, he felt a terrible need to see her, talk to her.

After leaving a good-sized tip (he'd once worked as a busboy at a summer resort; he knew how many people, surprisingly, didn't leave tips at all), he went up front to the pay phones.

She surprised him by answering on the second ring. It was barely six o'clock. That she was home this early on a workday probably meant that she was planning to go out that night.

As soon as she recognised his voice, a certain tension began to play in hers. "Hi," she said.

"Don't get excited. I didn't call up to hassle you. I just wanted to say hello."

"That's nice of you."

"How're things going?" He realised how foolish and pathetic he sounded. So uncharacteristically pleasant and dutiful.

"Oh, kind of hectic actually. I'm afraid I'm in a little hurry."

"Oh."

"A professional women's meeting tonight."

Right, he thought. You like women so much and hang around them so often. He shook his head, depressed about her lies. He wondered if he knew the person she was seeing that night. Miserable as he was, he hoped it wasn't somebody from his agency. It would be like being a cuckold. "Yes, I know how much you like those professional women's meetings."

She obviously chose to ignore his sarcasm. "Maybe we could go out and have a nice dinner next week."

"I'd like that."

"Good. So would I. I just hope it can be pleasant."

"Pleasant" meant friendly, and friendly meant doing everything on her terms. "Of course," he said.

"Well, see you in the morning."

"See you," he said.

Behind him a teenage boy with zits and braces was waiting impatiently his turn at the phone. Maybe the kid had women problems of his own. Maybe there was a tenth-grade version of Kathleen, stony heartbreaker. He smiled at the kid: "Just let me look up a name here, and I'll get out of your way."

The kid nodded appreciatively.

Brolan looked up the name Charles Lane. Or rather, names, plural. There were six Charles Lanes in the Minneapolis-St. Paul directory. He wrote them down in his notebook and then turned the space over to the kid.

Predictably Richard Cummings's silver XKE was still in the parking lot when Brolan rolled in there forty-five minutes later. Cummings rarely left work before nine at night.

Ten years before, Cummings had taken on investors in his business, and this building was the result, a four-storey glass-and-steel curiosity that was all angles, pointing like a rocket ship to the sky. It was the sort of freak that only an architect – and people who pretended to know something about architecture – could love. There was no warmth, no romance, just pretence.

That night, however, its parking lot lights like the baleful eyes of an eldritch god behind the swirling fog and snow, the building had a certain obstinate dignity, its angles breaking up the fog, its interior lights glowing warmly in the cold mid-western night.

Brolan got out of the car and walked up to the building. It sat on its own lot just off Grand Avenue. The other buildings were far enough away that Brolan felt a great sense of isolation.

In the lobby he pressed the lone elevator button that would take him to the fourth floor. He and Foster had worked in this building for three years before they'd had their final falling-out with Richard Cummings. The cleaning people had already done their work for the night, and a memory of scents came back to him as the elevator bore him up to the top floor. They were using the same cleaning solvent. The memories reminded him of his son, who was still in grade school then, and of his wife and how painful their split had been. Time rushed at you and ultimately made no sense. You just got older, and if it meant anything, its meaning was well hidden.

The top floor housed the executive offices. Unlike the days of his tenure, you now needed an electronic card to have access. He stood outside the door wondering what to do. The obvious.

There wasn't much else to do.

He knocked.

He knocked many times but got no answer.

From down the hall he heard a vacuum cleaner burst into operation. Following the sound, he walked down the deeply carpeted hall, around the corner, and down another long hall.

A grey-haired woman with a backside too broad to quite fit into her tight jeans moved a vacuum cleaner back and forth, back and forth. Over the roar of the machine she hummed something faintly familiar. Brolan was careful how he approached her. He didn't want to scare her.

But he scared her anyway. As soon as he touched a finger to her shoulder – she'd seemed unable to hear his three different greetings – she lurched as if shot, whirling on him.

He saw instantly why she hadn't heard him. She carried a Walkman strapped to her belt. Tiny grey earphones stuck out from her head like growths. She took them from her ears with obvious reluctance. "Jes?"

"I was wondering if you could help me get into the offices."

"You a frien' of Mr Cummings's?" She spoke with a heavy accent.

"I worked here for many years. My name's Brolan."

"Oh." She assessed him. She looked as if she couldn't quite make up her mind what she thought of him. He seemed to offer her reasons for dislike and reasons for like.

"I'd really appreciate it," he said as he watched her work through her assessment process.

She stared at him a moment longer, shrugged, then yanked the vacuum cleaner plug out of the wall. She had one powerful arm.

She disappeared for the next few moments. Far down the hall and around the corner he could hear her letting herself into the main office.

He stood there reminiscing. He thought of all the campaigns he'd worked on in this building. His first Clio. His first network spot. His first self-obtained client. Cummings was definitely a prick – no doubt about it – but he was also a genuine ad genius.

92

He regarded advertising the way Hitler had regarded his armies – as his vehicle for taking over the world. He could write copy, direct spots, scope out a print ad layout, create a product song, and design a billboard. He'd had four wives and several children and dozens of clinging, nubile girlfriends, but none of them had ever been as real to him as the ads he created. Hardly a wimp – he was, in fact, an almost psychotic weightlifter – Cummings could stand in front of people and weep openly at one of his own sentimental commercials. He loved showing beautiful little mid-western kids and beautiful mid-western sunsets and beautiful mid-western old folks, all made even more overwhelming by a Cummings musical score, a weepy melange of violins and gorgeous female choruses. He was a man of many and conflicting parts. He was, by turns, brilliant, generous, loving, as well as vindictive, spiteful, and treacherous. Nobody ever left his employment on good terms. He always threw them out – or so he made it appear – even if it had been their intention to leave anyway. He was notorious for punching out employees and clients alike. If he didn't like you, he didn't much give a damn who you were; you were treated to his infamous fist. Indeed on the very night – here in this very office building – that Brolan had resigned, Cummings had finally leaped over the desk and taken a hard swing at Brolan. Only ducking in time had saved Brolan from serious injury. When he lost his temper, Cummings was a crazed fool.

"I won't tell you what he tol' me to call you. If I do, I have to confess it to the priest, you unnerstan'?"

The Hispanic woman was back and shaking her head. "I don' think he likes you too much, you know?"

Brolan grinned. "No, I don't think he likes me too much, either." He leaned in and patted her on the shoulder. "Sorry you had to hear such vile language."

The woman smiled at him. "It's not the language so much. It's his face."

"His face?"

"Yes. When he is angry, he has terrifying face. You know?"

"I know." The woman wasn't exaggerating. Cummings was a

93

man whose face could clearly – almost oppressively – convey his feelings. You never had to worry about where you stood with Cummings. All you had to do was consult his face.

"Thanks again," Brolan said. He walked back around the corner and started up the hall.

Near the elevator the office door opened, and suddenly there was Cummings. He wore a fitted white shirt with a loosened red necktie and blue pleated trousers that obviously belonged to a suit.

"You've got balls, Brolan, I've got to say that for you." Brolan had the impression that this was the old West and that the meanest man in town had just announced his intention to draw down on him.

"How are you, Richard?"

"Don't give me any amenities, you jerk-off. What the hell are you doing up here?"

"I'd prefer talking in your office."

"I'd prefer not talking to you at all." Cummings's jaw muscles bulked. His eyes flared. As Brolan drew closer to him, he could feel Cummings's rage come off him like waves of heat. "Anyway, I figured you'd be out celebrating the account you took from me."

Brolan smiled. "That was a few nights ago."

He had the impression that Cummings was going to swing on him. Instead the man moved backward to the door, smashed it open, and stepped back for Brolan to go inside. "I still want to know what the hell you're doing here."

But before Brolan had a chance to speak, Cummings turned and led the way through the executive offices to his own office far in the back.

The place had changed a great deal since his last days there, Brolan noted. Dark panelling and even darker wainscoting gave the place the air of an exclusive lawyers' office. You wouldn't know the office was in the ad business at all except for a few discreetly placed framed print ads, all of them Clio winners. The buff blue carpeting seemed to get thicker the deeper you went into the place. By the time they reached Cummings's office,

Brolan had glimpsed half-a-dozen offices standing empty, each with a miniature American flag standing on its desk. Cummings must have gotten an extremely right-wing client and wanted to impress the man with the executives' patriotic fervour – exactly something Cummings would do, and without seeing anything ironic or cynical about it at all.

If the other offices looked as if they belonged to lawyers, Cummings's looked as if it were a judge's chamber. The dark panelling continued here, but it was joined by massive built-in bookcases and leather furniture that had recently been polished. It smelled pleasantly of oil. Mounted ashtrays sat next to each chair. They were made of marble and had claw bottoms, the sort of thing you would have seen in a men's club back when Victoria was still chiding Englishmen about their morality. A faint trace of cigar smoke lay on the air. Cummings probably still indulged – two a day, and good Cubans at that, never more.

Cummings hit him directly on the jaw.

It was a sucker punch because Brolan hadn't been expecting it at all, and it was, as you'd expect from Cummings, a hard punch. One moment Brolan had been standing there checking out the cushy office, and the next Cummings was slugging him.

Pinpoints of light – red, yellow, faint green – danced across the sudden panoramic darkness that cloaked Brolan's vision. It wasn't so much the pain as it was the disorientation, the rushing coldness in his nostrils, the wobbling of the knees. Blindly he put out a hand, grasping for anything that would help keep him on his feet. He didn't want to give Cummings the satisfaction of seeing him pitch to the floor. Why help Cummings gloat?

His fingers touched the leather of a chair. He steadied himself.

"Pretty mean punch, wouldn't you say?" Cummings said. He sounded as if they were boys talking about athletic prowess.

"You son of a bitch," Brolan said, his vision beginning slowly to return.

"Me, son of a bitch? You steal one of my biggest accounts, and you call me a son of a bitch?"

Cummings put out a hand to Brolan's elbow. He was going to help Brolan sit down. Wasn't that sweet? Brolan jerked his arm away. He didn't want Cummings to touch him. All his hatred for the man – the man's preening, the man's arrogance, the man's psychotic temper – rushed back to him now. There were times when he could be almost sentimental about Cummings (the man's larger-than-life qualities could sometimes be endearing when viewed from far away) but now Cummings's presence was too real and overwhelming.

Brolan went over and sat down in one of the high-backed leather chairs.

"You want a cigar?" Cummings said.

"No, I don't want a cigar."

"You want some sherry?"

"No."

"I'm trying to be nice. I feel a lot better about you now, Brolan."

Brolan said, "I want to know where she is."

"Where who is?"

"The girl on the playing card. The one in the S&M get-up."

Cummings had been on his way around the desk. He stopped now and jabbed a finger in Brolan's direction. "You sent that, you bastard?"

"Where is she?" The playing card was what Brolan had sent over earlier that afternoon by messenger.

"What the hell's going here, buddy boy? How did you even know I knew her?"

Brolan waved Cummings's anger away. "You're not answering my question."

Cummings went around the desk and sat down. The leather squeaked as he moved around in the chair, getting comfortable. His broad mahogany desk was clear except for a framed photograph of his children and a blank tablet and pen sitting in front of him. Cummings was an anal-retentive where neatness was concerned. He was famous for popping unexpectedly into someone's office and raging at the person for having a cluttered desk. Sometimes Cummings would clear the desk right then, sweeping everything to the floor, even breaking some things with the heel of his shoe. This was Cummings at his worst – the spoiled-little-boy temper, the unfathomable rage – and it was one of the reasons Brolan and Foster had left.

"What the hell is Emma to you?" Cummings said.

Brolan had decided on the way over there to use the story the pimp had unwittingly provided him. "I've made a bad mistake. I've fallen in love with a hooker." He shrugged, keeping himself nonchalant. He rubbed his sore jaw. He was tempted to fly across the desk and punch Cummings a few times before Cummings gathered himself and beat him into a crumpled heap. But he had more serious things to worry about than his ego. A murder charge, for one.

"I thought you were supposed to be making a fool of yourself over the beautiful Kathleen," Cummings said. He smirked. "The stories I'm hearing just aren't like you, old buddy. You were the one who always gave women a run for their money. But Kathleen is humiliating you every chance she gets, in the office and out of it." He laughed. "That's the sort of story I hate to hear. I think of you and Foster like my own sons."

"Have you seen Emma in the past three days?"

"No, I haven't. But why don't you ask Culhane?"

"Tim Culhane?" He decided to play naive, see what Cummings had to say on the subject.

"The one and only. Emma told me about him."

"What about him? That he sees her?"

"That he sees her and that he's into violence."

Cummings opened his desk drawer. In a moment he produced the playing card Brolan had sent him. Brolan's hope had been to rattle Cummings, make him reveal something useful about his relationship with Emma. But he'd forgotten how ably Cummings could defend himself. He was a past master at shifting blame. Now he was blaming Tim Culhane.

"That's quite a deck of cards, isn't it?" Cummings said.

With a great deal of ceremony and violence, he tore the card in half, letting the two pieces fall on his desk. "Stuff like this makes me sick."

"Then why hang around hookers?"

Cummings stared at him. "You mean you hadn't heard?"

"Heard what?"

"About my... problem the past few years."

"I don't know what you're talking about."

He smiled and pointed a stubby finger down to where his crotch was. "I've been having trouble making Harold stand up tall and proud."

"Ah."

"Better to embarrass yourself in front of women you're paying than women you're trying to impress. If you're paying them, they tend not to laugh. At least until you close the door on your way out." Then, obviously uncomfortable with appearing vulnerable in any way, Cummings said, "What're you here for, Frank?"

"I'm looking for Emma."

"Why?"

Brolan shrugged, forced a smile. "I told you. I fell in love with her."

"Then I pity you."

"Why?"

"You'd really want a hooker for a lover, Frank?"

Brolan leaned forward to the desk and stared at the photograph of Cummings's kids. They'd be early-college age by this time. "How're they doing?"

Cummings followed his gaze. "Damn well. Missy's at the university here, and Ted's got a job in a car wash. Good for him. He got sort of messed up on drugs during high school and dropped out. We had him down at Rochester for a while. Now he's doing a lot better. This is the first job he's ever held. As far as I know, he's really off the drugs. And his mother makes sure he gets up every morning for work. He's slowly putting it back together."

Brolan could never recall seeing Cummings quite this laid-back, quite this human. His ego wasn't even apparent in all this talk. Just concern for his children. What a perfect disguise – the ultimate nice guy – if you had something to hide.

Cummings came roaring back into character. "So, how're things with the Down Home Bakery folks?"

"Fine."

"You have no scruples." Ah, yes, there was the more familiar Richard Cummings. Spite in his voice, rage in his eyes. "You started bird-dogging them two years ago, and you've kept it up."

"In point of fact they came to us first. They wanted us to try a project."

Cummings jumped to his feet and brought down a mallet-like fist against the desk. His handsome face was now ugly with anger. "You don't know what the hell's going on, do you Frank?"

"Meaning what?"

"Meaning maybe you won't like what you find out."

Cummings had sat down. He was still angry but not quite so angry. He set his fists on the top of the desk as if they were weapons he was temporarily giving a rest. "I don't know how you two've done it."

"Done what?"

"Gotten the accounts you have." Cummings studied Brolan's face.

"We know what we're doing. We're good ad people."

Cummings challenged him with a glare. "You really think that's it, Frank?"

"Sure. What else would it be?"

"You really believe Foster went out and got those accounts himself?"

"Who else would have gotten them?"

Brolan sighed. It was odd that even after all these years apart, the two men found themselves arguing about the same things. Back when Brolan had worked there, Cummings had always said that Foster was not too smart, just cunning.

"Well, he did it, and he did a damn good job, too."

Cummings shifted subjects again. This was one of his techniques. He was able constantly to surprise you this way. "Tell me, Frank, why're you really looking for this hooker?"

Cummings leaned forward, his eyes fixed on Brolan's face. Brolan recalled a time in eighth grade when he'd made a terrible mistake while serving mass as an altar boy, causing the other altar boy to laugh out loud uproariously, right there on the altar. Father Banyon, big, fleshy, white-haired Irishman that he was, had called Brolan in to his study afterward and proceeded to sit there and stare the young boy down. Not say a word. Just stare. By the time he spoke, Brolan had been so unnerved, he probably would have admitted to anything. He'd never noticed it till that moment, but Father Banyon and Richard Cummings had a lot in common.

"You going to tell me the real reason, Frank?" Cummings said. A smile was tucked into the corner of his mouth, and his eyes were huge and malevolent.

Did he know that she was dead? Was that what this was all about? That Cummings knew that she was dead and had decided to put the pressure back on Brolan? But if Cummings knew, that meant he was the killer.

"What's your real problem here, Frank?"

Brolan sat up straight in the chair, trying to look and sound composed. "I was told you knew her."

"By whom?"

"Somebody I met."

Cummings smirked again. "You always did like being mysterious." He nodded at Brolan to continue. "So, somebody told you I knew her. So what?"

"So, as I said, I've been trying to find her."

Cummings sat back in his chair, knitting his hands behind the back of his head. He looked like an ageing matinee idol who had recently been touched by a bad case of malice.

Cummings said, "You want to hit me, don't you? You're still pissed that I punched you, and you weren't able to. do a damn thing about it. That really galls you, doesn't it, Frank?"

Brolan stood up. Any time a conversation with Cummings degenerated into bullying, the conversation was over. Cummings could snake-charm himself into such a mood, but he was rarely able to snake-charm his way out of it.

Brolan started to walk away. "See you, Richard."

Brolan turned his back to Cummings and took three more steps to the door.

Behind him he heard the rustle of clothes and feet actually trotting across the carpeted floor. Was Cummings going to sneak up behind him and hit him?

Brolan turned just as Cummings aimed another punch at his head.

This time Brolan ducked. The punch missed him by several inches.

"You shouldn't have done that, Richard," Brolan said, surprising both of them. He then sailed a hard fist into Cummings's midsection. He was surprised at all the flab his hand encountered. Cummings looked to be in much better shape than he was.

"You son of a bitch," Cummings said, face red from pain and embarrassment. But he was still doubled over. The punch had taken its toll. "You son of a bitch," he said again, clawing out a hand and trying to reach Brolan.

Brolan simply moved out of his way. "You're getting older, Richard. People are going to start taking advantage of that. People are going to start hitting back."

"You son of a bitch," Cummings said.

"You already said that," Brolan said. "Many times."

Cummings, standing erect now, cocked a fist, as if he were going to strike Brolan. But a hint of leeriness showed in his eyes. Not fear. Just wariness, as if Brolan had dimensions that Cummings had never before suspected.

Brolan walked to the door. "It's always a pleasure to see you, Richard." There was no need to trowel on the sarcasm. It was inherent in the words themselves.

He closed the door gently behind him.

16

THE BUS RIDE TO St. Louis Park took nearly an hour. During it the sky turned from dark grey to black, the oppressive winter-black that Denise hated so much sometimes. It got so dark so early in the late fall and winter, it was as if there were never any light at all, especially during the months of November and December. She always wondered how Eskimos got used to it.

The closer the bus drew to St. Louis Park, the larger and more impressive the homes became. When she was still living with her parents, she'd liked to watch sitcoms from the fifties and sixties. The homes in those – at least to Denise's farm girl eye – were like palaces. She recalled especially the Beaver's. What did the Beav and his dorky brother have to complain about anyway? Living in a home like that. God.

Glancing around her, inside the bus, she felt out of place. The other passengers tended to be much older, mostly women toting home various packages. None of them looked particularly friendly, either. She knew she looked out of place. She wondered if they suspected who she was, what she'd been doing with her life the past eleven months. Going with the men still embarrassed her. No matter how she tried to rationalise it, the word was always the same: whore.

That's the word other people put upon her anyway. She could not quite bring the word upon herself.

The bus driver had told her he'd tell her where she should get off. Sure enough, he kept his word. He turned around and said, "This is it, hon," and pulled up to a dark corner. She took a moment to note how he'd called her "hon." Actually, it made her feel good. She knew it was foolish. To put too much on somebody's calling her an affectionate name. But it made her feel good anyway.

She nodded her thanks and got off the bus, standing on the corner until it pulled away in an invisible cloud of diesel fuel.

She looked around. She felt as if she'd just been dropped off at the last outpost of civilisation. Despite all the big houses, she still felt isolated. Hunching down into her coat, she crossed the street and began looking for the address that was on the wallet card.

It took her nearly twenty minutes to find it. The place was large, angular, and set in a copse of elm trees up on a shelf of a hill. The place was also dark. Completely. It stood out in contrast to all the well-lighted homes on either side of it.

The first thing she did was check out the garage. She walked along the snow-encrusted side of the attached garage and looked to see if there were any cars. Pressing her nose up to the window, she peered inside. Empty. Without knowing why, she felt relief. She also felt cold. The temperature had to be nearing zero. Her nostrils felt glued to the bone in her nose. Her cheeks were already numb.

Having no skills whatsoever as a burglar (actually, a few months back, there'd been a street kid who had a crush on her who'd wanted to teach her about such things), she decided the only thing she could try was smashing a window in the back and climbing inside. She might have no skills as a burglar, but she had the appetites. Maybe the guy had stuff worth stealing. Portable stuff that could be easily sold in pawnshops.

Pale moonlight gave the snow on the hill in back an eerie flat gold colour. She could see occasional dog turds and yellow snow. Either the guy had a dog, or neighbourhood dogs had elected his yard the communal toilet. Dogs scared her. She looked with new fear at the dark windows facing her on the back of the house. What if she got in all right, only to be jumped on and torn about by some pit bull lying in wait? She'd seen a *60 Minutes* report on pit bulls that had made her forever petrified of the animals.

She stood there for a time saying an odd prayer or two for good luck and then realised that this was about the worst thing you could do – ask God to help you become a good thief.

She went up to a window to the right of the door, made a fist of her gloved hand, and then smashed her hand through the glass.

She held her breath, waiting for a burglar alarm to sound. She heard a car hissing by on the street out front, a big aeroplane lost somewhere in the rolling silver clouds above, a lonely dog yipping and yapping in the far distance, and an even more distant train roaring through the white mid-western night.

But she did not hear a pit bull, and she did not hear a burglar alarm.

Even though she knew she was being sacrilegious, she offered a silent prayer of thanks.

Then she set about trying to get into the house.

The first thing she realised was that she was too short to reach the hook inside that locked the window. She had to go into the oil-smelling garage and get a plastic milk case and bring it back to the window and stand on it to give herself enough height. The second thing she realised was that she had to break yet another window and fiddle with yet another hook to actually get inside. So, she had to go through all the terror again – waiting for the sound of a pit bull, waiting for the sound of an alarm.

In all it took her seventeen minutes to get inside. She stood in a large and largely empty dining room. The whole place – from what she could see from there – sort of looked like that... curiously empty. Oh, everything looked nice and expensive, what there was of it, but it appeared that the guy didn't have the money (or something) to finish the job of furnishing the place.

Still leery of a pit bull springing on her from nowhere, she set about searching the house. Once, just as she was standing in the centre of the living room, headlights splashed through the curtains and across the wall. She stopped, frozen, heart pounding, a glaze of sweat covering most of her body.

The man was home.

What was she going to do?

But then, miraculously, the headlights withdrew, a transmission whined in reverse, and the car was going back down the street.

Just turning around. Nothing more.

Her next stop was the basement. She'd found a flashlight sitting on a kitchen counter, and she used it then, easing her way down the basement stairs. A furnace blasted on when she got about halfway down, startling her. The flashlight picked out a large family room that, like the upstairs, gave the impression of crying out for furniture. Instead of curtains, for instance, the windows were covered with sheets and pillow cases.

In other parts of the basement she found a bathroom complete with shower, a formidable workshop area, and a large freezer.

For some reason she was curious about the freezer and was

ready to open it when the phone started ringing upstairs. Suddenly she heard a male voice filling the darkness above her. An answering machine telling people that he wasn't home. She let her hands slide from the lid of the freezer. She decided to go back upstairs, to the bedrooms. Most people kept cash on hand somewhere in the house. Thus far she hadn't found any, true, but the bedrooms were probably a more likely place to hide cash anyway.

On her way through the living room to the staircase, she thought again of sitcom families. Just a little more furniture, and this place would be a palace. How nice it would be to live there instead of a cramped, five-room farmhouse, where every night she'd had to listen to… She thought of her older sister Janice. How Janice had looked that last time in the hospital.

But there was no time for that. She wanted to find some cash… She went up the stairs.

There were three bedrooms on the upper floor. In the beam of the flashlight, the upstairs looked even more desolate than the rooms downstairs. In one she found clothes that still were packed in boxes, along with odds and ends such as hairbrushes and cuff links and shoe trees. In another, she found boxes of books. Here was a man who obviously liked to read. She pulled up one of the books and looked at it, an expensive hardcover entitled *The Great Gatsby* by F. Scott Fitzgerald. She had seen the movie version of this with Robert Redford and hadn't liked it.

In the third bedroom she found a double bed askew with twisted sheets and covers. The electric blanket was still on, its controls still glowing orange in the darkness. The windows were rimmed with frost; she wanted to climb into the bed and get under the covers and luxuriate in long hours of uninterrupted sleep.

In a four-drawer dresser in the west corner of the bedroom she found a small red box that had once contained chequebooks. It now contained cash. More than two hundred dollars. She put the money in her coat pocket and started downstairs.

When she got halfway down, the phone rang again. The sounds were loud, almost eerie, in the big, dark, empty house.

She heard the man's voice say he wasn't home but would call back as soon as possible, and then she heard another voice, the live one, describe how badly he wanted to talk to the man who lived there. The caller said that he knew the man could take his messages off this machine from a long ways away, so would the man please come over to the caller's house ASAP. Then the caller hung up.

Standing in the pooled shadows at the bottom of the stairs, streetlight and frost turning the white curtains to silver, Denise searched her mind for what ASAP meant. Then she remembered; it was an expression her mother had used frequently when Denise was younger. You clean that room up ASAP, young lady; you get your bike into the barn where it won't be rained on, and I mean ASAP.

As soon as possible.

In the echoes of the caller's voice, she could hear desperation and trouble. The caller wanted the man to come to his place right away. Which is probably what the man would do instead of coming back home, especially if he had one of those deals where you could snag your phone messages with one of those little black jobbies.

Which meant that if Denise wanted to confront the man, and tell him how much money she wanted to keep quiet, she was going to have to do it at the caller's address. If, that is, she could find the caller's name and address in the phone book.

At first she thought of the incredible hassle it would be to get back on a bus and be taken to God knew where. It could literally be another three hours. But then she remembered the cash in her coat. She didn't have to rely on a bus. She could call a cab. She had plenty of money.

Keeping the caller's name fresh in her mind by repeating it over and over to herself, she took the flashlight and started looking for a phone directory. After a ten-minute search, she spotted one in a kitchen drawer. By then she'd repeated the caller's name so many times, it was gibberish, the way you could say the word *spoon* or *clock* so many times, it ceased to have all meaning.

106

She found the caller's name and address with no problem, writing them down on a paper napkin she found in the same drawer.

Putting the flashlight back where she'd found it, she drifted toward the back door. In the moonlight the shards of broken glass looked terrible, spoiling the nice, if empty, look of the place.

Shrugging, feeling guilty about making such a mess, she rummaged around in the kitchen closet till she found a broom. Having no luck finding a dustpan, she went over to the green plastic garbage receptacle and fished out a TV dinner cover. She folded the cover in half and went over and swept all the glass up into the fold. It made a fine dustpan.

In ten minutes she had all the glass swept up. All that bothered her then were the holes in the window; bone-chilling night air flowed through them. Ultimately the wind would make the whole house cold.

She realised how weird it was, of course, feeling driven to patch up the same place she'd broken into, but she couldn't help it. Her mother had always taught her to lend a hand when a hand was needed, and one was certainly needed there.

She found some heavy tape in a drawer and then dug out a carton container from the garbage, fashioning two pieces of material that would cover both holes. When she was finished, she stood back and assessed her handiwork. All in all the patches didn't look so bad. The trouble was, they wouldn't last too long. Cold air would freeze the adhesive surface of the tape, and soon enough the patches would fall off.

But at least she had tried.

Going to the back door, she took the receiver from the wall phone and dialled a cab number. She was pretty familiar with cabs. Sometimes johns would pay the cab fare to bring you to different places to meet them. And she liked cabs. You felt kind of regal or special – or at least a country girl did – riding around in the backseat of what was really a chauffeur-driven vehicle. Or at least that was how she imagined it.

The guy at the cab company sounded kind of grouchy. He

said that with this weather, all kinds of cars weren't starting, and so it would be a while. She said okay.

While she waited, she looked in the refrigerator for something to eat. It was a huge new fridge, and all the guy had in it was a dried-out apple, some cottage cheese that was already three weeks beyond the fresh date and smelled like it, and one lone egg that sat pathetically in the back, like a deserted child.

Disappointed, she closed the door and started searching the cupboards. Unless she planned to dine on salt and sugar, she was out of luck.

Then she remembered the freezer in the basement, the long white chest model, like the one her father had always been promising to buy her mother.

Maybe in the freezer she'd find something she could pop into the microwave oven. Something that would fortify her for what would probably be a long night ahead.

She went over to the door leading to the lower level and started descending the stairs, the flashlight chasing away shadows the way a cat would chase away mice caught in a barn.

All she could think about was the freezer and the great stuff that might be inside. Maybe he'd have a few of those burger-and-fries deals that took just four minutes (the way they were advertised on TV) before they sat, steamy and succulent, before you on the table.

She headed straight for the freezer, ready to throw back the lid.

17

FOR DINNER GREG WAGNER FIXED HIMSELF a cheeseburger, cut himself a piece of pumpkin pie, and poured himself a glass of skim milk. As if the skim milk would compensate for the pie and the cheeseburger.

But for once he wasn't worrying about his weight. He was too excited over what he'd found that afternoon on one of

Emma's computer directories, one he'd never seen before. He hated to think about it, but maybe Emma hadn't been quite the "intimate" friend he'd always imagined. After he read this directory, it was obvious that Emma had kept secrets from him. Important secrets.

Just before eating, he'd called Brolan — twice, in fact — both times leaving anxious messages.

After finishing his meal, he wheeled his chair into the living room and put on a new videotape he'd bought from a mail order house in Missouri, run by a mysterious man who wrote very good and very disturbing horror fiction. The man's second book had given Wagner nightmares for several weeks after he finished it.

The name of the tape was *The Falcon in Danger*. Even though the Falcon movies of the forties had been dismissed by the critics of their time to be little more than B-movie action fodder, Wagner found them endlessly fascinating and nearly always charming. He especially liked the ones with Tom Conway, who had replaced his more famous brother, George Sanders, halfway through the series run. Conway was more boyish and vulnerable than the somewhat cynical Sanders, and for all of Sanders's drollery, Conway was the more believable ladies' man of the pair. The only thing Conway couldn't do with much credibility was throw a punch. In *The Falcon in Mexico* he knocked out a man with the worst movie punch Wagner had ever seen. Without meaning any disrespect, Wagner had laughed out loud when he'd first seen the punch. It was that memorably bad.

He watched the new Falcon tape the way he watched all his tapes at night, with all the lights out and only the TV screen providing illumination. He liked the warm glow the screen gave off. Knowing that it was snowy and cold outside and that he was safe and warm inside with a fine movie to watch always made him feel snug and cosy. He supposed it all reminded him of his early boyhood, when his parents had bought a twenty-one-inch Sylvania monster with a glowing frame around the screen. He could still recall how whitely the frame radiated, how soft and pleasant its radiance had seemed in the *I Love Lucy* darkness.

He never would have seen the girl if he hadn't needed to go get another Diet Coke. He had no idea how long she'd been standing on the kerb across the street, leaning against a tree, staring at the duplex.

On his way back from the kitchen he saw her out the front window, through the part in the curtains. She couldn't have been there too long. The bitter temperature wouldn't have permitted it.

At first he tried to dismiss her. She was probably waiting for a ride. She was probably staring at the duplex because there wasn't anything else to stare at. Anyway, she was just a girl, a teenage girl, and she didn't have anything to do with him at all.

The Falcon in Danger proved to be a real treat. It was better than a locked-room mystery; it was a locked-aeroplane puzzle. The associate of a leading industrialist was found dead after the plane on which he was riding crash-landed at an airport – without anybody else aboard, including a pilot. Where had everybody gone? As usual, Wagner made mental note of all the character actors. He liked most of them even more than he liked the big stars. For one thing, character actors usually had juicier roles, and for another, they were fun to follow from one picture to another. The same man might play, in 1942, say, a Mexican assassin, a Nazi spy, and a notorious western gunslinger. His favourite character actor of all was Elisha Cook, Jr., who usually stuck to film noir roles.

After a trip to the bathroom and after pouring another Diet Coke, Wagner came back to the living room for act three. He liked to know how long the running time was in advance and divide by three. It was amazing how most films – especially B-movies – broke down into the three-act pattern.

Before pressing the freeze-frame button off, Wagner pushed over to the window and looked out. He hadn't forgotten about the curious girl standing there, so solitary in the bitter cold.

She was gone.

He looked up and down the street-light traffic going by, exhaust pipes emitting grey-blue plumes behind them-but he didn't see her anywhere.

So, he'd been right. She hadn't been watching his place at all. She'd just been waiting for a ride.

Then he did forget about her. He went back to the third act of the *Falcon* and had himself a very good time. This time he'd even brought along a small bowl of popcorn to munch on. The popcorn had been air-popped and was therefore low in calories. He congratulated himself on his remarkable self-restraint.

The only thing he wondered about was when Brolan was going to call. Wagner was excited. He had some hard facts to offer Brolan, hard facts that might lead to the real killer. He had decided that Brolan wasn't the villain after all. Wagner knew it was foolish to go on a hunch like this, but when you came right down to it, what did you have to rely on but your instincts about somebody? You trusted him, or you didn't trust him. Simple as that.

The third act was a doozy. It was by far the most complex mystery Wagner had ever seen in a B. There were four leading suspects, and they kept Wagner guessing right up to the very last. It all reminded Wagner of a John Dickson Carr plot, Carr being a mystery writer he liked particularly, especially the atmospherics.

Just as the movie was ending, Wagner heard the noise on the back porch.

A less suspicious man might have put the sound down to wood creaking and groaning in subzero temperature. Houses made the same kind of complaints human bodies did in cold weather like this.

But somehow Wagner didn't think this was the case. Hair bristling on the back of his neck, he clicked the TV set off. He sat there in the darkness and the quiet. The only sounds were of electric appliances humming and of a car going by on the street out front.

He listened.

The sound came again. This time he knew for sure that it was not merely the house creaking and groaning.

Somebody was on the back porch.

He wheeled into the kitchen, where, in the centre drawer of

111

the cabinet, he kept a fancy .45, one beautifully blued and pearl-handled. He had always wondered what it would be like when the day finally came – the day when he'd have to use the gun to protect himself – and now he was about to find out.

He eased his wheelchair up to the kitchen door. He listened, waiting; the gun felt both odd and comforting in his small hand.

Denise knew she'd made a mistake as soon as her shoes crunched through the ice on the back porch. They made such a noise, it sounded like a section of wall pulling loose or something.

There on the shadowy moonlit back porch, she stopped, heart pounding. She wished she were back in the big empty house she'd left an hour ago or so. She'd been about to open the freezer and get herself something yummy to eat when the cab horn started blaring. She'd had no choice but to hurry out of the house before the cabbie informed too many neighbourhood people of his presence.

And she was here, at the address given by the man on the phone machine.

When she'd first stood across the street, she'd thought nobody was home. There were no lights apparent on either side of the duplex. But once she'd reached the back porch, she saw the glow of the TV set, faint but warm and inviting.

She wondered if the man who tried to kill her was inside already. But she didn't think so. She didn't see his car in either front or back. She wished idly that she'd taken Polly's advice and forgotten the whole thing. She was too young and too dumb to pull off something like blackmail. It was one thing to think about something like that; it was another actually to do it.

Calmer then, convinced that nobody inside had heard her after all, she turned and started to leave the small screened-in porch. She still had quite a bit of cash in her pocket, even after paying for the expensive cab ride. Enough left to buy a few really good meals and some warm clothes for winter. And then that'd be that; she'd never see the guy again, and good riddance. He'd go back to being one more creep and she'd go back to… she wasn't sure what she'd go back to being, but that didn't bother her so much. She just wanted to get away.

She was just putting her hand out for the screen door when the back door inside was flung open, and a small male voice said, "I've got a gun pointed right at your back. Don't think I'm afraid to use it."

The quality of the voice baffled her. It was male and mature, but it didn't seem to have as much... volume as most mature male voices.

The voice said, "Turn around."

She heard her teeth chattering, and she knew it wasn't from the cold. It was the idea of a gun. Within the past twenty-four hours one man had tried to strangle her to death – or something like that – and another man was pulling a gun on her. She was just a simple little Catholic farm girl. Why were so many people picking on her all of a sudden?

"Do you really have a gun?" Denise heard herself say.

"I really have a gun."

"But I mean, you wouldn't shoot me, would you?"

"And why wouldn't I? I found you on my back porch. I assume you were about to break in."

"But I'm a girl."

"Girls can be dangerous, too."

"I'm from a farm."

"So?"

"Farm girls aren't like that."

A hint of amusement played in the small voice. "Oh, they're not, eh?"

"Huh-uh. Honest."

She realised suddenly how weird this conversation was. She was standing on a stranger's back porch looking out on a backyard silver with ice and moonlight in a neighbourhood she'd never been in before, talking to a guy with a little voice, who (a) held a gun and her, and (b) seemed to find her funny in some strange way.

"If you're from a farm, what're you doing here?"

That was a good question. She wished she had a good answer. She panicked, thinking maybe she'd gotten the wrong address or something. "I, uh, was looking for somebody."

"Who?"

"Just a guy."

"Oh, a guy, huh? You don't sound old enough to have a guy."

That remark kind of irritated her. "I'm sixteen."

"That isn't old enough."

She wanted to ask him what was he, a priest or something? But she kept thinking about the gun. "Do you really have a gun?"

"Right in my hand."

"Will you put it away?"

"Why would I do that?"

"Because guns scare me. My brother shot himself in the leg once, when he was messing around with one of my dad's pistols."

"I'm sorry to hear that."

"So, would you?"

"Would I what?"

"Put the gun down. I'm not dangerous. I promise."

The amusement was back in his voice again. "I guess you don't sound particularly dangerous."

"Really I'm just a farm girl, like I said."

"A farm girl who stands in front of people's houses and then sneaks up on their back porches, eh?"

"Well."

"Maybe does a little B&E on the side."

"What's B&E?"

"Breaking and entering."

"No, huh-uh, honest." She shivered. "Also, I'm getting real cold."

"You weren't cold standing across the street all that time?"

"I kept walking back and forth. I wasn't standing still like this."

"How does some hot chocolate sound?"

"What?" She couldn't be sure she heard him right. One minute he was holding a gun on her and talking about B&E, and the next minute he was asking her how chocolate sounded. "It sounds great."

"Well, I'll make you a cup if you promise me."

So, here it was; the old trade-off. You promise me you'll do all these nice moist things to my body, and I promise you I'll give you something. In this case a cup of hot chocolate. "Promise you what?"

"Promise me that you're not dangerous."

"That's all?"

"Of course. What else would I make you promise?"

"I guess I was just thinking of something else." He paused. "Why don't you put your hands above your head?"

"Like this?"

"Exactly."

"Just like on TV," Denise said.

"Just like on TV."

"And then what?"

"And then turn around very slowly and face me."

"Like this?"

"Like that."

So, she turned all the way around and faced him.

And then – shocked – she saw why his voice was so small. Here was a man sitting in a wheelchair, holding a gun in his hand.

Then he said about the goofiest thing he could say, considering the gun. "You like marshmallows in your hot chocolate?"

18

CULHANE SOMETIMES DRANK in a bar out by the airport. It was a place where the middle management level of advertising people went to sulk about how bad the top level of management was. A nautical motif lent the place the look of a fashionable steak house in the 1950s – a little long on cute, a little short on taste.

Brolan and Foster had come here many times back in the days when they'd been employees and not employers. But as soon as they departed Cummings and Associates, they were no longer viewed by the gang here as reliable. They'd sold out. They were bosses. It was never anything as formal as a dig or a punch in the mouth… but soon enough they detected the subtle but certain way the boys viewed them. And so they started hanging out where top-level management folks were supposed to go. It was a caste system rigid as India's, except nobody would admit it existed.

Brolan found Culhane's ten-year-old Mercedes sitting in the lot. Despite the recent cleansing snow, the silver car still needed a wash.

Brolan got out of his car and stood for a moment taking fresh night air into his lungs. Several times that night he'd thought of giving this all up and just calling the police and telling them what had happened. Maybe they'd believe him after all. The problem was that having a woman in his freezer did not increase his credibility as a witness.

Taking the fresh air deep, he thought again of Emma's portrait. He was beginning to wish he'd known the woman. Some intimate knowledge of her might help him as he tried to figure out who'd murdered her.

Feeling refreshed, even a little mean in the face of all the forces against him, Brolan went inside.

The nautical decor was covered up with holiday decor. An electric Santa Claus peered out from a buoy, and mistletoe hung from an anchor. This was from last year. The place smelled of cigarettes and whiskey.

Brolan had a straight scotch while his eyes adjusted to the gloom. He didn't see Tim Culhane anywhere. After a time he went to the men's room. The big clean white room was empty, nobody at the urinals, no feet sticking out beneath the stall doors.

He went back and had a second scotch. This time he asked the bartender – who looked somewhat familiar – if he'd seen Tim Culhane.

The bartender winked at him. Brolan hated winks. "Think he got lucky."

"Oh?"

"Brought some real babe in here; then they took off."

"His car's still out in the lot. That's why I asked."

The bartender winked again. "Probably took her car. Is Tim boy lucky or what?"

Brolan decided to finish his drink slowly. Sometimes it felt good to stand alone at a bar and think about things. There was humanity all around you, reassuring in its way, and yet you weren't forced to be a part of it. He listened to an ancient Beatles ballad, Lennon slightly too sweet for Brolan's taste but the song – "Norwegian Wood" – comforting in its smooth line of melody. At this moment even the corny decorations looked nice. He allowed himself the luxury of forgetting the spot he was in. He wanted to stay all night like this. There'd be other old songs on the jukebox. He could forget .

He felt the cold air on his back when the front door opened. A young couple came in. They had snow on their heads and shoulders. They looked enviably happy. The cold air reminded him again of what lay ahead. He no longer paid attention to the Beatles; he downed his drink and started for the front door.

Earlier the snow had been light, scattered flurries. By this time it was a serious snow, making the Expressway slick, sticking to the contours of parked cars. Oddly enough it did not seem quite as cold.

He was just looking over Culhane's car – wondering where Culhane might have gone – when he saw headlights start down the steep incline to the parking lot. He thought nothing of them, just continued on to his own car.

After brushing off his front and back windows with his hand – the moist snow was heavy and white as paste – he slid in behind the wheel and closed the door. And it was then he got his first good glimpse of the car that had just pulled in.

It was a new silver Cougar. It was Kathleen's car.

Obviously the occupants hadn't seen him – neither Kathleen nor Culhane – and so they sat in her car talking and smoking cigarettes. Arguing, really. Or that's what it looked like anyway.

He sat there feeling stupid and embarrassed for all three of them. He should have known that eventually Kathleen would

117

get around to the office heart throb.

In high school he'd dated a girl ('serious' dating for him; something less for her obviously), and one night, with no warning, he'd been walking along a river path and found her making out passionately with a senior boy. He'd never forgotten the sick and helpless feeling of that terrible moment. It had taken long and solitary weeks to recover, and even then he no longer trusted women the way he once had. He saw the power they had over him, and he knew he had to be wary.

At some point their argument ended, the one Kathleen and Culhane were having, because she leaned over and pulled him to her gently and kissed him.

Brolan could smell her perfume, taste her lipstick, feel the silk slip beneath her dress. He dropped his head, unable to watch anymore.

After a time he heard a car door open. He looked up. Culhane was leaving. He still leaned half-in, half-out of the Cougar. They were talking now. Intense talking. She took his hand and kissed it, something she'd done many times with Brolan. Even in the wan interior light she looked beautiful, far more beautiful than Brolan wanted her to.

Culhane went over to his car, got a scraper, and proceeded to clean the windows. She gave him a little beep and then left the parking lot. Brolan waited till she got to the top of the incline that lead to the access road and then the freeway. Then he went after her.

It took him twenty minutes to be sure where she was headed: home. A house in the North Oaks area. In the meantime they both slid around on the snow and ice. Brolan must have passed ten fender-benders. For all its vaunted winter Minneapolis went to hell during the season's first bad snow, as if its citizens had never seen the white stuff before and had no idea how to drive on it. Miami couldn't have responded much worse. Unlike Miami, however, what made Minneapolis tolerable was that it was one of the world's great cities, big but not too big, modern but with traces of its prairie history and dignity still in evidence, proud but not disgustingly so à la San Francisco. Wherever he went on vacation, Brolan was always happy to be back in the loving arms of the Twin Cities.

Even after they left the freeway – Brolan keeping a quarter-mile behind her – the fender-benders continued, red-and-blue emergency lights splashing bright light on white snow. The cops looked fatigued already. They'd have a long night, probably one or two fatalities.

Only when she reached her own block did Brolan speed up, his car sluicing through the heavy slush. As she pulled into her garage at the side of the Victorian that she was house-sitting all these years while some rich college friends of hers 'did' Europe, Brolan came right in behind her.

Anger overwhelming him, he twisted off the ignition key and jumped from the car. He didn't get far. Just as he was about to enter the garage, the automatic door started descending in jerky fashion.

He had to stay out in the night until she left the garage. With only moonlight as illumination, the neighbourhood took on an appealing, Christmas card look. Other Victorians could be seen silhouetted against the dark blue, starflecked sky, their towers and gables and patterned masonry chimneys nostalgic symbols of a gentler time.

She was as angry as Brolan. "Did you used to follow your wife around this way?" she said, emerging from the garage.

In the gloom he could not make out the details of her face, But he smelled her cologne and saw the appealing shape of her body inside her dark coat.

"Why the hell didn't you tell me about Culhane?" he said.

"Probably because it isn't any of your business."

So, there you had it. She wasn't even going to deny anything. Offer any excuses.

She said, "I want to go in." She seemed beat. "Alone." He wanted to strike something. Curse something. He wanted to tell her how betrayed he felt, but what was the sense of whining, when she so obviously didn't care. He also wanted to tell her about Emma.

When he thought of Emma, he realised how dangerously he

ED GORMAN

was giving in to himself. He should be trying to locate Charles Lane, the man who'd bought the painting of Emma from her pimp. Surely a man willing to pay for a painting could tell him something about Emma.

She said, "I'm sorry, Frank."

He had never heard her apologise before, for anything, and the sound of it surprised him.

She came over three steps, her heels cracking a membrane of ice as she moved. She took him by the coat and tugged him gently to her. In the moonlit gloom, both of them dark figures against the white snow, she kissed him tenderly on the lips. He tried not to think about her kissing Culhane less than half an hour before.

"Some things just don't work out," she said. "It's not anybody's fault particularly. It's just – they don't work out."

He had no idea what to say.

"I don't blame you for being angry with me, Frank. I don't even blame you for hating me. But I wish you'd try to believe me that I put everything I had into this relationship. It's just – we're different people, Frank. You want to settle down and get married again, and I understand that. But I'm younger than you, and I'm not ready for that. Not yet anyway. Maybe if we'd met a few years later –"

She left the thought unfinished.

At the mention of age Brolan felt foolish. Rather than her lover, he now felt as if he were merely some foolish older man who'd been pestering her, one of those pathetic men who embarrass themselves over young women.

He turned and started back to his car.

She grabbed his sleeve. "I'd like you to come in."

"What?"

"For a drink. I don't want to leave it like this."

"I don't think so."

But when she pulled him closer, he felt overwhelmed, felt love and lust equally, unable to stop himself.

"Please, Frank. Just this one last time."

He was trying not to read too much into her tone, but he

120

couldn't help but feel that she was inviting him to go to bed with her.

He started to say no again, but this time she kissed him full on the mouth, and he knew there would be no backing away. He felt helpless again, the way he had with his first high school girlfriend. It was a perfect fusion of pleasure and pain.

19

DENISE NOT ONLY HAD HOT CHOCOLATE, she also had a powdered doughnut and a ham sandwich on rye bread, with hamburger dills and mustard, and she had a tall glass of fresh skim milk. During all of which – or around which, actually – talking with her mouth full, she told him all about it. Everything. The guy in the wheelchair. Which was real weird because not even with the counsellor at the runaway shelter had she told everything. She'd skipped over the part, for example, where her dad got her older sister pregnant and where the sister had a breakdown and went to a mental hospital, where she wrote forlorn letters; and then Dad tried stuff on Denise, but Denise wouldn't let him, though she finally had to leave home to stop him, and how Dad always said it was Mom's dying that had made him this way, that he wouldn't have touched either Denise or her older sister if only he had a regular wife, like every other regular farmer he knew, and how it wasn't wrong anyway, really, because it was about love, it wasn't about rutting, groaning animal sex; it was about love, and who loved you more than your father (of course he was shit-faced whenever he started rolling along on that particular rationale), and by the time he was done trotting out his explanation for why he behaved the way he did, you started to get the idea that maybe by humping his own daughters, he was doing them a favour or something, for God's sake.

Anyway, Greg Wagner, the guy in the wheelchair, listened to it all, never once getting glassy-eyed with boredom or smirking with superiority the way most people did. She even told him about the sleeping room she had and how everybody around her was a junkie – throwing up and sobbing on those long black nights when they'd had too much or not enough – and how, even though she didn't exactly believe in God anymore, she still said her prayers.

He said, "That's what I do, too."

"You don't believe in God, either?"

He shrugged his shoulders. "I guess not."

"But you still pray?"

"Yep. Because I figure it can't hurt."

And for some reason that cracked her up – she felt giddy, as she had the few times she'd smoked marijuana – just the way he said it.

And then he said, "You know something?"

"What?"

"I really like you."

She grinned. "You know what?"

"What?"

"I really like you, too."

"But guess what you could do to make me like you even more?"

"What?"

"Tell me what you were doing on the back porch."

She rolled her eyes. "Looking for this dude who tried to kill me."

"Kill you? Are you serious?"

"Yeah." She hesitated. "You know how I told you that I sometimes – you know, like, do the street-walking thing."

"Right. I remember that."

"Well, last night this dude picked me up and – well, he takes me out into the country, see, and I think he's going to try and do something really kinky, but what he does is, he tries to kill me. Tries to get his hands around my throat and choke me."

"God. Weren't you scared?"

"Terrified."

"So, what did you do?"

122

So, she told him all about it. Admitted lifting the guy's wallet; running till she was safe; talking to Polly about should she squeeze him for some money.

"What's the guy's name? In the wallet, I mean?"

"Brolan," she said. "Frank Brolan."

"Oh, it couldn't be!"

She was almost shocked by Greg's adamance. "Really?"

"He's a very nice guy," Wagner said. He kind of scootched himself up in his wheelchair. She could see that he was excited. But not in a good way. "What'd he look like?"

"The guy last night?" Wagner nodded.

"Oh, I don't know. Kind of ordinary. He had a beard."

"Brolan doesn't have a beard."

"Oh, well this guy did."

"See," Wagner said. "I told you it wasn't him."

She decided, at least for a time, to change the subject. Let Wagner calm down a little. It was as if she'd called one of his best friends a dirty name.

She looked around the room at all the mementoes of thirties movie stars. She loved stuff like this. Whenever she was staying somewhere that had cable, she always watched the Fred Astaire and Ginger Rogers movies. She loved how they danced. Ginger was so elegant, the way Denise wished she herself was.

There on the glass coffee table was a press book for a Betty Grable movie called *Mother Wore Tights*. Next to that was a colour postcard that showed the Cathay Circle Theatre in Beverly Hills on the night of April 4, 1936. How beautiful and sleek the fancy cars looked; how beautiful and sleek the movie stars themselves looked. The beams of floodlights criss-crossed against the soft spring night. Hundreds of people stood swooning as movie stars emerged from limousines to the bursting intensity of flashbulbs.

"Boy," Denise said. "You've got a neat place here."

"Thank you."

"And I've never seen so many tapes." She nodded to his videotapes. "Do you have Ginger Rogers?"

He smiled possessively at his tape collection. "Do you prefer Ginger Rogers the singer-dancer in *Shall We Dance*? or do you prefer Ginger Rogers the serious actress in *Kitty Foyle*?"

"She was a serious actress?"

"Yes, and a good one."

"Really?"

He smiled again. She got the feeling that he thought she was kind of naive, but that he found it endearing. He wasn't like a john. She wasn't trying to please, but she seemed to be pleasing him anyway. "Really," he said.

As he arranged himself in his chair once more, getting comfortable, she said, "Would you mind if I asked you about – you know, why you're in the wheelchair and all."

"Be my guest."

"I'm not trying to be rude."

"I know."

"Were you born that way?"

"Yes. And I was lucky."

"Lucky?"

He laughed. "Well, not lucky-lucky but luckier than the people who had spina bifida before I did. People like me didn't used to live very long. Not until thirty years ago."

"What happened then?"

"Somebody was kind enough to invent the brain shunt, which drains the cerebral spinal fluid. It allowed us to be reasonably self-sufficient and to live a lot longer."

"I'm glad they invented that, then."

He shook his head. "I keep thinking about Brolan."

"You really like him, huh?"

"Yeah. He seems like a real nice guy – and he's in a lot of trouble. Somebody's really trying to make him look guilty." He sounded as if he wanted to go on, say more, but he didn't.

She said, "You really don't think it was him last night?"

"Who tried to kill you? No."

"But why would somebody do that, then? Pretend to be him, I mean?"

"I'm not sure. Neither is Brolan."

Unable to help herself, she yawned. The warmth of the place, the comfort of the recliner in which she sat, had made her tired after such a long day of tension.

He said, "Would you like to watch a movie?"

"Right now?"

"Sure. We're waiting for Brolan to contact me. We may as well have some fun doing it. What kind of movie would you like to see?"

"You want me to choose it?"

"Why not? You're my guest, aren't you?"

"Then you're not mad at me – for being on your back porch?"

"Not anymore. I was. But not anymore." He nodded to the tape library. "Why don't you go pick one?"

"God, you're really nice."

"So are you."

She got up and went over to the tapes. You could tell by the way that he had everything alphabetised and colour coded that these movies were his life. He was a lot more than just a guy in a wheelchair. He was warm, and he was funny, and he was smart, and he was generous. Somehow, being in this place was like being in a retreat of some sort, a place where people couldn't get to you and hassle you and hustle you. And it was because of him – because of the careful, loving way he'd put this place together, layer after layer of things he loved, to protect him from a world that saw him as a freak. Having always felt like a freak herself, she knew just what he was doing.

"Hey, you've got *Cat People*," she said.

"You like that?"

"Yeah. It's really spooky. I saw it on cable."

"The man who produced it was named Val Lewton. He made some great horror pictures."

"Could we see that, *Cat People*, I mean?"

"Simone Simon? You bet."

"How come she had the same first name and last name?"

He laughed loudly at that one. "I'm afraid that's one of those great Hollywood mysteries that we mere mortals will never know."

She took down *Cat People* and handed it over to him. He zipped across the hardwood floor and put the tape in. "They

125

really screwed it up when they remade it," he said. "Lots of blood and guts. And for no good reason. Did you ever see it?"

"I wanted to. This was back when I still living at home. But my dad wouldn't let me. He thought it would be too sexy."

Greg Wagner looked at her, hitting the pause button on the VCR. "When's the last time you saw your sister?"

Denise felt sad. Whenever she thought of her sister, all she could imagine were stark white walls and bars on the windows and long, long hypodermic needles and people in small rooms lying on beds and sobbing and sobbing.

"They took her to a mental hospital. I've only been there a couple of times."

"How come?"

"Rochester's a long way away, I guess."

"Would you like to see her?"

"Sure."

"Good. Why don't we go up there next week?"

"Are you serious?"

"Sure, I've got this friend who's got spina bifida, too, except he's got this big Buick specially laid out so he can drive it. He loves to drive. He'll give us a ride. How would that be?"

"That would be great!"

"Good, consider it done." He turned back to the VCR and punched up the tape. "And now," he said, "for the mysteriously-named Simone Simon."

Denise plopped herself down in the recliner again and prepared herself to watch one good movie.

20

THE MOTEL WAS out past the University, where Washington Avenue intersects with University Avenue. It was modern and brick, with more than a hundred units, and designed to resemble an apartment house. On the west side was a small bar where a sing-along piano (which told you something about the age and the inclination of the clientele) was played five nights a week by a chunky woman in a sequinned gown and at least five huge costume jewellery rings. She preferred songs of the forties (having always had a mad crush on Dick Haymes), but usually relented and played stuff from the fifties, Fats Domino ballads such as "Blueberry Hill" being the most popular.

He knew all this because he'd been inside a few times himself.

That night, however, he was standing in the shadows beneath the overhang by the parking lot. In the blowing snow, the red neon sign over the bar's door was blood red. He had been there fifteen minutes, waiting for her, the hooker who came there on the nights when she wasn't working. The people inside didn't know she was a hooker, of course. They were too respectable even to think about things like that except in a joking way. No, they spent more time contemplating dentures and trusses and support hose than they ever did hookers.

Around nine-thirty she came out. She was tall, and she was drunk, which made for an interesting combination, because instead of just walking, she tottered, like a too-tall building that was soon going to fall over. She'd be just the kind of driver you'd want on slippery roads. She'd probably kill half a dozen people, including herself. Hell, he wasn't going to commit murder. He was going to perform a public service.

He left the shadows of the overhang and fell into step with her. "Slippery out here, isn't it?" he said, taking her elbow.

She had tried dutifully to cover her age with makeup, but the eye pouches were getting too pouchy, and the cheeks too cheeky for that. For somebody as drunk as she was, she sure looked sad. What the hell had ever happened to happy drunks anyway, the sort who wore lampshades and kissed everybody in sight?

"Am I s'posed to know you?"

"I'm just a gentleman trying to help a lady."

She stopped, sliding a little before coming to a complete stop in the icy parking lot. He knew which car was hers, the ten-year-old Ford over in the east corner beneath the purple glow of the sodium lamp.

"I'd like you to take your hand off me," she said. "Like you said, I'm a lady."

"Oh, yes, you are. A lady. A very special lady. A lady for hire."

"Wha's tha s'posa mean?"

From inside his coat he took the crisp new hundred-dollar bill. Even in the blowing snow – which was now beginning to freeze on both their face – she could see what it was. If you drove a car like hers, you obviously weren't used to seeing crisp new hundred-dollar bills very often.

With a gloved hand she made a pass at the hundred. "I get the money first."

"Of course." He nodded to her car. "Why don't we walk over there?"

She eased up a little. Apparently knowing what he actually wanted made her more trusting. "You shoulda come inside."

"Oh, why's that?"

"Doris was playin' a buncha Hawaiian songs. You know, like a lotta songs Elvis sang in *Blue Hawaii*. Stuff like that. You like Elvis?"

"Very much."

They reached her car. Even from there you could hear the piano bar. From this distance the red neon sign looked even bloodier through the tumbling snow.

She leaned over to open the door, and once again she almost slipped and fell.

He grabbed her by the hips. By now his face was frozen. He had the sniffles.

"Why don't you let me do that?" he said.

"'S my car."

He didn't pay any attention; He put his hand on the door handle and opened up the car. "Why don't you sit down? I'll clean off the windows for you."

"I ain't knockin' nothin' off. Full price."

She was such a dignified woman. "I wouldn't expect you to knock anything off."

She glared at him and got inside, cracking her head on the door frame as she did so.

He smiled to himself. Maybe he wouldn't have to kill her.

Maybe she'd kill herself.

At first he tried to scrape her windows off with just his glove, but that didn't work because the snow was freezing into clumps of ice.

"Excuse me," he said, leaning in past her and grabbing a scraper-brush she had on the back seat.

He went back to work. It took him five minutes to do all the windows. When he was done, he was breathless and freezing.

He went around and got in on the passenger side of the car. She had the heater going. It was as loud as a B-52. She had Jerry Vale on the radio. She was smoking a cigarette. Despite the freezing temperature the car smelled damp and mildewy. He suspected it had been burned once and then tricked up to sell on the used car market.

"This is some beast," he said.

"You don't like it, you can always get out."

"Just making a joke."

"Well maybe I don' fin' your jokes so funny."

"My apologies."

"You wan'me to blow you or what?"

"Just like that, huh?"

"You wanna fall in love or somethin'?"

"Here."

He guided her hand to his crotch. Or almost did.

She put out her hand, palm up. "Cash, buster."

He stared at her for a long moment. Cash, buster. Jesus. Did people still really say stuff like that? He reached into his coat and took out a ten.

"Hey," she said. "That was a hunnerd when we were outside."

"Inflation."

The interior of the car was dark. He couldn't see anybody anywhere in the parking lot. The wind was a pisser. It was like being on the tundra. He wished he was with somebody he really wanted to hump. It would be fun to snuggle up and do it with your clothes on and then get really sweltering from body heat.

He came up very quickly with the knife and put it exactly in the centre of her right eye.

She cried out and writhed as if she were a madwoman that no number of men could hold down. When he jerked the knife out, she covered her eyes with her hands but blood was gushing so fast and hot that it ran through her fingers.

He next put the knife where he judged her heart to be, twisting the blade as he put it in her. His gloves were already soaked. A smell of hot metal – the taint of dark red-brown human blood – filled the car. He thought she might also have already started evacuating her bowels, too. This was no fun at all. He wanted to get out of here as soon as possible.

She grabbed him by the shoulder and sank her teeth into his neck, shrieking as she did so.

My God, he wondered as he turned around to get some leverage and push her away, what was this bitch anyway, a vampire?

She broke the skin.

He knew this right away.

Broke the skin. My God. He thought of all the diseases he could get.

He grabbed her by the hair and tried to yank her head back, get her teeth out of his flesh. But no matter how hard he yanked, her teeth were still in there.

Pain now started radiating from his neck down through his shoulder and into his arm.

Frigging bitch.

It was difficult to get any purchase in the cramped car but after wriggling around, he was able to cock his arm and then land a strong one right on the side of her head.

She slumped over instantly, and he knew she was dead. Biting him had taken all her waning life force.

The stench was incredible.

Jesus.

He was about to open the door and flee when the headlights swept over him, coming up on his side of the car. His first impression was that the big-ass Cadillac was going to slide right into him, unable to stop on the ice.

He braced himself for the collision. Then he started thinking of all the implications of a crash, even a fender-bender. Police reports being chief among them.

The Caddy came seven, six feet away. Still sliding. He could see faces inside it. Two fat guys wearing Shriner fezzes. Two fat women in the backseat shouting warnings to the driver.

Four, three feet. Still sliding.

He closed his eyes and looked straight ahead, waiting for impact.

He counted to five and opened his eyes again.

The Caddy had stopped maybe a foot from his door.

He could see the people really well. They looked even fatter and even drunker. The men looked even sillier in their fezzes.

Their headlights, on downbeam, still splattered a warm gold glow over the side of the dead woman's car.

On the edge of that glow he could hear a car door opening, and see a tall, portly man come struggling his way across the ice up to the car.

"Darn close call there," the man said. He looked to be in his fifties. He was loud. "Darn close. Sorry if I scared you."

Now that the man was leaning in a little ways, he had to sit just so, so that the man couldn't see the dead woman in the front seat.

"It's all right," he said.

The man nodded to the bar. "Why don't you come inside? We'll buy you a drink."

"Not necessary."

He could see that the man was sniffing around. The dead woman reeked. Maybe he couldn't see her, but he could smell her.

The man sniffed once more and then stood up straight.

His fez clung to his balding scalp at a precarious angle.

Through the opaque effect of the snow, the man resembled Oliver Hardy. Maybe he wasn't a Shriner at all but a son of the desert.

"You sure fella? Hell, we'll probably buy you a lot more drinks than one. We really shook the girls up in the backseat. Our wives, I mean."

131

"No, thanks. That really won't be necessary."

"Up to you." He gave a jaunty fat-handed salute off his fez. "Night, then."

"Night."

He took his fez and went back to his Caddy.

The Caddy was moved down closer to the entrance of the bar. Four of them piled out and went inside. When they opened the door, the piano bar sounded very loud on the snowy midwestern night.

His breathing came in ragged knots. He was saturated with her odours. He wanted to vomit. He reached a gloved hand up and touched the part of his neck where she'd sunk her teeth in. It hurt badly. He was worried about infection.

When he could see that nobody was coming, he got out of the car and walked around to the driver's side.

When he opened the door, he could see in the dim light from the overhead that her blood had soaked through the seat cover entirely on the driver's side. He pushed her over and then slid behind the wheel. It was like sitting in a puddle. My, oh, my.

His original plan had been to leave her and the car right there in the parking lot. Nobody would have seen him. But the stupid bastards in their fezzes had changed all that. He would have to park the car in an alley somewhere and walk back to get his own car.

Before he forgot, he took the cuff link and tossed it on the floorboard on the passenger side. It was platinum, and it had on its plain surface the inscribed initials FB. Frank Brolan.

He put the car in gear and drove carefully away from the parking lot.

21

"DID I EVER TELL YOU that I wanted to be a nurse?"

"No."

"When I was in high school."

"Oh."

"I suppose you can't imagine that, can you?"

"It's not that."

"It's all right. I know how you think of me."

"How do I think of you?"

"You know."

"No. How?"

"A stereotype yuppie. A lot of cunning and greed but no scruples."

"That isn't how I think of you."

"It really isn't?"

"No."

"Then, how do you think of me?"

"As confused about what you want."

A pause. "Maybe I am. But I don't want to start talking about us again. I'm tired of it, Frank. I can't help it. I'm just tired of it."

"Believe it or not, so am I."

For a time neither of them said anything. They were in the master bedroom upstairs. In keeping with the Victorian motif of the house, the room was filled with such things as a canopy bed, a George III kingwood inlaid Pembroke table, and a nineteenth century mahogany display cabinet in Chinese Chippendale style. Not a graceful man, Brolan was always warned by Kathleen to be careful in the house.

Wind rattled the windows; a faint silver light from the street painted one wall, cross-hatched by the intricate shadows of tree limbs.

"I really did want to be a nurse, Frank."

Whenever they argued, whenever he implied that she couldn't be faithful to anybody, that she wanted too many material things and not enough spiritual things (though who was he to talk?), she found a way to work into the conversation proof of what a good person she was. That was always her justification for herself – for whatever she did – something she'd learned in six struggling months of analysis shortly after she left college. That no matter what she did, however many men she might fuck over, she was basically a "good person."

ED GORMAN

Kathleen was the fourth daughter of a dumpy little man who'd owned his own dry-cleaning business, one that was never quite successful. He managed to put his girls through college, Kathleen being the last – and shortly after that dropped dead of a heart attack while pressing trousers for some impatient customer who stood waiting in the shabby fitting room.

Whenever Kathleen spoke of her father, it was with great anger and bitterness. Not directed at him but rather at the world that had treated him so badly. She often said "They never gave him a chance." Well, it was obvious she was going to get her chance from the world. She wanted to be the best-looking, most successful woman anywhere she went. And she was well on her way.

Most of the time Brolan felt sorry for Kathleen. Hers had been a harsh and unloving background. Her mother had pushed and pushed her father constantly, almost never being gentle or tender with the man. Kathleen often recalled how, when her father had suffered an early heart attack, she had run alongside the stretcher that the ambulance attendants carried her father on. As she ran along, her mother said, "Well, he'll miss two weeks of work over this. I'll have to go in and run the place." About all Kathleen's mother ever did was watch soaps, smoke Kools, drink Cokes, and talk on the phone with her girlfriends about how pretty she used to be back when she was young ("Before I met Chester") and what a limp-dick Chester was in the sack ("He doesn't even know how to fondle my breasts; it's like he's kneading dough").

It was no wonder that such a marriage had produced such a sad, confused, and angry little girl. One who had a great deal to prove to the world at large. One who had a great deal to prove to herself.

But what Kathleen couldn't seem to understand was that she was crushing Brolan, just as her mother had crushed her father.

Kathleen rolled over and kissed him. "I really like you, Frank."

"But you don't love me."

"I – I've tried."

134

"You really think we should be friends instead of lovers?"

"I really do."

He was tired of supplication, of hearing his whining. She owed him nothing. If she chose not to have a relationship, that was her choice alone to make. He had no right to ruin her life.

He lay next to her, his eyes open.

"Need to pee," she said. "Be right back."

He saw her naked backside in the faint light from the window. She was a beautiful, beautiful woman.

He wanted a cigarette, had in fact bought a pack earlier. Given the situation he was in, worrying about his health did not seem like much of a consideration.

He reached through the gauzy curtain hanging down from the canopy top and got his cigarettes. He found a package of matches next to them. The matches must have been there all along. He'd forgotten his in his sport coat. As he lighted his cigarette, he idly noted The Paramount Motel signature on the red, fancily embossed match cover.

Then he realised what he was looking at.

Kathleen, a jogging fanatic, didn't smoke.

The matches belonged to one of her recent guests. A man who'd obviously been staying at the Paramount Motel.

Jealousy struck him with the force of a seizure. He felt all sorts of irrational, self-pitying, violent things.

He was glad for both their sakes that she wasn't there at that moment. Nothing would be served by his blowing up once again. He'd humiliated and debased himself enough already.

He lay back once more and smoked his cigarette.

He was already re-addicted. At some point he'd have to go through the whole cold turkey process again.

The toilet flushed. In the quiet gloom it sounded like a car bomb exploding.

He heard her size 4 AA feet against the floor. She had dear little feet. She really did. It was one of those helpless sentimental thoughts he always had about her. Dear little feet. God, he made himself sick sometimes.

When she slipped into bed with him again, her whole body

135

ED GORMAN

felt cold. On her arms he could even feel goosebumps.

She said, "Foster said you were taking some time off." As usual, when she mentioned his partner, she sounded as if she were describing something filthy and deadly with germs.

He forced a laugh. "It would be nice if someday you two would get along together."

She returned his laugh. "Getting along with one of you is difficult enough. Getting along with two of you would be impossible." She hesitated, as if nervous about asking him her next question. "So, why the time off?"

He had an easy enough excuse at hand, and he used it. "I think I need some time away from you. It'll make it easier for us if I take some time off. Anyway, God knows I've built up enough vacation time."

"That's probably a good idea. I was thinking about taking a vacation myself. Maybe go to Jamaica for a week. Work on a tan."

He tried not to think of her on the yellow beaches of Jamaica, in the mauve string bikini she'd worn last summer. So many men...

He slipped out of bed and started the process of dressing. She said, "I'm sorry about the way things worked out."

"I know."

"Do you really believe I'm sorry?"

He thought a moment. "Yes."

"Come here a moment."

His trousers on but not buckled, one sock on, the other foot cold from the hardwood floor, he knelt on the edge of the bed and met her as she rose naked to kiss him.

Her mouth was cool and tasted of toothpaste. She'd brushed while in the john.

He tried to keep everything platonic. No sense of getting turned on again. He felt as if this house – and even her arms – had become a tomb. Anyway, his crotch felt as dead as his heart.

"After a while I hope we can be friends again," she said. He said nothing, withdrew from the wonderful tangle of their kiss.

As he was tugging on his other sock and reaching for his

136

shirt, she said, "I appreciate how you're handling this."

"That's me, all right. Exemplary behaviour."

"I know it's not easy for you."

He hung his necktie under his collar, but he didn't tie the two ends. "Good night."

"Should I walk you downstairs?"

"No. That's fine."

"Take care of yourself."

"Thanks."

The shoes were the last to go on. Then he was ready. He wanted to leave very quickly, yet something made him linger, too.

He had to say it. "If you change your mind –"

He left the rest unsaid. She was a smart girl. She could figure that out. If she changed her mind, he'd be happy to take her back.

"Good night," he said again.

He went through the dark house, with its antiques and high ceilings and its Persian rugs.

He went out the same side door he'd come in. The cold air seemed to freeze his nostrils on contact.

He went out to the bottom of the drive, careful of how he was walking because it was so icy, and opened the door of his car and was just putting one leg in when he noticed it – a car across the street, a dark shape behind the wheel, clearly watching him.

He recognised the car right away.

A silver XKE was not the kind of car you should use if you were trying to keep yourself hidden.

He wondered what his ex-boss, Richard Cummings, was doing there anyway.

He closed the door on his own car without getting in and then started down the steep slope of the drive. Moonlight gave the ice and snow a silver surface.

He was about halfway to Cummings's car when the XKE's lights suddenly shone like awakening eyes, and the car pulled jerkily from the kerb, heading in the opposite direction.

What the hell was going on – had Cummings been following

him, or was he there to see Kathleen?

Brolan raised his head to look at the Gothic house outlined against the moon. It was dark, forbidding, unknowable. And inside was a beautiful young woman just as dark, just as forbidding, just as unknowable.

Shaking his head, he walked back to his car, got inside, and left.

22

THE LAUGHTER STARTLED BROLAN. Music, a voice from the television, maybe even a conversation – all of these would have seemed reasonable coming from Greg Wagner's duplex. But somehow laughter seemed odd.

Brolan raised his hand and pushed in the doorbell. This late at night, there were just a few yellow-glowing windows along this prosperous-looking middle-class street. People up late watching Letterman or Arsenio Hall, most likely. On the slopes of some lawns you could see plump, happy snowmen, scarves wrapped around their thick necks, top hats cocked at jaunty angles. Maybe they were standing sentry, keeping ill from their owners' houses. In a few yards sleds had been left on lawns, which made Brolan flash back to his own kids, their cold red cheeks as they frolicked in the snow, the way they'd moved so cumbersomely and cutely in their little snowsuits. It was near midnight; the snow was blue, the tranquil and ideal blue of a sentimental Christmas card, and blue-grey smoke coiled up from chimneys to make everything seem that much cosier. Brolan wanted to be one of those people sitting at home watching Letterman, a bowl of popcorn on his lap and a Diet 7 Up in an ice-clinking glass. And no dead women. No; no dead women at all.

Inside the laughter stopped abruptly.

Brolan could hear Greg Wagner's wheelchair coming across the hardwood floor.

Apparently a trusting man, Wagner didn't ask who it was. He simply pulled the door back.

"Hey, Frank, c'mon in!" Wagner called.

The festive mood, like the laughter, surprised Brolan. The last time he'd seen Wagner, the man had been lamenting Emma. Something had obviously happened in the meantime...

As soon as he got inside and closed the door behind him, Brolan saw the girl. She was maybe sixteen and very pretty in a sad sort of way, one of those wan beauties who seem to be all the more appealing because of their very wanness. She wore a blue button-down shirt and a grey pullover sweater and designer jeans, and very white tube socks that made her seem very comfy on so cold a winter night.

Brolan noticed immediately how anxiously Wagner was watching the girl. Almost as if he were awaiting some kind of answer from her.

"Well?" Wagner said to the girl.

She looked Brolan up and down, so carefully and obviously that he felt self-conscious standing there.

"So, what do you think?" Wagner said to her.

But the girl wouldn't be rushed. She continued to tilt her head this way and that, considering Brolan from a variety of angles.

Finally the girl said, "He isn't the one."

"I'm not the one what?" Brolan said.

"Not the guy who tried to kill her last night," Wagner said.

"Gee, am I supposed to tell her thank-you?" Brolan said.

"Hey, Brolan," Wagner said, spreading his hands in an gesture of friendship. "It wasn't anything personal."

The girl said, "You want some hot chocolate?"

Before Brolan could say anything, she said, "He's got these little teeny marshmallows. They're really good."

Brolan felt as if he'd walked into the middle of a very private and very intimate party, where outsiders could never possibly know the ground rules.

"Yes," he said hesitatingly. "Hot chocolate sounds good."

"Great," the girl said, half jumping to her feet and snatching up both her own white ceramic cup and Wagner's as well. "I'll get us all another round."

She put out a slim little hand. Brolan took it. "I'm Denise, by the way."

"Hi, Denise."

"Be right back," she said.

Instead of merely walking across the hardwood floor, she got a little steam up and slid across the well-varnished boards. Her sudden enthusiasm played nicely against her young-Garbo countenance.

After watching her disappear into the kitchen; Brolan glanced down at Wagner. Glowing was the only word that could possibly do the look in his eyes justice.

"Where'd you find her?" Brolan asked.

Wagner, love-struck or what ever the hell he was, looked up from his reverie and said, "Oh, Denise, you mean?"

"Yes, Denise."

"She tried to break in."

"She tried to break in?" Brolan shook his head, still feeling as if he'd landed somewhere in the middle of Alice's adventure down the rabbit hole. "Maybe if I'm a good boy and take off my shoes on this throw rug and go over there and sit down – maybe you'll explain all this to me."

Wagner stared at him, as if really taking note of his presence for the first time. "It's not that difficult to understand, Frank. Not if you really sit down and give everything a fair hearing. And by the way, you'll like Denise. I promise."

Brolan got his shoes and coat off and went over to sit on the end of the couch. As he crossed the room, he noted that on the outsize TV screen was an image of Laurel and Hardy in cowboy duds from *Way Out West*, his favourite of their movies.

Greg was smart enough to start the conversation on exactly the right note. "You know," he said, "if we can figure out who tried to kill Denise last night, we can figure out who killed Emma."

Then he told Brolan all about his wallet's being in the back pocket of the killer. Then he told Brolan everything.

Half an hour later Brolan finished his second cup of hot chocolate. The room was deeply shadowed, thanks to Greg's turning on a lava lamp ("I'm just a hippie at heart") on the far end of the long coffee table.

Brolan, relentless, had had Denise repeat her story three times. Each time she came up with a few more details. He supposed he could learn even more if he sat there and questioned her all night. But from her tone he could tell that she was tiring quickly, even getting somewhat irritable.

"You're not sure if the beard was fake?"

She sighed. "I told you. It seemed real to me."

"He was heavy?"

"Yes. Chunky."

"With brown hair?"

"Right."

"And his eyes?"

"Blue, I guess."

"Earlier you said you were positive they were blue."

"I can't be sure. Not absolutely. You know, some people have kind of blue-grey eyes. They could've been like that."

"But they weren't brown?"

"No; they weren't brown."

"You're sure?"

"I'm sure."

"And you didn't notice any scars anywhere or any tattoos."

"No."

"I'm sorry I have to keep asking you questions." She sighed. Glanced at Greg. "I know."

"Could we talk about the car again?"

"I'll try."

"You said it could've been a Chevrolet."

"It was something new anyway."

"Why did you say Chevrolet?"

She shrugged. "My dad used to go to all the auto-dealer showrooms. He always liked to get all the free stuff they give away when they've got their new cars in. You know?"

"And you've seen a car like that before?"

"Something sort of like it, yes."

"And it was a Chevrolet?"

"Uh-huh."

"Now I've got to ask you some questions about what you do."

"What I do?"

He nodded. "You know, when you go over to Loring Park."

"Oh. Right."

"Where will the kids go tonight?"

"Because of the snow and everything?"

"Yes."

"Oh, I hear there're couple a places off Hennepin. They work the corners, but they can stay close to these bars, so they go in there and get warm when they need to."

"So, if this guy wanted to find you again… you think he'd look there?"

"I guess."

"What if he wasn't a regular john. Could he find out where the kids work?"

"Sure. He could ask a cabbie or somebody." She looked at him curiously. "You think he's still trying to find me?"

"Possibly."

"Why?"

Brolan hesitated. "Maybe he wants to finish what he started."

She smiled at Greg Wagner. "Greg said I can stay here for a while. Sleep on the couch."

Brolan avoided Wagner's gaze. He remembered the man's saying that some men with spina bifida – himself included – tended to fall in love with somebody impossible to attain. And who could be more unattainable than a sixteen-year-old street girl who spent part of her time hooking and the other part of her time concocting blackmail plots?

"You'll be safe here," Brolan said. "But I don't know how safe you'll be when you go back to the streets."

"Why does he want to hurt me?"

"I don't think he does."

"He sure gave me a different impression."

"You, specifically, I mean. He's trying to hurt me through you. That seems to be his main purpose. He selected you purely at random."

"Why does he want to hurt you?"

"I don't know."

"You really don't?"

He laughed gently. "Hey, Denise, I'm not an all-around loveable guy, I admit. But somebody killing women and then trying to blame me for it? Now that's somebody who really hates me. The last time I looked, I wasn't that bad a guy. I really wasn't."

"And you don't have any idea who it was?"

"Not any idea at all. Nothing substantive anyway. Just some guesses at this point."

Without any warning at all Denise leaned back in the couch and yawned. She was a kid at this moment – a sleepy kid. "Boy, I'm getting tired."

"Why don't you go in and lie down on my bed?" Greg said. "I'd planned to sleep on the couch tonight anyway."

"Gee, I hate to put you out, Greg," she said. "Why don't you let me sleep on the couch?"

Greg grinned. "And miss one of my few chances to be gallant? I wouldn't hear of it."

Greg turned to Brolan. "Are you done questioning her, Frank?"

Brolan nodded. "Yes. And I appreciate your spending the time with me."

Standing now, Denise yawned again and stretched. "Hope you catch him."

"So do I."

She eyed the hall leading to the bedroom. "Well, I guess I'll see you guys later, then."

"Good night, Denise," Greg said.

She walked over to him, took his face in her hands, and kissed him tenderly on the nose. "I really appreciate everything, Greg. I haven't felt this good in a long time."

Greg Wagner started blushing. Brolan smiled.

"You, too, Frank," she said. "I enjoyed meeting you, too. Only maybe next time you won't have so many questions."

"G'night, Denise," Brolan said, and watched her disappear down the hall.

As soon as she was out of sight, Greg said, "So, what do you think of her?"

"I guess I don't have to ask you what you think of her."

"You don't approve."

"I just don't want to see you get hurt. Or ripped off."

"Ripped off? She's not that kind of kid."

"She came here to blackmail me, didn't she?"

"You're making too much of that."

Their eyes met. Brolan didn't want to ruin the other man's hope. "Maybe you're right, Greg. Maybe I'm just too cynical."

Greg said, "Even though I suspect that's a deeply insincere comment, I'll take it at face value."

"Good."

"And now I'll go on to tell you about our friend Charles Lane." He shook his head. The glee put in his eyes by Denise was gone now. This was how he'd looked when Brolan had first met him. "Maybe Emma and I weren't the friends I thought we were."

"Meaning?"

"Meaning that there was a lot she didn't tell me."

"You're sure of that?"

Wagner nodded. "This afternoon I decided to go over to the other side of the duplex. See what Emma had left behind." He tossed a leather-bound book about the size of a paperback novel over to Brolan. "She kept two diaries – the way dishonest businessmen keep two sets of books."

"Why would she do that?"

"Probably didn't want to hurt my feelings. Or just resented the fact that every private thought she wrote down on the computer could easily be seen by me anytime I cared to tap into it." He smiled without humour. "Can't say I blame her, can you?"

"I guess not. Everybody needs privacy."

"Exactly. And she had her privacy. That diary."

"Charles Lane's in here?"

"A great deal. I suspect that her friend the pimp was telling you the truth, Frank."

"About what?"

"I think that over the past six months, she was working a lot for Lane on the side."

"You mean he became her pimp?"

"Apparently. You'll find a lot of references in there about Lane's setting her up with this man or that man. None of the names mean anything to me. I thought you might look it over and see if it made any more sense to you."

"I appreciate it."

This time there was a little humour in Wagner's laugh, but it was sour humour. "You remember how I told you that some men with spina bifida make fools out of themselves with women? Well, you're looking at one, I'm afraid. After I read her diary and the way she talked about me, I don't think Emma felt much more for me than pity."

Brolan let him talk. That was obviously what the man needed.

"When you came in here and saw Denise, I know that's what you thought."

"I'm sorry I'm so cynical."

"No, no," Wagner said. "You're probably right. She came in here and saw a good thing and decided to latch onto it." He shrugged. "That's why being handicapped and having money at the same time is a bad combination. It leaves you open to people who don't mean you any good."

"I shouldn't have been so adamant about Denise. She may be just what she seems. A very nice girl who's got some personal problems and nothing more sinister than that."

"I shouldn't have offered to put her up."

"You're going to ask her to leave?"

"I'm going to think about it."

"Greg, I repeat: I'm a pretty cynical guy. I always tend to look on the dark side. That's a pretty inhibiting attitude sometimes. And sometimes you have to disregard it. I'd give her a chance."

Wagner stared at him. "You're not just saying that? You'd

give her a chance?"

"Sure. Let her stay here a few days. You two seem to get along. See how things go. She's too young to have a romance with, so you don't have to worry about that. All you have to see is how you get along as friends. If she just wants your money, that'll be obvious pretty quickly. She'll start hitting on you for all sorts of things."

"I guess you started me thinking when you mentioned the fact that she came here to blackmail you."

"She's young. And she doesn't strike me as very sophisticated. Remember what she said – 'I was going to ask him for a couple of hundred dollars.' With that kind of attitude blackmail wouldn't be a very remunerative field. I think she's just reaching out. Trying to make some sense of her life and not finding much to be optimistic about. I don't think it was a very serious attempt."

"We've kind of reversed positions."

"Not really, Greg. All I'm saying is, wait and see what happens. She seems like a decent enough kid."

"What about you?"

"I'm going home and read the diary. I'm going to the office tomorrow."

"Thought you were going to take a few days off?"

"Now I need to see our art director." Brolan told him about the pornographic playing cards. He said, as gently as possible, "Emma was in one of them."

He'd expected Wagner to be shocked or at least angered by this, but the man just sat stared at his small hands. "She mentions that in her diary. She also mentions a videotape she's got hidden somewhere. Whatever was going on with Lane, it was starting to scare her."

"Any idea where the tape is?"

"Not yet. But I'll bet it's somewhere in her side of the duplex."

"Does she mention who set it up?"

"Our friend, Charles Lane."

"I can't wait to talk to this guy."

"I'm starting to think he's our killer," Wagner said.

"Does she mention anybody else's being involved in the

photographs?"

"Like I said, she mentions names throughout the book, but none of them mean anything to me. No city fathers or leading model citizens or anything like that." He indicated his tape library. "But this isn't my world, Frank. I don't know a lot about the honchos of the Twin Cities. I get my cheque from my inheritance every month, and I get new videotapes sent to me every week, and when dealers have something really collectable, they call me. That's my world, Frank. I don't move in the same circles you do."

Brolan stood up, dropping the diary into his suit coat pocket.

"I'll get back with you tomorrow sometime," he said.

Wagner said, "She didn't really care about me, Frank. Not the way she said she did." He sounded as if he were very close to tears.

"I don't believe that, Greg, not from what you told me about her. Maybe she didn't love you romantically, but I'm sure she cared about you as a friend. If she'd been faking that, I think you would've known it."

"I'm just sitting here and getting embarrassed about the stupid things I did." He looked up at Brolan with silver tears shining in his eyes. "You know, I actually asked her to marry me. Pretty goddamn crazy, right?"

Brolan went over and put his hand on Wagner's shoulder. "Greg, if I had the time to sit here and tell you all the foolish things I've done with women, we'd be here till dawn."

"Really?"

"Really, Greg. Just before I came over here, my former girlfriend told me to get lost. She was more polite than that, but that's what she meant."

Wagner laughed. This time it was a hearty and pleasant sound. "You know something terrible?"

"What?"

"That makes me feel better, Frank. Knowing guys like you get dumped, too."

Brolan smiled. "Glad I could be of service, Greg." Then he got his coat and left.

23

DENISE WASN'T SURE what woke her.

It was four hours after Brolan left and two hours after Greg, exhausted from the pleasant turmoil of the evening, pitched himself on the sofa and fell asleep watching a Pete Smith short subject.

At first Denise thought the sound was something in a dream. Her dreams were always vivid, especially the bad ones. Her sister used to get up and shake her hard, just to help her escape the nightmare images that had plagued her since she was a little girl.

It took a while for her to understand that the sounds were not in the fervid, sweaty cages of her nightmares but were rather – real.

Her first thought on waking was: Where am I?

Her second thought was: What is that noise?

Quickly the hours she'd spent with Greg Wagner returned to her. Nice images. Nice times. At first she'd been pleasant to the man because she'd been afraid that he was going to call the police. But then she genuinely started liking him, especially his sly, off-the-wall sense of humour. The only times she didn't like that was when he made fun of himself. There was too much pain in his remarks, too much disappointment. And if they ever became better friends, she'd tell him that, too. That he shouldn't make fun of himself. That he was a beautiful man. From what she'd learned on the streets, real ugliness was on the inside, not on the outside. He had wit, generosity, warmth, and compassion to boast of – which was a lot more than most people had to congratulate themselves for.

Then she realised what the noise was.

Next door, in the duplex just beyond the wall that separated the two places, somebody was wandering around.

Stumbling into things.

She came up from the bed feeling naked and vulnerable in her bra and panties. She should have asked Greg if he'd loan her a pair of pyjamas. She was sure they wore about the same size.

She slipped into her clothes quickly. Against the drawn blinds she could see the nimbus of alley light and ring of crusty ice on the window. Greg must have turned the thermostat down for sleeping. The hardwood floor was cold.

She went out into the hallway, feeling her way along the walls with her hands, moving toward the light at the front of the house; the streetlights gave the living room a faint glow from the sodium vapour lamps.

Greg looked like a child curled up inside a tangle of covers. As she leaned down to him, he smelled of sleep. She touched him gently, not wanting to frighten him. He made deep, groggy noises, but at first he didn't wake up at all. She tapped him softly on the forehead.

"Greg," she whispered.

"Huh?" he said, stirring at last.

"Sh," she said, putting her finger to his lips. "Whisper; otherwise he'll hear you."

"Who'll hear me?" Greg whispered.

She could tell that he still wasn't quite fully awake yet, but he was getting there. "Whoever's next door."

As if to oblige her, the person next door now stumbled into another piece of furniture. It wasn't a big sound, but in the stillness of the winter night, when only the creaking wood and the furnace made noise, it was a significant sound.

Hearing it, Greg sat up immediately.

Even in the shadows she could see that he had trouble manoeuvring. She felt sorry for him. She wanted to hug him.

"I'm going to get my gun," he said, still whispering.

"Why don't you call the cops?"

He shook his head, then pawed at his face. "Brolan and I don't want to get the police involved just yet."

"Involved in what?"

He patted her hand. "No time to explain things now, Denise. I need to get my gun."

He manipulated the wheelchair deftly, moving himself up into it in a single near-spectacular motion. Without pause he rolled the chair down the hall and into his bedroom.

She heard a drawer squeaking open and then closing. She heard him moving quickly back down the hall toward her. He was lost completely in the darkness.

Then he sat before her, the .45 in his hand. "I'm going over there," he said. "No!" she said. And violated her own rule about whispering.

They both stood there listening to hear if the person next door had heard her. But apparently not. The undercurrent of sound – things being moved around, drawers opening and closing – continued.

"I'll go over there," she said.

"God, Denise, you can't go over there with this gun. You'd end up shooting yourself."

"Then I won't take a gun."

"What've you got in mind?"

"Just see who it is. He probably drove a car. I can get his licence number and maybe get a good look at him."

"He could kill you."

"Not if he can't see me."

"Aren't you getting tired of whispering?"

She laughed; she couldn't help it. He sounded so crabby when he said it, like a little kid awakened in the middle of the night by a parent. A grouchy little kid. "Yes, I'm tired of whispering, but if we talk any louder, he'll hear us."

He took her hand. "I don't want you to get hurt, Denise. Maybe we should just forget it."

"I'll be fine."

"Maybe you should take the gun."

"No, you're probably right; I'd just end up shooting myself." She nodded toward the other duplex. "I'd better hurry while he's still in there."

"I'll say a prayer for you," Greg said.

She leaned over and kissed him on the cheek. Then she grabbed her coat and knit hat and went outside.

She figured it couldn't be a heck of a lot colder at the North Pole. She had been out there maybe three minutes, and already her whole face was frozen, as if an invisible dentist had just given her an extra-strong shot of Novocain, and her leather gloves weren't doing much for her hands, either. Her fingers felt like frozen fish sticks.

The backyard was absolutely still. It was the kind of night that is so cold, it's breathless. The alley light cast a purple glow and purple shadows over the three-foot drifts of sparkling snow. In some places you could see where dogs had roamed past and peed yellow in the white snow. In other places you saw where snow was capped by ice; the surface glittered.

Her present vantage point was behind an orderly row of garbage cans next to the garage. She was approximately ten yards from the back door. Her first goal had been simple enough: get out the back door without being heard and then find a place to crouch and wait while she got her bearings.

It was time to get to work, and the first thing to do was to find his car. It was very unlikely he'd parked out front. Too easy to spot by anybody passing by, cops especially. No, more likely he parked in the back somewhere.

Keeping her eye on the back door of the duplex, she started easing herself away from the protection of the garbage cans.

Then she was in the alley, her rubber-soled boots making vague farting noises against the hard-packed snow. Farting noises; God, she always had weird thoughts like that. It was just one of many reasons that she considered herself so weird and unworthy. Other human beings – real human beings didn't have thoughts like that. She was sure she was alone in that and so many other things in the world.

It didn't take a genius to find the car. He had parked it several yards down the alley, parallel with a garage. From inside her coat she took the small tablet and pencil she'd copped from Greg and wrote down the licence number. Then she went over and peered inside the car. She had no idea what she was looking for.

She tried the driver's door. It was unlocked. Since she was

looking for stuff, it would probably make more sense to open the door and start looking around that way, wouldn't it?

She opened the door and started rooting around inside. She could tell immediately that the owner of the car smoked cigarettes. The damp tobacco smell was almost foetid. She could also tell that the owner of the car was rich. The seats were real leather. They smelled that way, and they felt that way.

She found, among other things, a paperback novel, an unopened pack of cigarettes, a black pocket comb, a map of Milwaukee, some kind of brochure about the trucking industry, an empty 7-Eleven coffee cup with a lipstick smudge at the top, and a candy wrapper, which made her hungry. God, she was hungry all the time. In some ways that scared her. All her aunts and uncles were real porkers. Was she going to turn out that way herself?

She was just about to start on the glove compartment when the man grabbed her. She knew it was a man because no woman (unless she was one of those ripple-bodied steroidal bodybuilders) could ever have this much strength.

He grabbed her, yanking her out of the car, and then he struck her a mighty blow on the back of her neck. She assumed in that instant of totally blinding pain, in that instant of terrible warmth rushing up her spinal column to her neck and then exploding inside her head – she assumed that she was dying.

Then she struck the ground, her cheek smashing against the snow the man's boots had just turned into small ruts.

She thought of her sister in the mental hospital; of her first dog, Peachy-Keen; of the way sunlight and shadow played on the surface of Henderson creek in the summertime. These were weird things to think of, probably; but then, she was a very weird girl indeed.

And that became her last thought: how odd she was, how different from all others.

Then there was nothing. Nothing.

24

Friday

THE MAN WAS PLUMP. The man was bald. The man was astigmatic. The man wore a black leather jump-suit; the man was about sixty-three years old. The man was an asshole. The man was a client.

"So, when're you going to line me up with that chick back in the art department?" Harold McAlester said.

"Soon as she gets a little older," Brolan said.

McAlester, a fat, evil child despite his years, winked over at Foster. "Brolan here doesn't approve of me. Never has." He looked at Brolan. "Fuck 'im."

They were in the main conference room. They had been in the main conference room for nearly two hours. All the time with McAlester. Though he had ostensibly come here to discuss advertising, McAlester really wanted to tell them about all the women he'd screwed on his recent trip to Vale. Or said he'd screwed. Or would like to've screwed. McAlester, who a long time ago had been a famous college running back, was the owner of a dozen gourmet shops that did windfall business in upscale malls. He had a woman whom he badly underpaid actually run all the day-to-day stuff, while he went out and gave pep talks to high schools about capitalism and positive thinking.

Once, there'd been an incident when he'd gotten a little over-smitten with this sixteen-year-old Nordic ball-buster whom he'd tried to lure out into his Mercedes following some kind of pep-club deal. Just because she was a small-town Lutheran didn't mean she didn't know what the old bald fucker had in mind. She told the small-town Lutheran principal, who, in turn, told the small-town Lutheran mayor, who, in turn, told the small-town Lutheran newspaper editor. This guy, a mean Republican in a county of mean Democrats, started out his editorial by noting all Harold's contributions to the Humphrey and Mondale campaigns over the years, and then without a fare-thee-well, mentioned the fact that Harold, in addition to giving his positive-thinking sermons, also spent an undue amount of time sniffing around the small-town Lutheran daughters of all the small-town Lutheran men who read this here particular paper. Harold spent the next fourteen months eating bag after bag of shit and trying to come up with the right gimmick that would turn his image around.

Which was when he'd come to Foster and Brolan and which was when, together, they came up with the idea for The House of Sunshine, the big rambling mansion where terminally ill kids could come and spend up to five days a month in luxury and privilege while they went back and forth to the university hospital to have their tests and whatnot. Now, no reporter wanted to come right out and say this was a despicable, low-down publicity ploy fabricated by one despicable, low-down, Vatican-loving son-of-a-bitch-they couldn't, not without sounding awfully cynical themselves. And so they let it slide, and every night there was old bald McAlester on the six and ten o'clock news (on the tube he always wore conservative three-piece suits and put some kind of jazz on his shaved head to cut down the glare; no kidding), tub-thumping the shit out, The House of Sunshine, sounding for all the world like a guy who was probably related in some way to Mother Theresa. The heat off, McAlester was back to Vale trips and European trips and Vegas trips and Jew York trips (as he was so fond of calling them), and most especially, he was back to trifling with chicks who probably couldn't buy legal beer yet. All Brolan could figure out was that the asshole had everything. All that was left to him was the risk of jailbait. Maybe it was the only way he could get it up.

"She's got this peach coloured skirt that's so tight, you can see the crack in her ass when she first stands up," McAlester said. "You ever notice that, Brolan?"

"No, I never noticed that."

Another wink to Foster. "You ever think there's maybe something wrong with Brolan here, Foster? He doesn't notice the crack in her ass when she stands up."

"Come on, you guys," Foster said, playing his inevitable

role of scout leader. "Let's talk some fucking advertising; how'z about it?"

Around eleven that morning a cold air mass from Canada brought new snow. By eleven-thirty three new inches of the white stuff had been added to downtown Minneapolis. The overcast sky lent everything the air of dusk, including the fuzzy look of stoplights and department store windows seen behind the haze of falling snow.

Brolan was in his office. He had to pretend everything was all right, which meant actually getting some work done. His meeting earlier with Foster and McAlester had left him angry. He didn't like working with clients who were essentially bullies, who saw all your female employees as potential chattel, and your personal values as something to smirk about.

Three of the writers had left copy on his desk for approval. He was fortunate to have three very good writers who could turn out solid work in a variety of styles. This stuff on his desk was fine and required little revision.

He was halfway through a slide-show script when somebody knocked. Foster walked in. He smiled. "I hope you and McAlester aren't ever marooned on the same desert island together. One of you wouldn't be alive after twenty-four hours."

"Sorry if I was shitty."

Foster walked over to the coffeepot and poured himself a cup. "He's my client and my headache. I shouldn't have dragged you in there. There really wasn't any reason."

"I'm not sure what you mean by *my* client. I guess I was under the impression that they were all *our* clients." He was aware of how paranoid – angry – he sounded. Right now he didn't give a damn.

"Hey, my friend, cool out a little, all right?"

Foster came over and sat in a chair on the other side of Brolan's desk. "All I meant, Frank, was that I went after him personally."

"You went after all the biggies personally. All five of them."

"Yes, that's right. Is there something wrong with that, Frank?"

155

"I guess I just don't like your proprietary tone is all. You may have gone out and hustled them up, but if we didn't give the right kind of creative edge, we wouldn't keep them very long. That's what you always tell me anyway."

In the silent office, snow streaking the window, cars in the distance starting to slip and slide, Brolan knew how tired and crazed he sounded.

Foster sat there and stared at him. He took a couple sips of coffee. "You know something, pally?"

"What?"

"You're coming apart."

"You think I don't know that?"

"What're you going to do about it?"

"What can I do about? I've got a dead woman in my freezer, remember?"

Foster sipped some more coffee. In his brown three-piece suit, his post-Beatles hair neatly combed, he looked like the ultimate Jaycee, one given to goofy party hats and drunken speeches about brotherhood. He said, "Maybe it's time to go to the police."

"Right."

"I'm serious."

"I know you are."

"You can't go on much longer like this." Foster paused. "I'll grant you that McAlester is tough to deal with sometimes, but you didn't even try this morning."

"You going to give me one of his positive-thinking speeches, Stu?"

"No, but I am going to give you the best advice I know."

"And what would that be?"

"Contact a good criminal lawyer, and go to the police."

"It's too late. It was too late when I found her in my freezer."

"You're forgetting something, pally."

"And what would that be?"

"That I'm your witness. You don't seem to understand that. I'm your witness, Frank. I can testify that she was already in the freezer when you and I got there. I can corroborate your story."

"You're the one who's not thinking it through."

"No?"

"No. All the cops have to say is that I put her in the freezer myself and that I then dragged you up there so it would look as if somebody else put her there." He shook his head and looked angrily across the desk at his partner. "I'm still in a hell of a lot of trouble, Stu."

Foster sighed. "Frank, I want to help you. That's why I came in here."

"I know you do."

"Going to the police is the only thing that makes sense at this point."

Brolan sat forward in his chair. "Maybe I'm putting some things together."

"Oh?"

"I've found out a lot about this woman, Stu. There are some very good reasons some people would have wanted her dead. And there are some people who look as if they'd have been happy to do it."

"Then turn all your evidence over to the police."

Brolan sat back in his chair. He felt exhausted suddenly. He wanted to sit in this office alone and never move. Night would fall, balming night, enveloping him in darkness, and he would rest then. Rest. He said, wearily, "I'm sorry I didn't handle McAlester better."

"I know, Frank. It's just – it's just how you are at the moment. The dead woman, I mean."

"You know something?"

"What?"

"I've never figured out why he came over to us in the first place. Never figured out how you snagged him."

"He was in trouble, pally. Or don't you remember when half the papers in this state were attacking him as a lech?"

"I know that. But I mean, why us in particular? The agency he had wasn't doing a good job for him but he's so big and so powerful that he could have taken any big agency in the state. A lot bigger than us."

"Meaning?"

"Meaning I've never figured out how you pulled it off. Or gotten any of our five big ones, actually. You're damn good. But why us?"

Foster grinned. "Just lucky, I guess."

Brolan started to speak, but Foster stopped him. "You're still pissed, aren't you, pally? About the remark I made?"

"Yeah, I guess," Brolan said.

"I shouldn't have said that, Frank. About them being my accounts. They're our accounts. Because what you said about creativity is absolutely true. I went out and got them, but it's your work that's kept them."

"I appreciate you, saying that, Stu. I – I'm just paranoid about things."

"I know." Foster stood up. "Frank."

"You don't need to say it."

"I'm just trying to be your friend."

"I know."

"If you get the right lawyer, Frank, you'll be ahead of the game."

"Maybe you're right."

"The longer you wait –"

Brolan looked up at him. "You know, I didn't even go down to the basement and look at her last night. I was afraid of – of what she'd look like. You know?"

"I know. We're ad guys, pally, not morticians."

Brolan stared out the window. He thought about Greg and Denise. At that moment they were probably having lunch and planning which movies to watch that afternoon. He felt an odd pang of jealousy. They'd never have a romance, but they'd have an enviable friendship. Brolan knew this and felt excluded. Over the past twenty-four hours he'd started to call his daughters several times but always stopped himself. Why inflict his misery on them? They were college age, with their own lives. They didn't deserve to have them spoiled. He was alone, and he'd simply have to live with that fact.

Coming out of his brief reverie, Brolan said, "If I can just find

out who hired her to spill a drink on me, I can find out who the
killer is."

"The police could do it in half the time."

Brolan stood up. Went over to the window. Below, shoppers
kept their heads down, ploughing their way into the harsh wind
and snow. Brolan turned back to Stu. "I'll think it over, Stu. I
really will."

"If you want to talk, pally —"

"I know, Stu. I appreciate it."

Foster left.

Around noon Brolan went back to the production department.
Two young women stood in the hallway, exchanging rubber
boots for shoes and wrapping red scarves round their pretty
necks. "You look like you're getting ready for Alaska," he said.
They smiled so girlishly that he got sentimental about them and
might have given them a big raise on the spot if they'd asked for
it. "No, just down a couple of blocks over to Murray's. It's Jane's
birthday." Then they floated off on their laughter.

By the time he reached the production department, he'd been
able to determine that the place was empty. Except perhaps for
the only office that really interested him — Culhane's. The door
was closed, but a light shone behind the frosted glass. Maybe he
was in there.

Brolan knocked twice. When he got no answer, he turned the
knob and pushed inside.

Tim Culhane was there all right but his mind wasn't presently
engaged. He had his feet up on the desk and his eyes closed.
From his ears trailed two black snakes of cord that plugged into
the Walkman sitting in his lap. Tim Culhane was grooving to
some tunes.

Brolan closed the door behind him as he came in. He walked
over to the desk and pushed Culhane's feet to the floor. Brolan
had already decided that if it came to violence, he'd give it first
and hardest and without thought to anything as quaint as rules.
Culhane was a bodybuilder, after all, and Brolan needed every
advantage he could muster.

ED GORMAN

"Hey," Culhane said, as his feet slammed to the floor and his chair threatened to spill him on the desk. "What the fuck do you think you're doing?"

Brolan tossed the pornographic playing card on the desk. "Look familiar?" he said.

Culhane's prim little mouth grew even tighter. "What the hell have you been doing – going through my desk?"

"Emma," Brolan said. "Tell me about her."

"There's nothing to tell."

Brolan realised that if he missed, Culhane would likely break him apart. But he seemed to be in a good position to do it, so he readied himself and took his shot – kicking Culhane hard and square in the mouth. He could feel some teeth go beneath his foot, and Culhane immediately went over backwards in his chair, slamming his head against the wall as he went down.

Brolan went around the side of the desk quickly. Blood the consistency of ketchup covered Culhane's mouth. Culhane was moaning and putting his hands flat on the floor, apparently trying to get up.

This time Brolan kicked him in the chest, right in the heart. Culhane started to say something, but Brolan quickly filled his face with his shoe again, managing a kick that caught the man in the nose. Culhane's nose was now as big a mess as his mouth.

"Tell me about Emma," Brolan said.

Culhane reached out a hand and put it on the walnut finish of his desk, still trying to gain his feet. His hand was bloody from patting his mouth and nose. A long, smeary red hand print stained the desk finish.

"Emma," Brolan said.

He got Culhane in the ribs and so deftly that Culhane's face smashed against the desk in reaction.

Brolan went over and grabbed Culhane's hair and started ripping it out. For good measure, he slapped Culhane across the face. Culhane started crying.

Brolan took the chair that sat directly across from Culhane's chair.

Brolan sat down and lit a cigarette. There was a No Smoking

160

sign on Culhane's door. Brolan figured the poor dear would probably survive.

"I want you to tell me everything you know about Emma," Brolan said.

Culhane lifted his head from the desk. He looked almost comically injured; a creature from a horror movie.

"Emma," Brolan said.

Culhane stopped the blood with a handkerchief so he could talk. "Lane knows her."

The often-referred to but never-met Charles Lane.

"What does that mean exactly? That he 'knows' her?"

"Maybe they worked together or something."

"Where'd you get the playing cards?"

"Lane."

"He took the pictures?"

"Uh-huh."

"You have anything to do with them?"

Culhane glanced anxiously at the playing card sitting face up on his desk. "I helped with the lighting and stuff."

"Maybe you can enter this stuff for an Addy award."

"I know why you're doing this."

"Yeah?"

"You found out I was balling Kathleen, didn't you?"

Brolan was happy that this was what Culhane believed. "Yeah."

"She told you, didn't she?"

"Yeah."

"That fucking cunt."

"Where do I find Lane?"

Culhane struggled to his feet. His whole face was bloody, and blood had spattered his once-white turtleneck. He moaned and cursed. "You may think you got away with it, Brolan, but you didn't. You got your shots in first, and that was smart. But next time I'll get mine in first."

"Oh, goody. Threats."

"Yeah; we'll see how much of a wise-ass you are when I get started on you."

161

"Where do I find Lane?"

"I thought you were supposed to be a bright boy. And you don't even know where to find him?"

Brolan waited.

Culhane said, "Am I gonna get fired?"

"No. Why?"

Culhane shrugged. "Because my wife's pregnant, man. If you kick me out of here, I've got bad financial problems."

"You're not fired."

"I threatened you."

"Well, I kicked the shit out of you. Seems like you owed me at least one good threat."

"I appreciate it, not firing me, I mean. But I'm still going to beat your face in sometime. You can bank on that."

"Just make sure I'm wearing old clothes, all right?"

A knock came on the door.

"Shit, I don't want anybody to see me like this," Culhane said.

"I don't either. You look like shit." As a second knock sounded, Brolan said, "Where do I find Lane?"

"Why?"

"That's my business."

"Well then it's my business where you find him."

Brolan reached across and grabbed Culhane by the front of his turtleneck. This time Culhane had been anticipating it. He moved back before Brolan really got a chance to do anything.

A third knock came.

Brolan glowered, realising he wasn't going to get his answer.

He went to the door, trying to fill it as much as possible so the other person couldn't get a good look at Culhane behind him.

"Hi, Sara," Brolan said.

Sara was the secretary for the writers and the artists. "There's somebody in the reception area to see you, Frank."

"Oh, yeah. Did he say who it was?"

"He told me, but you know how I am with names."

"Do you remember who he's with?"

She smiled. She had a nice white mid-western smile. "Oh,

that part I can remember fine."

"Oh?"

"Yes. He's with the Minneapolis Police Department."

"He is?"

"Yes. He's a homicide detective. That's why I thought it was weird he wanted to talk to you. You know what I mean, Frank? Why would a homicide detective want to talk to you, anyway?"

25

BREAKFAST WAS A BACON-CHEESE-green pepper omelette accompanied by two pieces of wheat toast, a glass of orange juice, and a small container of skim milk.

The meal was served in the living room, on the couch, where Denise had been lying since finding herself in the alley and staggering back into the house.

Greg had kept her awake for two hours, trying to make sure that she looked, sounded, and felt all right. He was afraid she might have a concussion. She was convinced that her biggest problem was her stiff neck, where the guy had hit her. And her damaged ego. Denise liked to think of herself as self-sufficient – even with a lot of evidence to the contrary – and letting somebody sneak up on you the way he'd snuck up on her... well, she wasn't feeling really good about herself this morning.

Around dawn she'd fallen asleep despite the three cups of coffee Greg had given her and despite the fact that MTV, which she'd asked him to turn on, was playing some very good but very loud heavy metal (Greg was kind enough to pretend that he didn't exactly, uh, well, hate heavy metal).

He'd watched her sleep.

Just watched her.

Pulled his wheelchair up across from the couch after sliding in a Buster Crabbe jungle movie on the VCR and turning it low... and sipped hot chocolate and watched the movie (there was actually some rather good jungle footage in it) and every so often let his attention drift over to her.

She looked so young sleeping. Not innocent, because while she was naive, she wasn't innocent. But young. And definitely sweet. He felt a desire to protect her. That was the only way he could think of it. Protect her. Make her life better, help her forget all the things she'd suffered as so young a girl.

At one point he put Buster Crabbe on hold and wheeled over to her and put his hand against her cheek. Her sweet, tender cheek. And then he'd taken her young hand and held it as she slept... held it for a long and sombre time. And once more the desire to protect her came to him. And he resolved then that she would stay. That he would make arrangements with whomever required arrangements... and she would stay.

Around ten-thirty, as she struggled up from the fathoms of her sleep, and as he was immersed in a really crazy movie called *Gorilla at Large* with Raymond Burr and Cameron Mitchell and a beautiful and voluptuous Anne Bancroft (who had been, unlikely as it seemed, not only a babe in 1953 but a *very sexy* babe)... around ten-thirty he went into the kitchen and started fixing her breakfast, trying to time it so that by the time she emerged showered and fresh for the day, the breakfast would be there waiting for her.

Which it was.

He sat across from her in the living room – MTV back on the tube with Cyndi Lauper's new video, which he actually liked a great deal – and Denise shovelling it in. No pretence at delicacy. This kid knew how to eat and obviously loved to eat, and man, was she happy to eat.

He, of course, wanted to be complimented (who doesn't?), and she obliged every couple minutes by saying (with her mouth full usually), "Greg, I can't believe how good this tastes!" And then she'd sort of roll her eyes and shake her head in pure unadulterated appreciation and go back to scooping it up and shovelling it in.

Toward the end, when she was working on the toast and

orange juice, he started playing Dr Ben Casey (he always wondered what had happened to the guy who'd played Casey anyway), asking his questions.

"So, how's the old bean?"

"Old bean?"

"Your head."

"Oh. Fine."

"No headache?"

"Huh-uh."

"How's the neck?"

"Great."

"Not even stiff?"

"Well, a little, I guess. But not bad."

"You seeing everything all right?"

She looked over at him and crossed her eyes and said, "I think so, doctor."

"Smart-ass."

"Really, Greg, I feel fine."

"Up to shovelling a walk?"

"Huh?" She paused with her last piece of toast held halfway to her mouth.

"It probably wouldn't hurt you, and it needs to be done. Usually I have the kid down the block do it but –"

She looked at him kind of funny, and for a terrible moment he wondered if he'd made her mad. Maybe she expected to be treated like a princess, the way she would've in one of those old 1930s comedy romances where the pauper gets used to indolent luxury.

She said, "God, Greg."

"'God, Greg' what?"

"I can't believe you asked me to do that."

"You can't?"

"No. And it's –" And she put down her toast and kind of half jumped across the coffee table and threw her arms around him and hugged him, and he could feel warm tears on her soft cheeks, and she was apparently laughing and crying at the same time and saying, "God, it makes me feel like I really belong here; like you really care about me."

"Well, that's good, because I do care about you."

And then she sat back on her haunches, holding her hands in his lap, and she said, "I'd really be honoured to shovel your walk. Really."

"Boy," Greg said, "I've got to remember this for future reference."

"Remember what?"

"That whenever I want to make you happy I don't have to buy you anything or give you compliments. All I've got to do is ask you to shovel the walk."

She laughed. "Now who's being the smart-ass?"

So, while she got bundled up and grabbed the shovel from the back porch, Greg got on the phone to call Brolan and tell him all about the mysterious visitor they'd had in the middle of the night, and how said mysterious visitor was desperate enough to knock unconscious a sixteen-year-old girl.

26

"MR BROLAN?"

"Yes."

"I'm Tom Dodge with the Minneapolis Police Department." The men shook hands.

"Is there somewhere we could go to talk for a little while?"

"Sure."

"It shouldn't take long. In case you've got another appointment, that is."

"Right down here."

Brolan led the detective down a short corridor to where three small conference rooms were housed. It was lunchtime, and two of them were open. In the third two art directors were projecting a slide show and making notes on which slides had to be replaced. These were the two resident agency wise guys.

They could turn anything into dark humour. In general they were very funny, and all the funnier because they were often the butt of their own jokes.

Brolan opened the door on conference room number two, flipped on the overhead light, and then stepped back for Dodge to precede him.

"I can get us some coffee if you'd like a cup," Brolan said.

He was well aware that his voice was about half an octave higher than usual. He was also aware that beneath his undershirt was a glaze of cold sweat.

"No, thanks," Dodge said. "Coffee makes me want to smoke cigarettes. My kids convinced me to give up smoking about six months ago. I still haven't been able to go back to coffee." He glanced around the room. "This is a very nice place. I haven't seen this much mahogany since the days when my grandfather had his law offices."

"So, you come from a tradition of law?"

Dodge shrugged. He was a trim man with short hair going grey. His blue blazer, white button-down shirt, Oxford-stripe red tie, and grey flannel slacks had the air of a uniform. He looked fifty, perhaps, and very bright and very composed. He also looked enigmatic. His dark eyes and somewhat tight mouth gave no indication of what he might be thinking. Brolan imagined this was damned useful to a cop. "I guess I never thought of it that way before. The tradition of law, I mean."

"You work out of downtown?" Brolan asked. He was aware he was chattering. He didn't know how to not chatter.

"Yes. Criminal investigation division. Homicide."

"Really? Homicide?"

Dodge smiled slightly. "Homicide. Really."

"And this has something to do with me?" Brolan's voice was going up again.

"Would you care to sit down, Mr Brolan?" He smiled again. "I guess I shouldn't be asking you to have a seat in your own place but –"

"Of course," Brolan said. "Let's sit down right now."

They sat down. At one end of the conference room was a

folding table loaded down with video playing equipment. Somebody in production was taking inventory of all the electronic stuff the agency owned. Presumably it would all be traded in on better stuff.

"Have you heard the news this morning?" Dodge asked.

"Afraid I haven't."

"There was a murder last night. A prostitute."

"I see." Brolan had been dreading the man's mentioning a freezer and a house in the suburbs. What was this all about?

"Do you ever spend time with prostitutes, Mr Brolan?"

"I want to be as co-operative as possible, Officer Dodge."

"Sergeant Inspector Dodge. That's my official title anyway."

"Thank you." He gulped some air. "I want to be as co-operative as I can be."

"I appreciate that, Mr Brolan."

"But I don't know why you'd ask me a question like that."

"About visiting prostitutes?"

"Yes."

"I didn't mean to offend you, Mr Brolan. There was a good reason for me to ask you that."

"Really?"

"Really. One of your cuff links was found at the crime scene."

"My cuff link. My God."

From his pocket, Dodge took a small oval piece of platinum inside a clear plastic evidence bag. From where he sat Brolan recognised the cuff link.

Dodge held it up. "Is this yours?"

"Yes."

"You don't need to look at it more closely?"

"No. I can see my initials inscribed from here. The cuff links are real platinum. My ex-wife had them made for me at Enrique's in St. Paul."

"Enrique's was one of the jewellery stores we called in trying to track this down. They gave us your name."

"I see."

Dodge then told him about the killing. The woman had been stabbed in the eye then savagely cut up. Dodge described the area where the body had been dumped out. "Have you been in or around there lately?"

"No."

"Think a moment. Think back a month or two. Are you sure you haven't been in or around that area?"

He thought a moment. "No."

"When was the last time your wore these particular cuff links?"

"I'm not sure. Months at least. Maybe years."

"And being in that vicinity?"

"Maybe never. I just wouldn't have any reason to be out there."

"So, you weren't out there last night?"

"No. Absolutely not."

The detective sort of nodded. Brolan still couldn't read anything on the man's face. He sat there in his cold sweat, hoping his hands weren't twitching. It was like being afraid of farting at a fancy dinner party. You knew you were a weird and twisted wretch; you just didn't want other people to know that.

"Here's a photograph of her," the detective said, reaching inside his sport coat pocket and taking out a small photo and handing it over.

Brolan realised now that the detective did not necessarily believe his denials. No, I don't know any prostitutes. No I don't go out to that area ever. Fine, Mr Brolan, why don't you take a look at this photo anyway?

Brolan took the photo and studied it. A fleshy woman in a cheap green dress stood by a ten-year-old Chevrolet on a sunny spring morning in front of a crumbling three-storey apartment house. She gave you the impression that these were her Sunday clothes and that she'd just come from church. Her cheeky, middle-aged face also gave the impression of a kind of weary sorrow. Even at a distance the smile revealed dentures, and the hair revealed an unnatural henna tint, and the belly and hips revealed an iron girdle. She might have been somebody's slightly boozy maiden aunt except for a certain coarseness around the mouth, a coarseness put there (or so Brolan imagined in his somewhat moralistic way) by too much loveless sex. It was a mouth that had told and laughed at too many feeble dirty jokes for the pleasure of too many feeble johns.

"Not familiar?" the detective asked as Brolan handed the photo back.

"Afraid not."

The detective put the photo away. "Are you married, Mr Brolan?"

"Divorced."

"Lady friends?"

"I wish I could say yes. I'm afraid my lady friend and I are splitting up."

"I'm sorry."

"Thanks."

"So, you don't have any idea how your cuff link could have gotten there?"

"No."

"And you keep your cuff links where?"

"In a small leather box with some other stuff – tie bars and things like that – in a bureau drawer in my home."

"You live alone?"

"Yes."

"Does anybody else have access to your place?"

"By access, you mean, do they have a key?"

"Right."

"No. I'm the only one with a key."

"Have you had any suspicion lately that somebody might have broken in and taken things?"

"No."

"So, you can't account for this cuff link being where we found it?"

Brolan tried a smile. "Obviously I wish I could." He hesitated. "I take it, this cuff link makes me a suspect."

"Not necessarily, Mr Brolan. It could be a freak coincidence. Maybe somebody did break into your home recently, and you just weren't aware of it."

"That happens?"

"Certainly. Some thieves don't call any attention to themselves. They come in and take very specific things. Jewellery, for instance. The owner may not notice that anything is missing for several days. This gives the thieves a real advantage. They're way down the road before we even know that they took anything."

"So, this thief could have taken my cuff links and – what? Dropped them at the scene of the crime on purpose?"

"Perhaps. At this point we can't be sure. All we know is that, for some reason, one of your cuff links was found at a murder scene."

"And somebody could have dropped it there on purpose or by accident?"

"Right."

"And that could have been a thief. Or – me."

"Right."

"I wasn't there," Brolan said. "I wasn't there, and I don't know the woman. Never saw her before. I want to be emphatic about that."

"I can see that, Mr Brolan."

"And I certainly don't want to be a suspect in a murder case."

"Nobody does, Mr Brolan," the detective said. He sat up on the edge of the chair, obviously getting ready to leave. "But if you should remember anything, I'd appreciate it if you'd contact me. I'll leave you my card."

"Remember anything?"

The detective stood up – as did Brolan – and extended his hand. As they shook, the detective said, "Remember anything you might have forgotten to tell me." He stared directly into Brolan's eyes. "Maybe later on you'll recall that you actually met the woman somewhere previously. Maybe you just didn't recognise this particular picture. That happens sometimes."

"But I don't know her, and I'm sure of that."

"Well," the detective said, "just in case anything like that does come up, please feel free to give me a call."

He handed Brolan a small white card with very unfancy typeset information on it.

Brolan nodded and took the card and right then realised that somebody had very crudely – but very effectively – framed him for murder for a second time.

"Talk to you again, Mr Brolan," the detective said as he was leaving.

27

HE WAS FOURTEEN YEARS OLD the first time he ever hurt a girl. The funny thing was, he hadn't planned on it happening at all.

Next door there was a twelve-year-old named Jessica. He'd known for a long time that she had a crush on him. She followed him everywhere and wrote him letters and was always asking him to join various neighbourhood clubs she invented. She also frequently asked him to come over when *American Bandstand* was on and dance the twist with him. This was in the summer of 1961. Later he would try to figure out why he did what he did, if there were some certain inspiration for doing it. But he could find none. It was a typical summer, a humid and furious green in the wealthy neighbourhood where he lived, and a pastel blue where his family had a cabin and sailed – blue water, blue skies.

There were woods two miles from his house, and sometimes he'd ride his bike over there and go hiking. He liked the woods, the secret hiding places, especially, where he could sit and watch people walk by on the trails below that ran along the edge of the river. The secret hiding places made him feel powerful, and he needed that sense particularly this summer. His parents were getting a divorce.

They'd always fought, but now there was violence. His mother had a lover. His father could not get over this fact. Several times he'd seen his father very savagely slap his mother.

Curiously, though, it was his father who always cried after such violence, never his mother. She went downstairs and had a drink of bourbon and smoked several cigarettes and stared out at the vast rolling lawn kept in shape by a coloured man none of them quite trusted. His father always disintegrated, going into the den and sobbing, the way a boy would sob. He always wanted to go in and put his arm around his father, but he couldn't because his mother would get angry and accuse him of taking his father's side and not hers.

Sometimes he would go downstairs and talk to his mother before she got drunk. "You don't have to go away with that other man, Mother. You can stay here. Things can be like they were. We can be happy again, just the three of us." "Oh, baby," she'd say, touching his face gently, "baby, you're just too young to understand. But Dad loves you," she'd say. "Dad loves you. That's the only reason he hits you." Then she'd smile and say, "You've got to give Gil a chance. You'll like him once you get to know him. He played for the Vikings one year; did I ever tell you that?"

"You tell me that all the time, and I don't give a shit. I don't want to live with him!"

"Baby, you hurt me when you talk like that; you really do."

Then he'd go upstairs and stand outside the den and listen to his father stretch out on the leather couch. Usually his father would fall asleep. It was as if he could no longer face consciousness, and he'd just tune out.

By nightfall, she'd be dressed up and gone, moving through the summer dusk in the aqua Thunderbird with the white hardtop.

He'd make his father dinner. Oh, no gourmet dining to be sure – usually a chili dog with potato chips and maybe baked beans, the sort of stuff they always ate at the cabin. Then he'd take it up to the den, and he'd knock softly and his father would wake up and let him in. His father's law practice had pretty much gone to hell over the previous four months. He'd heard his father arguing bitterly with one of his partners on the phone about how his father wasn't carrying his load.

So, in the den they'd eat and watch TV shows, such as *Perry Mason* and *Lawman* and the Jack Benny and Andy Griffith programs. Both his father and he were big fans of Don Knotts. Whenever Don, as Barney, was called upon to hold down the fort while Andy was off doing something else, you just knew it was going to be a great episode.

And his father would try to explain. Ultimately he understood or thought he understood anyway. Impotence. "Do you know what that means?" his father would ask. "Sorta," he'd say. "Sorta."

They'd been to doctors, and they'd been to psychiatrists, and they'd tried all sorts of methods and techniques, but it hadn't seemed to help. His mother started drinking then and saying that in some way it was her fault, and then things just kept getting worse and worse until now .

Sometimes his father would start drinking, too, and that was the worst, because his father was an even worse drinker than his mother. After several drinks he was like a stranger, angry and violent – his handsome face distorted in rage – smashing things up with his fists and always ending up on the couch crying, crying.

When his father got like this, all he could do was watch. His father's temper was so bad that he was afraid to go up to the man. Afraid of really getting hurt. Sometimes the booze would make his father more or less unconscious. When this happened, he'd turn off the light and stand in the doorway listening to his father snore and then he'd say, "Good night, Dad. I love you." Then he'd close the door and go to his own room.

He usually didn't sleep till his mother got home. Deep into the rolling black night he'd hear the T-bird's engine on the drive below and see the wash of its headlights across his window, and then he'd hear the automatic garage door go up.

She always came in and kissed him goodnight. She always smelled of hard liquor and what he would later recognise as the moist scent of sex. He always pretended to be asleep. He didn't know what to say to her. He wanted to say, "You whore, you whore." But he wasn't sure that was true. He didn't know if it was her fault his father was impotent… or if it was his father's fault.

Six weeks before school was to start, his father made things easy for everybody by driving his new Chrysler straight into a bridge abutment at more than ninety miles per hour. Officially the word was accident, but of course he'd been drunk, and of course he'd meant to do it.

Three weeks later the incident with Jessica took place in the woods.

He had no idea how she'd found his hiding place near the clay cliffs above the water. He was sitting in the shade of a clay overhang, trying to escape the ninety-six-degree heat, when he looked up, and there she was. Dressed in a T-shirt and cut-off Levi's and a pair of white tennis shoes. Hands on hips. Very bold.

"You probably didn't think I knew about this place, did you?"

He shrugged. "Guess not."

"Well, there're a lot of things I know."

"Oh."

He closed his eyes, willing her out of existence. The air was heavy with humidity and butterflies and mosquitoes and bluejays and wrens and robins. Close by, the air smelled of spruce and maple and redbud; of wild ginger and ginseng and bloodroot. He often wished he were a deer and could bound through the bluffs and caves and mineral springs; the lakes and gorges and forests. That was his most profound wish – even more than being like Steve McQueen or Marshall Matt Dillon – to be an animal, to appreciate nature and know nothing of the human heart.

"Is it all right if I sit down?" Jessica asked.

"Guess so."

As she took two steps toward him, he realised again that Jessica was blooming suddenly. Small but distinct breasts played against the white cotton of her T-shirt, and her summer-tanned legs were getting long and shapely. Even her blue eyes had changed somehow – were more knowing, inscrutable. She used to be just a kid. But now she was something more than that, even if she wasn't quite a woman yet.

She brushed sand from a nearby rock and sat down. "I haven't told you how sorry I am about your father."

"Thanks."

"I know how much you loved him."

"Yeah."

She watched him. "You don't want to talk about it, do you?"

"Guess not."

"Are you mad I came here?"

"Guess not."

"I'm not trying to bug you."

"I know."

"You do?"

He looked at her. "Yeah."

After a time she said, "My parents were wondering how your mother is."

"She's doing all right." Both of them were aware of the sudden anger in his voice. "She's with that creep all the time."

"My dad said that her boyfriend used to be a Viking. Is that true?"

"Yeah, but so what?"

"I was just asking. I didn't mean to make you mad." He raised his eyes to hers again. "Why don't you come over here?"

"What?"

"Come over here. Closer to me."

"Really?" She sounded very young just then, as if she couldn't at all believe her good luck.

"Yeah."

"How come?"

"You want to come over here or not?"

"Sure," she said, and with not another word she raised her shapely bottom from the rock and plopped it next to him on the cool grass beneath the overhang.

But at the moment that her venerable dream was at last fulfilled, she found herself not knowing what to do.

For a long time they sat next to each other, silent. There was no more than half an inch between their bodies, but it might as well have been a yard.

Without any warning he slid his arm around her shoulder and pulled her to him. He kissed her directly on the mouth, lips closed.

He could feel her squirm like a joyous puppy against him and hear happy sounds deep down her windpipe. She was so happy, it was almost embarrassing.

"Oh, God," she said when he took his face from hers. "Oh, God."

"Did you enjoy that?"

"Are you kidding? I loved that." She hesitated, looked embarrassed. "Did you enjoy it?"

"Guess so."

"Couldn't you say it kinda better than that?"

"What?"

"You know, say it nice. Like, 'Boy, I really enjoyed that.' You know. Enthusiasm."

"You know I enjoyed it."

"Well, I'm glad."

"You going to tell your parents?"

"Are you kidding? I'm only twelve."

"You going to tell anybody else?"

"Not if you don't want me to."

"Good."

It was then he took the pocket knife from his jeans. It was a Boy Scout knife with a black handle. He opened the longest blade.

As they'd been kissing, he'd been aware that his groin was dead. A lot of times, just lying on his bed and thinking of this girl or that, he'd get so aroused, he'd have to leap up, put a chair up to the door so nobody could break in, and masturbate. He'd close his eyes and imagine the girls he'd glimpsed in *Playboy*, those swaying breasts and mounds of pink buttocks.

So, he should have been doubly aroused with a real girl in his arms, even if she was only twelve and his next-door neighbour.

But he hadn't been aroused, and he knew that something was wrong. He thought of his father.

"How come you took out your knife?" she said. "It was kind of poking me in the leg."

"You want me to kiss you again?"

"Do you want to kiss me again?"

"Guess so."

"You'll have to say it better than that."

"Guess I'd like to kiss you."

"How about 'Jesse, I'd really like to kiss you.'"

"Okay."

"Will you say it?"

He shrugged and said it.

She smiled, and he put his arm around her again and kissed her.

This time he pushed his tongue into her mouth. He felt himself begin to tingle. Breath coming a little faster. But still — nothing in his groin. Nothing. Was he going to be impotent, too?

His hand cupped her breast. He felt silken flesh and a little nub of nipple.

But nothing in his groin; nothing.

He wanted to be an animal and run away. Fast. Far.

And then his hand found the knife and almost without realising it he… cut her and he… pulled the knife a quarter inch down her arm.

She cried out, pushing away from him, furious and baffled and terrified of him now.

"What're you doing?" she shouted, scrambling away backward. "What're you doing?"

It wasn't much of a cut, really. You could get a lot worse than that just getting scraped by a branch.

But it had worked.

At sight of her blood, his crotch had swollen and pained him with a monumental erection.

At sight of her blood…

"It was an accident," he said.

"An accident?" But she was crying then and barely coherent. Somehow she sensed what this was all about, and there was frenzy about her...

He went over to her and sat by her and began to stroke her. Once he had hurt her, once he could see blood, he could be tender with her.

He took her in his arms and held her until her crying stopped, until she turned her face up to his and they kissed again

He was never to see her intimately again. Apparently she never told anybody about that afternoon, because her parents never said a word to him. In the autumn she fell in love with a boy she would ultimately – after breaking up and making up many times – marry and have four children with (this was after the whole family moved away when she was a junior).

But he never forgot the afternoon; nor did he forget the lesson. The sight of dark red blood on soft white flesh, dark red blood on the soft golden down of her arm, dark red blood...

Stu Foster recalled all this on the way over to Brolan's place. When he looked back, there was a direct line running from the afternoon with Jessica to how he'd treated certain women all his life. Certain women. There was a euphemism for you. Whores. Those were the "certain women." He had married well, a really darling if plump girl who'd been a Tri-Delt and a beauty queen runner-up, and whose father had made and lost a fortune in petrochemicals down in Kentucky – and of course he kept his preferences secret from her. Oh, once or twice he'd been tempted to hurt her a little – disguised, of course, as playfulness – during their lovemaking. But he'd been afraid he couldn't stop. So, he'd visited whores. The late sixties and seventies had been a boon for people like him. Sex was everywhere. Everything from weekend clubs to outcall massage parlours, when you were in a strange city and didn't want to leave your hotel room. And almost always when you explained to them what you wanted, what you really wanted, you paid them a little money, and there you were. Commerce, just like anything else. Commerce.

Only once had there been real trouble. New Orleans, it had been. Too much rich food, too much hard liquor, too many women who gave you the impression they'd do absolutely anything if you had the good green Yankee cash. A mulatto woman asked him if he'd ever shaved a woman down there before and he'd said no, that he hadn't really even thought about it. So, she gave him this straight razor and a shaving mug and brush and she lay back on the bed and spread her legs and told him to go ahead. She had some kind of blues on the radio, and she was smoking a joint, and she closed her eyes as if he weren't even there at all. And there he sat on the edge of the bed, looking at the juicy pink meat between her legs with a bone-handled straight razor in his fingers, and then a darkness came over him, and he wasn't even sure what he'd tried to do. All he knew was that soon she was screaming and holding her hands over her sex, and that there was blood, blood streaming between her fingers.

…And he was apologising and saying he was sorry – "My God, listen, I'm really really sorry; I'll leave you extra money; so sorry; just drunk; please, please just take this money and quit screaming, please." And for a full year he'd been afraid to go back to a hooker. Afraid of what he might do.

But then, the following spring, he met some hookers in Des Moines who knew how to deal with men like him – who knew how to let him get his kicks without ever going too far…

In the backseat, in a brown paper bag, were the clothes he'd worn with the whore Emma and with the whore at the piano bar the other night. You could still smell the blood. A kind of steely tang. Also in the bag was the knife he'd used. Same knife on both occasions.

As he approached Brolan's street, he thought of how his partner had looked when he saw the detective waiting for him in the reception area. The thing was, he didn't really dislike Frank Brolan. So, he'd felt a little sorry for him, seeing that Brolan realised that he was trapped, that forces beyond any of his powers were working against him.

He took the alley. Given the time of day, there were no

children around playing.

He drove to Brolan's garage, got out, grabbed the bag, and carried it quickly inside the garage.

Even in winter the interior smelled of car oil from stains on the floor. Sometimes Frank liked to putter around on his own car, finding such work relaxing.

The garage was orderly, almost empty. On one wall hung a manual lawn mower, three rakes, and a lawn seeder. Against the opposite concrete block wall was a tall stack of corded firewood, a kerosene heater, an aluminium stepladder, and several fifty-pound bags of salt for ice. None of these lent themselves to his purposes. He looked around, finally raising his eyes to the two-by-fours that criss-crossed the ceiling. A few pieces of plywood had been laid across the two-by-fours so that things could be stored up there. You could see where the plywood sagged in the middle from the weight. This would be an ideal place for what he had in mind.

He went over and got the ladder and carried it to the centre of the garage. He took the paper bag with the clothes and the knife in it and took it up the ladder. He set the bag far back on the plywood, as if somebody had tried very hard to hide it up there, and then he came back down the steps.

That should work.

Within another minute, the ladder put back, the side door of the garage closed snugly, he was in his car and sluicing through the deep snow in the alley.

Ten minutes later, at a drive-up phone, he stopped and deposited thirty-five cents and called the office. He asked for Kathleen. She came on the line in a minute or so.

"Are you someplace you can talk?" he said.

She hesitated. "Not really."

"Well, I just wanted to let you know that I made my little trip to his garage."

"No problems, then?"

"None."

"Good."

"In about an hour I'm going to call the police and tell them that as an anonymous good citizen, I feel duty bound to tell them that I think he's hiding a body somewhere in his house. That I think I saw him carrying one in the other night." He sighed. "Poor bastard. You should have seen his face this morning."

But he was being sentimental, and Kathleen was almost never sentimental. From all this, she would gain half the agency, taking over Brolan's role. That was all she thought about. Two years before, Foster and Kathleen had been forced to accompany each other on a business trip to Denver. One snowy night, the client's plane unable to land, they'd endured a dinner together. They genuinely disliked and distrusted each other. Foster saw her as all ambition and cunning; and she saw him as everything she hated about the men's club that still ran most of advertising. But drinks had led to sex and sex to a peculiar relationship. She seemed to hate men in much the same way he hated women. She'd even sensed – that very first night – that for him pain was a part of pleasure. She'd started biting him, hard, almost angrily, to the point of drawing blood. And that night he'd had an orgasm that nearly blinded him with its pleasure... They let people, including Brolan, continue to think that they still hated each other. It lent their real relationship a protective coloration. And after a few months Kathleen started talking about how they could get new clients for the agency. Good, blue-chip clients that so many other agencies were always hurling themselves against uselessly .

"I'm going to have a little talk with Lane first. Brolan's been poking around. He may have figured out some things about our friend Charles," Foster said.

"Good," she said.

"I'll see you at your place around six," he said, and hung up.

In another minute, he was driving again, enjoying the sparkling white snow and the dark branches swinging in the wind.

28

BROLAN WAS NOT ABLE TO STOP SHAKING.

Fifteen minutes after the detective had left, he sat behind his desk, his office door closed, trembling as if he had been left out in a farm field over night.

He felt the weight of the past three days and nights on him – paranoia about the woman in the freezer, not enough sound sleep, wild suspicions and surmises about nearly everyone around him.

One way or another, he knew, it would be over with soon. He simply didn't have the stamina for much more.

He had put his head down on his desk, the way he once had as a grade-school boy. Had he ever been sleepier than he'd been trying to survive an afternoon of history and maths?

It was no different now. All he wanted was sleep. Given all the trouble he was in, the desire was almost perverse.

But he didn't care.

He slept.

He had no idea what time it was when his intercom buzzed. His head came up quickly, as if somebody had poked him with a pin.

"Yes?"

"Line two."

Rubbing sleep from his eyes. "Do you know who it is?"

"Somebody named Denise. Sounds young."

"Oh. Right. Denise. Thanks."

He picked up. "Hi."

"Greg asked me to call you."

"Fine."

"He – we – wanted to know if you knew anybody who drives a silver XKE."

"I sure do."

"Well, he came here last night – over in Emma's apartment – and he pushed stuff around pretty good, and then he knocked me out."

"What?"

So, she explained. "So, you know who he is?"

"His name is Cummings."

"Greg thinks you should find out what he's up to."

"I think that's a very good idea." He paused. "How do you feel, Denise?"

"Neck's kind of stiff is all."

"Otherwise all right?"

"Otherwise fine."

"I'm going to check him out. And right now."

"The man who hit me?"

"Right."

"If you get a chance, punch him for me, will you?" Then she laughed. "I'm just kidding. I hate to see anybody get punched."

"I'll try and get over there around dinner time. Maybe the three of us can order a pizza or something."

"Greg wants to show me a serial called *Jungle Girl* tonight. Maybe you can watch it, too."

Actually that sounded nice. Pleasant. Relaxing. He said, "Hope so, Denise. Hope so."

From downtown Brolan went to the Chichester Country Club, which lay in a wooded — and now virtually snowbound area — south of the city.

The snow, the freezing temperature, and the brutal winds hadn't kept many members from lunching there. The parking lot was full. A man in a hunting outfit on a mobile snowblower was scraping the parking lot. He waved when he saw Brolan.

Chichester was by no means the most exclusive club in the city, but in a peculiar way it was the most difficult to get into. The men who founded the place following World War II looked for like kind only — hunters, fishermen, sports fanatics. That was the measure there — what type of man you were, and not social background or wealth. Of course, if you were impoverished and living on food stamps, it was unlikely the Chichester boys would take you, even if you knew how to catch fish with your bare hands.

The ranch-style building stretched over a deeply sloping hill down to a small wooded area of pine and fir. It was made of native stone and rough timber, lending it the hoped-for look of rustic sophistication. The creek that ran downslope was frozen over and silver. A white-haired man in a long dark overcoat skated across the ice, holding himself erect with military decorum. At his age Brolan would be lucky to be able to get out of bed every morning, let alone do a few miles on a frozen creek.

A chunky man in a good suit one size too small greeted Brolan just inside the door. "May I help you?"

"I'd like to see Mr Cummings."

"I see. I'm afraid he's swimming right now. Maybe you'd like to wait in the bar."

"Fine."

The man pointed to the bar and stepped back for Brolan to walk in front of him.

Brolan had a scotch-and-water and a cigarette. Then he had another scotch-and-water and two cigarettes. Toward the end of the second one, he started coughing. Wonderful.

He had been in the bar twenty minutes when he started looking around. The northern wall was solid glass and overlooked steep downslopes that a few people were using for skiing. The other walls were the same native stone as the exterior. Deep leather chairs and dark wooden trundle tables took up the rest of the space – except for the bar. All the linen was very white and very well pressed, and none of the glasses had any water stains on them, and the preppie-looking bartender was careful to call you sir without any irony in his voice whatsoever.

Brolan decided to go looking for Cummings. He could sit there a long time. Cummings was a swimming freak. When stress got too much, he often came out here and swam all afternoon. Anyway, there was at least a chance that the doorman had mentioned Brolan to Cummings. And an equal chance that Cummings had glimpsed Brolan and decided to take off so he wouldn't have to answer any questions.

Without having any idea where he was going, Brolan started searching through the club for the swimming pool. He found a snooker room and a den and a locker room. The pool was nearby.

Cummings was in there. Barrel-chested, his. arms and back and chest covered with white hair, he rose and dove, rose and dove like a porpoise through the green, chlorine-smelling water. He was the only one in the pool.

Steam misted the large window that overlooked the grounds. On the bottom of the Olympic-size pool you could see Chichester spelled out in a mosaic of blue and white tiles. Brolan walked along the edge of the pool. Cummings hadn't noticed him yet.

Brolan went to the far end of the pool and stood next to the silver-coloured ladder leading into the water.

After a minute or so, coming up for air, Cummings saw him. He said, spitting water, "What the hell do you want?"

"I want to know why you broke into Emma's duplex last night."

Cummings's answer surprised him. "How the hell'd you know about that?"

"The girl you knocked out told me about it."

"I didn't mean to hit her so hard. She shouldn't have been looking through my car."

Cummings finished his lap and swam to the ladder. Climbing out of the water, he shook his head and then sleeked back his hair. He grabbed a nubby white towel from a deck chair and started towelling himself off.

"So, what the hell're you doing here, Brolan?"

"I want to know why you were in Emma's duplex."

Wet, eyes red from the chlorine, white hair turned a dirty grey from the water, Cummings said, "Why the hell do you think?" He tugged his blue trunks up.

"I don't know. That's why I'm asking you."

Cummings began to work his jaw muscles. He narrowed his eyes and glared at Brolan. "What's going on here? You know damn well what I was looking for in her duplex. The nice little package I pay 'rent' on every month."

Brolan started to ask him what he was talking about, but just then the doorman came into the pool area. His voice echoed off the tall ceiling and the lapping green water. "There's a call for you, Mr Cummings."

"Thank you," Cummings said, poking a little finger into an ear and cleaning out some water. To Brolan, he said, "I've got to say one thing, Brolan. I'm surprised you'd have anything to do with this."

"With what?"

Some of the anger died in Cummings's eyes. His gaze was one of curiosity, then surprise. "You really don't know what I'm talking about, do you?"

"No, I don't."

Cummings's laugh bounced off the pool walls. "My God, Brolan, did you think it was because you two assholes are such great businessmen that you suddenly started picking off accounts?"

"Cummings, I want you to tell me what you're talking about."

Cummings patted his arrogant, handsome face with the nubby towel. "Go ask your partner, Brolan. Maybe it's time you started asking him about a lot of things."

Before Brolan could say anything else, Cummings's wide white feet began slapping the wet tile floor. He was heading for a wall phone about ten yards away. He was obviously finished talking with Brolan, even if Brolan wasn't finished talking with him.

But just before he reached the phone, Cummings turned around and said, "Tell the girl I'm sorry I hit her so hard."

He walked over to the phone, jerked up the receiver, and began talking.

Brolan stood there a long moment. What the hell had Cummings been talking about? What was he paying 'rent' on? And what did Stu Foster have to do with any of this?

In the lobby, furious without quite knowing why, he went over to a bank of pay phones. They weren't enclosed, so he knew that he'd have to watch what he said. He called the office and asked for Foster. Still at lunch, was the answer. He hung up.

As he walked to the parking lot, the cold finally dispelling the sharp, lingering scent of chlorine in his nostrils, his mind raced with possibilities of Stu's role in all this. But what would that be?

And what had Cummings been looking for the night before, when he'd knocked out Denise?

He got in his car and left the country club. As he made his way out, the man on the snowblower waved again.

Brolan waved back and then gave his car as much power as it could handle on the icy road.

29

HALFWAY THROUGH HIS SEARCH, he found the photograph. It looked as if it had been taken sometime during the sixties, because the little girl standing next to a 1967 Ford was not only dressed up in a Sunday blue dress but was also proudly hugging a Partridge Family album to her chest. The girl was very young and, in the sunny day, squinted up at the camera, which only made her look even more vulnerable than she would have naturally. The girl was Emma.

"Did you find something?" Denise called from the other room.

He had to clear his throat. Looking at the photograph had touched him in a way he hadn't wanted to be touched. Not by Emma. Not anymore.

"No," he said. "I'm still looking."

Over lunch Denise and Greg had speculated about what the man who'd broken in the previous night might have been looking for. Ultimately – because they had decided that the man probably had not found what he'd come for – they'd come over to Emma's and started looking for something that probably wasn't very mysterious at all... but something that was no doubt vital to the killer.

In a bureau drawer Greg had found the photograph, and he couldn't stop staring at it. In a way the photo put a curse on him. He had decided that he no longer loved Emma; that in her heart she'd seen him not as an individual or a man but as that abstraction known as a cripple. He had decided two days before to keep that in mind whenever he felt sentimental or sad about her. But staring at this photo… he wondered what she'd been like as a little girl. He wished he had a time machine and could go back to her on that sunny Sunday morning and talk to her. Help her, really.

If Greg had raised Emma, she certainly would have turned out to be a very different woman. Not hating herself; not lacking even the barest self-confidence. (She genuinely believed she was ugly and stupid; Emma – ugly and stupid!) He would have seen that she took her studies seriously, that she dated only the right kind of boys, that she went on to college… And then, of course, (in this time machine fantasy) she would have fallen in love with him. He would have offered her a wonderfully normal girlhood, and she would have returned the favour by seeing that no one loved her as well as Greg Wagner himself. And it would not have been pity, and it would not have been gratitude; it would have been pure love, an admixture of both the romantic and the more mature sorts of love, and they would have been bound up in this forever.

He had no idea that he was crying as he sat in the sachet-scented bedroom, slumped in one corner of his wheelchair.

But behind him, gently, Denise said, "You all right, Greg?"

And when he looked up at her, he felt very foolish, of course, and unmanly, tears silver on his cheeks. "I'm fine."

She grinned. God, she did have a cute, impish grin. "Yeah, that's just how you sound, too. Fine."

He had to laugh. He was sad, but she got him laughing, and he silently thanked her for it.

She came over and stood next to him and looked at the photograph. "Is that Emma?"

"Yes."

"Boy, she was really pretty."

"She sure was."

"You'll always love her, won't you, Greg?"

He smiled up at her. "Actually I'm trying to not to."

"Really? How come?"

"Because she didn't love me."

"From what you said, I'll bet she did."

"Well, not in the way I wanted to be loved anyway."

"So, why should that stop you from loving her in the way you want to love her?"

"Because it makes me feel weak and foolish."

She leaned over and kissed him on the side of the head. "You know what it is?"

"Huh?"

"It's your pride. That's all." Then she tousled his hair. "You men. You're all alike." She snatched the photo from his hand and said, "Now, give this to me, and I'll go get it framed for you tomorrow. This is a great picture, and you should keep it someplace special in your duplex."

She thumped him on the shoulder. "And forget about your pride, Greg. You've got enough problems without that hanging over your head."

By then, of course, he was laughing and laughing hard. She was treating him just like a child... and somehow making him understand (without hurting his feelings) that he was behaving just like a child.

From the back pocket of her jeans she pulled out a manila envelope and held it up. "What's Brolan's partner's name?"

"Stu Foster. Why?"

"Well, he sure sent Emma a lot of letters. Or not letters, exactly. Envelopes. And – oh, yeah – and this tape that was inside this box of candy."

"What?" Wagner said. Already he was trying to reason through what Denise was telling him and imagining how interested Brolan would be in this piece of information. Why would Stu Foster send Emma envelopes? Why would Stu Foster even know Emma to begin with?

"Here," Denise said, handing him the envelope. "There's a whole pile of these in a kitchen drawer. You want to go see them?"

Wagner, sounding as if he'd just discovered gold, said, "Lead the way!"

30

HE WORE AN EARRING. Foster had never quite gotten used to that, a guy wearing an earring. Much as he hated to admit it, the earring threatened Foster in some way.

But then, so did most everything else about Charles Decker Lane.

Lane was a thirty-seven-year-old man who'd inherited a small chain of ten motels from his father. That was back in the seventies, just as the Motel 6s and the other low-priced lodgings were moving into the mid-western market. Lane, an MBA from Northwestern, had been of the mind that people would ultimately tire of the low-enders. The average businessman wanted more than a closet-sized toilet that smelled of disinfectant and two double beds that were practically bunk beds, the way they almost piled on top of each other. Or so had been Charles Decker Lane's thinking in the mid-seventies, right before Jimmy Carter and the recession and stagflation happened and made Charles Decker Lane eat every foolish goddamn word he'd said. In February of 1977 he'd had 1416 rooms under his control. By April of 1978 he had fewer than 200 – three frigging motels left out of the ten he'd started with, and not a one of them within walking distance of an airport. Or did they even have airports in Terre Haute, Indiana, site of two of the motels?

Which was when he discovered cocaine, first as a user, then as a distributor. Back when he got in, the thing was like a big Amway deal. There was even a certain amount of fun in it, not to mention just ducky profits. The chicks liked it especially. Even the country club bitches he met at his brother's would finally give in and fuck him if he offered enough cocaine. (His brother's wife thought that Charles Decker Lane would someday die of a state-injected terminal drug and told everybody this.) The white stuff made him lots of green stuff, but then things started changing, and for once in his young but unsuccessful life, Lane knew when to get out of something. The first thing he did was go to a chemical dependency clinic and get himself clean. Talk about a bitch. He hadn't cried this much since he'd found his

ED GORMAN

first wife balling that nigger football player right in Charles
Decker Lane's bed. (Lane had broken her nose, knowing that
was the only satisfaction he was going to get, assuming that she
was going to soak him in divorce court.) The second thing he did
was tell everybody that he was clean and no longer dealing. He
even went to a downtown dealer and turned over all his names
and contacts free, gratis. (The guy was understandably suspicious
that Lane here might be a narc.) Then he took all the lovely
money he'd made dealing coke and put it in federally-insured
CDs all over the Mid-west. He kept one motel for himself and
used as his chief source of income the interest his ducky money
was making for him.

Six years before, Lane and Foster met at a party one wintry
night, got along, and started talking about all the ad execs who
used Lane's sumptuously decorated motel as a sort of
whorehouse. Foster, who was then in the employ of Richard
Cummings and Associates, didn't start thinking about this till he
and Brolan got fed up with Cummings's temper tantrums and
decided to go out on their own. There were many ways to go
about getting clients – you could wine and dine them; you could
marry into the right family; you could even actually show them
a few good ads you'd done over the years – but what with all the
competition, Foster started wondering if there wasn't maybe a
more interesting way to get clients. What if you had a motel
room, see, where ad execs had their little trysts... and what if
somebody had the room bugged with microphones and a
videotape camera... and what if you presented the execs you
had on videotape with the choice of exposure (no pun intended)
or turning their accounts over to you? Could there be any faster
way to get yourself five big-name clients in a very short time? All
you had to do was concentrate on which execs were (a) players,
and (b) liked some sort of kicks they considered shameful. They'd
be begging you to take their accounts once you showed them
the tapes. Thus was born the Foster-Brolan agency.

So, anyway, Charles Decker Lane's earring.
Foster had always been curious why a guy who wore Brooks

Brothers suits, a tie stick in every collar, cuff links, and a hundred-dollar razor cut would wear an earring. Wasn't that a little like a bank CEO wearing a bone through his nose?

That day, though, Foster tried to forget the earring. He sat with Lane in the motel's coffee shop, telling him about Brolan.

"You mean he's figured it out?" Lane said.

"I mean, he's trying to figure it out."

"And you think he's coming out here?"

"You can bet on it."

"I just won't tell him anything."

"You don't know Brolan. He's got one of those tempers."

"Well, there's always Ernie."

Ernie was the night bartender. He used to fight on one of the regular cards downtown. He had a smashed nose and wide, flat fists and a very bad temper.

"You'll need him," Foster said.

Lane shrugged. He had cornflower-blue eyes and blonde hair, and a tiny moustache that made him look like a danceband leader in a thirties musical. "Right now I'm more concerned about Emma."

"What about her?" Foster said. He had to be very, very careful.

"I can't get hold of her. I've left about twenty messages on her phone machine, and she hasn't gotten back to me in three days." He shook his head. "Waybright is asking for her again." Waybright was one of Foster's largest clients and a man who had a fairly serious crush on Emma. "You haven't seen her?"

"No."

"Or heard from her?"

"No."

"I wonder where she is."

Immediately an image of Emma stuck inside Brolan's freezer came to Foster. As soon as he left Lane, he was going to call the police and tell them where they could find Emma.

"She'll turn up," Foster said.

He glanced around the coffee shop. The place was all got up as a forties diner. Art deco meets blue collar. The waitresses wore hair nets out of the *Rosie the Riveter* era and little buttons that read "Buy War Bonds." Lane often talked of wanting to produce dinner-theatre musicals there. He took his frustrations out on his coffee shop.

"So, expect him anyway," Foster said. "Fair warning."

"You sure are uptight. Relax, for Christ's sake, Foster. Everything's going to be fine."

"Yeah, I suppose."

"I'll call you as soon as Brolan leaves. Just to let you know that everything's okay. All right?"

Foster stood up. As he did so, he bit at the nail on his forefinger. He hated it when he started biting his nails. It was such an unbecoming habit. "And let me know if you hear from Emma, too."

Lane stared at him for a long time. "Sure, Foster. I'll call her again, see if I can scare her up." The way he was looking at him, Foster had the uncomfortable feeling that the man had become a mind reader.

Maybe in Foster's mind he could read the image of Emma lying dead and rigid inside the freezer.

"Talk to you in a while," Foster said, and left the coffee shop.

In the lobby he watched as two very good-looking stewardesses checked in for the night. As people came in from the outside, they made loud noises stamping their feet on the big rubber mats over by the row of newspaper vending machines.

Foster found a phone booth. He went inside and closed the door. Then, as an afterthought, he opened the door again and checked out the booths on either side of him.

Back in his own booth again, the door closed, he deposited thirty-five cents, looked up the number of the downtown police department, and placed his call.

When the receptionist answered, Foster asked for Homicide. "Anybody in particular?"

"No, sir." Foster had a handkerchief over the receiver. An old trick, to be sure, but an effective one.

"Then you can talk to me. I'm Sergeant Inspector Nordengren."

"All right." He paused.

"What is it you'd like to tell me, sir?"

"About a murder."

"About a murder?"

"Yes, sir."

"Well, what about a murder?"

"There's a dead woman in the freezer."

"I see. And where would this be?"

Foster gave the man Brolan's address.

"And would you know how she got there?" the detective asked.

"I think so."

"And how would that be?"

"He put her there."

"He?"

"The man who lives there."

"Ah. And would he possibly also be the man who murdered her?"

"I don't want to say any more. I've said enough already."

"But —"

"I've been a good citizen. Now I just want to forget about it." And with that he hung up.

He imagined Inspector Sergeant Nordengren was going to be quite busy the rest of that evening.

31

AROUND SIX O'CLOCK, just as dusk was becoming black night, and snow flurries began to increase, and the winds from the north-west cranked up several miles per hour, Brolan pulled up in front of Greg Wagner's duplex. He had spent two dollars in change trying to locate Stu Foster by phone, trying the office again, Foster's home, and several downtown bars where Foster liked to go. Nothing.

Denise answered the door. She wore a bulky blue pullover sweater that he suspected belonged to Greg. The jeans he

ED GORMAN

recognised from the previous night. She had her blonde hair
tied in a ponytail with a red Christmas ribbon. She looked
younger and even prettier than she had before.

"You look like a guy who could use a straight shot of hot
chocolate," Wagner said. Behind him the TV was rolling into the
six o'clock news. It was the usual team of hair-sprayed and
lacquered TV news people.

"Yeah, I could," Brolan said, sitting down on the edge of the
couch, pawing at his face with a big hand. He frowned at Wagner.
"I figured out who killed Emma."

"What?" Wagner, whose attention had been drifting to the
news, snapped his head back in Brolan's direction.

Brolan nodded. "My partner. Foster."

"Then the envelopes make sense."

"What envelopes?" Brolan said.

First Wagner told him about the videotape showing various
men in the same hotel room at different times with different
women (including Emma), and then he told him about the
envelopes Emma had received each month from Foster. Just as
he was finishing his explanation, Denise said, "Look, Frank."

Brolan switched his attention to the screen. A reporter in a
trench coat stood screen left with a microphone, while in the
background there was a night shot of Brolan's house. Red
emergency lights flashed blood-red in the gloom. Bundled-up
neighbours stood watching fascinated as a large, boxy ambulance
backed up to the side door.

The reporter said: " …At which time, about an hour ago,
police were notified by an anonymous caller that a body could
be found in the freezer downstairs. Police, who've been in the
house, have now confirmed that this is indeed the case.
Repeating: A body has been recovered from a chest-type freezer
in the basement of a suburban Minneapolis home. Police also
confirm that the body is that of a young woman. So far there has
been no identification."

"I'm dead," Brolan said. "He's set it up perfectly."

Wagner snapped off the TV set. "Why would Foster do this
to you?"

196

"I'm not sure exactly, but I think I know somebody who might be able to tell me." He took the hot chocolate Denise carried over to him. "Charles Lane. Somehow he ties in to all this." Brolan felt his stomach knot, felt acid sear his stomach lining and oesophagus. His mind kept returning to the screen – the reporter grim, the emergency lights flashing off the otherwise unremarkable white house. There was no way the police would believe his story of merely storing the body in the basement until he could find out who had killed her...

Wagner said, "If I say something, will you promise not to get mad? I'm just trying to help."

Denise stood next to Wagner's wheelchair, her arm hanging loosely around his shoulder.

"I'll be happy to listen," Brolan said, trying to keep his eyes from the TV screen.

"How about calling that detective and telling him the truth?" Wagner said.

"An hour ago that might have worked," Brolan said. "But now that they've found the body –" He sighed, dropped his head into his hands. Then, abruptly, angry at Foster for having set him up so elaborately, he raised his head and said, "I'm going to see Charles Lane."

Wagner nodded to the TV. "The police will be looking for you now."

"I know." Brolan stood up "But right now I don't have any choice but to risk it."

Wagner said, "Somehow you've got to get Foster to confess."

"Maybe I could just write a confession for him, and he'd sign it?" Brolan was immediately sorry for the undue sarcasm of his tone. "Sorry, Greg."

"If we could just figure out some way to smoke him out."

Brolan smiled bitterly. "Well, if you come up with any brainstorms, let me know." He glanced around the duplex. The place looked comfortable. He'd planned to stay here a while, relax, figure out what to do next. The live TV report changed all that, of course.

Denise said, "Maybe I've got a brainstorm."

"What's that?" Wagner said.

"What if I call Foster and tell him I'm the girl he tried to kill Wednesday night, and that I want him to bring me some money tonight, or I go to the police?"

Brolan shook his head. "If you saw what he did to Emma, you wouldn't want to get anywhere near him. You're lucky to be alive as it is." He nodded to Wagner. "I don't want to have to worry about her," Brolan said. "Just make sure she doesn't do anything stupid. All right?"

Wagner patted Denise's hand on his shoulder. "She'll be fine."

Brolan said, "I appreciate your trying to help me, Denise."

She sounded young and defensive and hurt. "I was just trying to –"

Brolan leaned over and kissed her on the forehead and gave her a hug. "I know what you were trying to do, Denise. And I appreciate it, I really do. But I'm going to have to handle things this way. All right?"

She sighed and returned his hug. "Good luck, Frank." Then he was gone, back into the cold, dark night.

32

THE MOTEL DIDN'T HAVE MUCH STYLE, but its three sections stood angled against the night, offering, at the very least, comfort from the screaming wind and the biting snow. Snow was starting to pile up on the slanting red roofs and in the parking lot. Already several cars looked as if they would be buried till a snowplough came and started earnest work. People bent their heads into the whipping wind and ran from their cars to their respective sections and rooms.

Brolan stood in the blast of snow, finishing his cigarette and staring in the motel's front-office window. He was freezing, but somehow the cold only made him all the more resolute about dealing with Charles Lane and then with his partner, Stu Foster. He flipped his cigarette into the wind, which promptly slammed it, tossing and turning, against the rear end of a canary-yellow Buick with a JESUS LIVES! sticker on its bumper.

In the office Brolan went up to the counter. A man in a blue cardigan and a blue button-down shirt and a red-and-blue holiday bow tie stood watching him. The man was white-haired and wore rimless glasses. He was probably sixty. He was applying chapstick to his somewhat prim mouth. There was something obscene about this to Brolan, as if it were a dirty secret the man should not be so willing to share with others.

"Hi," Brolan said.

The man nodded, continued what he was doing.

"I'm looking for Charles Lane."

"Do you have an appointment?"

"Afraid not. But I'd still like to see him."

The man did Brolan the favour of putting his chapstick away. "Then, I'm afraid you can't see him. He's very strict about appointments." The man raised serious blue eyes to a clock on the wall behind Brolan. "Especially after hours."

Though Brolan wasn't experienced at this sort of thing, he slid a ten-dollar bill from his pocket and laid it on the desk. "I'd appreciate any help you could give me."

The man smiled. "You must be a bad-movie fan."

"I beg your pardon?"

The man nodded to the ten-dollar bill on the counter. "Bad movies. Somebody's always trying to bribe somebody else."

"You don't want it?"

"I'd rather have my job than ten dollars, my friend."

Feeling foolish, Brolan picked up the ten. "You sure?"

"Positive."

Brolan said, "You're an asshole, you know that?"

"I've been called a lot worse than that. Asshole is almost a compliment."

And with that the man turned his attention to a small portable TV set on a desk behind him. On the screen Pat Buchanan and Michael Kinsley were calling each other names on *Crossfire*.

Shaking his head, sliding the ten back in his pocket, Brolan slunk back to the parking lot.

He stood in the blast of wind and snow wondering what to do next. The desk clerk had given the impression that Charles Lane was definitely somewhere inside. Therefore, instead of standing out there feeling sorry for himself, Brolan should be inside, combing the halls and looking for the guy.

That wasn't too hard to figure out.

So, he went inside and started combing the halls and looking for the guy.

Brolan hated motels. Walking the narrow hallways, no windows in sight anywhere, always gave him the claustrophobic feeling of being in a submarine. At least the carpeting was new and the corridor paint recent, so the place didn't look grungy on top of everything else.

He moved toward the centre of the place, where the three buildings merged, assuming that there he'd find the places where guests congregated. He was right. The first thing he found was the swimming pool. Two small kids swam quickly and smoothly up and down the water lanes, spitting silver water at each other as they moved and laughing about their ingenuity. A sour woman in a lime-green one-piece swimsuit that revealed too much hip and too much cellulite watched the kids with a kind of smouldering, nun-like authority. The next place he found was the workout room, taken up by two wonderful-looking young women in leotards who were being shown the weight machine by a curly-headed guy who couldn't have been half as neat as he obviously held himself to be. Brolan leaned in and said, "Excuse me, I'm looking for Charles Lane."

The curly-headed guy shot Brolan an irritated expression, turned slightly from the ladies, and said, "What?" He happened to glance at his formidable biceps as he said this.

"I said, I'm looking for Charles Lane."

The muscle boy looked at the girls and winked and said, "Good for you."

Then he went back to demonstrating the equipment.

Brolan's next stop was the aerobics room. There were maybe twenty women working out. Some of them looked pretty tasty.

The instructor was a very serious-looking redhead in a mauve leotard and a lot of sweat. Parts of the mauve looked almost black. Brolan went on down the hall. Halfway along he saw a man who wore a blue blazer and a white shirt and a red regimental-striped tie and grey slacks and black loafers with big tassles and a lot of TV-minister hair spray. He had a little dealie on his breast pocket that read 'Manager'.

"May I help you, sir?"

He sounded as hearty as a Jaycee trying out a new pitch. He was big, maybe six two, and chunky, and there was a certain operatic quality to his manner.

"I'm looking for Charles Lane."

The manager frowned only slightly. "I probably should refer you to the front desk."

"You mean, you don't know where he is?"

And then the manager gave Charles Lane away. Just the way he glanced down the hall to an office marked Private. Maybe in time Brolan would have figured this out for himself, but the manager had done him the favour of confirming the obvious suspicion.

"I think he's gone home, sir." He made a big deal of thinking hard for a moment – sort of like an eighth-grader in a play about Einstein contemplating nuclear energy – and then said, "Yes, now that I think about it, I'm sure I saw him pulling out of the lot about twenty minutes ago."

"Darn," Brolan said. "I'll just have to try again tomorrow."

"Is there a name you'd like to leave, sir?"

"No. I'll just try him again tomorrow."

"Well, see you, then."

"Thanks," Brolan said, waving goodbye.

He went back down the corridor, glimpsing the babes in aerobics, sneering at muscle boy, who was still demonstrating the weights to the two helpless damsels, and then sucking up the odours of chlorine as he passed the swimming pool.

The manager was not around. The door marked Private stood unguarded.

Brolan put his hand on the doorknob. He was surprised to

find it unlocked.

He turned the knob and pushed inside.

The office was spacious, done in earth tones with mahogany wainscoting and mahogany furnishings. A long row of filing cabinets stood on one wall; a smaller desk with a phone and adding machine was pushed against the other. The overall effect was of a serious rather than simply decorative place.

One other thing: The office was empty.

This confused Brolan. The way the manager had looked nervously at the door, Brolan had expected to find Charles Lane in there.

A few seconds later a noise came from inside the closet door at the rear of the office. At first Brolan thought it might be a furnace kicking on. But then the faint but unmistakable noise came again. Inside the closet something was swaying against the wall.

Brolan walked across the office to the back. He leaned carefully to the door and listened.

He heard somebody saying, "Go, babe. Give it to her, babe."

What the hell was going on here?

Brolan pulled the door open and found out for himself.

Inside the small closet a videotape camera had been set up flush against a piece of one-way glass. On the other side of the glass, an old man was humping a frail young girl who was probably not much older than twelve.

Brolan recognised the man immediately. Say hello to Harold McAlester, the client with the bald head given to leather jumpsuits, the man Brolan had seen earlier that morning in the office with Foster. The motel room was a mess of whiskey bottles and food trays.

The man operating the camera – the man urging McAlester on – turned, abruptly aware of Brolan's presence, and it was just then that Brolan hit him hard enough on the side of the face to draw blood from his nose. The man slammed against the wall, and the camera fell in a noisy heap as the man started to stumble.

If McAlester, on the other side of the glass, heard anything, he didn't let it deter him.

He turned the little girl over on her stomach so he could back-door her. Even in a glimpse a naked McAlester was an obscene sight, white chest hair and sagging little titties. The little girl looked virginal as an eight-year-old on First Communion Sunday. Brolan wanted to go in there and kick in McAlester's face.

But right then Charles Decker Lane was closer, so Brolan proceeded to kick in his face.

33

IT TOOK FOSTER AN HOUR to find Greg Wagner's place. Not that it was hidden or anything, just that the roads were getting that bad.

He parked across the street and sat there for a time thinking about winter, how it howled, how it raged, how it made almost anything going on seem insignificant. You could lose yourself in winter and its furies, and that's just what he did for a time. Shut off the engine. Listened to the trees above creaking with ice. Listened to wind rattle shutters. Watched a city snowplough moving down the street like a giant yellow electric monster. Thought of his mother and father. His father, especially. Sometimes he imagined himself reaching out across the black gorge separating life from death. Touching his father's hand. Comforting his father. As his father had comforted him. Somewhere his mother was still alive. He hadn't talked to her in fifteen years and didn't plan to; he had not even gone to her when that heart condition showed up, and she pleaded with him to come to Rochester and see her there in the hospital. No fucking way, bitch. Why don't you count on your football player now? The man who'd been such a cutie and such a celebrity and such a hunk was now a lard-ass alcoholic who spent his time talking about what pussies the new generation of ballplayers were. Yeah. Hope you're enjoying yourself, Mom. Nobody deserves it more than you.

Then he didn't think of anything at all. Just sat there with the wind rocking the car and cold air seeping in through the doors, and the windows fogging up a ghostly grey.

Finally it was time. Go across the street and push the gun in the door and demand that the cripple tell him where the tape was.

On the seat was the .38 he sometimes took out to the gun club when he wanted to relax and zone out. There was something about the feel of a weapon clutched in your hand – you could easily imagine that the targets were really people. Starting with Mother. Dear, fucking Mother. Blam, blam, blam, Ma. Blam, blam, blam.

Five minutes later he stood on the doorstep, hunched over because the wind was like a thousand tiny razors cutting his face and neck. The way the wind whined, he wondered if they could even hear his knock. Faintly he could hear a TV set going. He knocked again, let his eyes rest on Emma's part of the duplex. In a peculiar way he'd liked Emma. She was like a kitten. So gentle, even when you were pushing her around. He knew she hadn't liked him, not ever. She was one of those women who'd sensed instinctively who he really was and what he was really about. So, he'd been forced to pay her very well indeed for his various favours over the past couple years. Because otherwise she wouldn't have worked with him.

The door was opened by the young girl he'd tried to kill Wednesday night. "Yes?" she said, making it sound as if he were trying to sell them unwanted Boy Scout cookies or something. She didn't recognise him. He saw that instantly. No recognition whatsoever.

"My car," he said. "It stalled across the street. I wondered if I could come in and use your phone so I could call a service station."

"Oh, sure," she said. She smiled then. It was a very healthy, clean-cut smile. She was very good at hiding the fact that she was a little whore. "We'll even give you some hot cocoa."

"Gee, I really appreciate this," he said, standing back so she could push the front storm door open and let him come inside.

He took two steps across the threshold, glancing over at the man in the wheelchair; then he jerked the .38 from his overcoat pocket and put it dead against the girl's temple.

"You're Foster," the man in the wheelchair said. "You're the killer."

Foster saw recognition in the girl's eyes.

"Do I look a little different from Wednesday night, Denise?" he asked, smiling.

Before she got a chance to respond, he cracked her hard across the mouth, knocking her backward to the couch.

He pointed the gun at the man. "I want the tape, pally. I don't want any lies, any excuses, any stalling. Either I get the tape right now, or I kill her. Do we understand each other?"

Wagner said, "I don't have the tape anymore."

Foster leaned down and grabbed the girl by the hair and jerked her to her feet. She cried out from the pain and tried to kick out at him. He just yanked on her hair all the harder.

Finally he yanked the girl close to him – so close he could smell the sudden sweat on her body and feel the slight clamminess on her skin – and put the gun once more to her head.

"You know how it's going to be, pally?" Foster said. He nodded to the east wall where framed photographs of long-dead movie stars were neatly and reverently arranged. "You're going to lose two ways. Because her brains are going to spray all over that wall and spoil your nice fancy photographs. Now, no more bullshit. I want the tape."

"It's in my room."

"Get it and bring it to me."

Wagner glanced anxiously at the girl. "Don't pull her hair anymore."

Foster smiled. "Kind of sweet on her, huh?" He laughed, thinking of his father. "Bet she's safe with you, isn't she? All these other guys sniffing around her little teenage pussy, but not you, Wagner. Not you. You couldn't do anything if you wanted to." He gave the girl's hair a final twist and then shoved her back on the couch. Her knee struck the coffee table as she fell forward. Once again she cried out. He waved the gun at Wagner. "Now, go get the tape."

Wagner looked at the girl. You could see he was sharing her pain. Afraid for her.

"Don't touch her," Wagner said.

"Anything you say, pally," Foster said.

Wagner rolled his wheelchair out of the living room and down the corridor to a darkened doorway. He turned to look back at Foster. "Don't hurt her anymore. I mean it."

"You're a real tough bastard."

"You heard what I said."

Then he was gone. Inside. A light came on and made a yellow oblong of the doorway. After a moment or two Foster heard the wheelchair move across some more of the room. Then he heard a squeaky bureau drawer opening and closing. There. At last. The tape.

Foster looked at the girl and said, "Come here."

"Are you going to hurt me again?"

"I didn't ask you to talk. I told you to come here."

"No."

He pointed the gun directly at her face. "I want you in front of me when he comes back here."

"Why?"

"Because I don't trust him."

"There's nothing he can do to you."

"Oh, yeah? Well, maybe not. But I'm not going to take the chance. Now get your ass over here."

He leaned down and took her wrist and snapped her to her feet. Then he pulled her in front of him just as Wagner was returning in his wheelchair.

As Wagner rolled down the hallway toward the living room, Foster could see in the man's hand the outline of a videotape. There it was. Without the tape Brolan would spend many weeks trying to convince the police that he was not the killer after all. By that time Foster would be in South America with plenty of cash – enough to buy a new identity.

Foster kept the gun at the girl's temple. He said to Wagner, "Put the tape down on the edge of the coffee table."

"Let the girl go first."

"You're a real macho little bastard, aren't you?"

"The girl. Or I don't set the tape down," Wagner said. Foster laughed at the absurdity of the little man's being so tough. But he was. He really was.

To the girl Foster said, "Now, when I let you go, you walk over to the couch and sit right on the end of it and keep your hands in plain sight. Do you understand me?"

"Yes."

"Good. Then you're going to do what I say?"

"Yes."

Foster kept looking to see if Wagner and the girl were exchanging any messages through their eye contact. He was getting increasingly paranoid, and he knew it.

He let the girl go, shoving her toward the couch.

She did as he'd told her. Sat right on the edge. Almost primly. Watching. Waiting.

"The tape," Foster said, snapping his fingers and pointing to the coffee table.

Wagner held up the videotape. "This isn't going to help you now. I hope you know that. The police will no longer believe that Brolan is their man."

"Oh, no, pally? Well, I guess we'll see, won't we?" He snapped his fingers again. "Put it down on the table and push it over to me."

"And if I don't?"

"Then I'll blow your fucking brains out right on the spot."

The girl sounded as if she were going to cry. "Please, Greg. Please do what he says."

"You better listen to her, Wagner. She's got the right idea."

Wagner said, "All right."

The way he laid the tape down on the table, you might have mistaken him for a poker player about to play his trump card.

He set it slowly, carefully, down.

"Now push it over here," Foster said from the other end of the long glass table. "Now."

Wagner pushed the tape toward Foster.

"Good little boy," Foster said.

When the tape reached his end, he started to lean over and pick it up, and that's when the gun appeared at the side of the wheelchair.

The little bastard wasted no time in firing.

Foster dove for cover behind a leather recliner. A bullet had nearly caught him in the shoulder just as he was jumping.

The first thing Foster did, once he got his bearings, was say, "You fucked up, little man. You really fucked up bad. I'm going to make you pay for what you just did."

With that he raised his head slightly behind the arm of the recliner and shot the girl once, twice, three times, in the chest. She had still been on the couch; she rolled off, in a mixture of cries and blood, to the floor.

Wagner cried out, too, and started blindly firing toward the recliner. He needed to use both hands, and he wasn't much of a shot – he was better at hitting the wall decorations than anything else – and about all Foster had to do was wait till the little pecker ran out of bullets.

Which came soon enough.

Knowing he was safe, Foster stood up in the echoes of gunfire and Wagner's sobs and went over to the man and slapped him hard across the face.

"I told you I'd kill her, you little prick," Foster said. "If you'd done what I said, she'd still be alive." He wasn't excited. His voice was flat and matter-of-fact, and his breathing was quiet and regular.

He had never heard a man sob the way Wagner was sobbing as he wheeled his chair over to Denise, who lay sprawled and unmoving on the floor. Blood was everywhere in small and large pools, in flecks that had spattered the furnishings.

Foster wasn't unsympathetic. He felt sorry for the little prick. "You should have listened to me," he said again. "I wouldn't have had to kill her if you'd just listened to me. Don't you understand that?"

Foster snapped up the tape, dropped it in the pocket of his overcoat.

And then he was gone, the door banging behind him, Wagner's sobs raging against the vast, empty night.

34

AT THE LAST MOMENT Kathleen decided to pack the doll, which was her way of admitting to herself that her flight from Minneapolis was probably not going to be temporary after all.

There was nothing special about the doll. It was a Barbie from the early sixties, one of the few expensive gifts her impoverished parents had ever bought her. She'd kept it with her all these years. Once, a lover who found her unfaithful had tried to smash the doll with his fist but before his knuckles reached its face, Kathleen had struck the man across the back of the head with a large clock radio. The pleasure she took in this violence almost shocked her. It felt good to strike the man, to feel the intersection of clock and skull, to hear his cry of pain and to see him sink in a heap to the floor.

She brought the doll in its blue taffeta dress to her face and kissed it as tenderly as she would a sister. Parts of the doll's forehead had started to crack. Kathleen smiled wryly about this. So, even Barbies got age lines.

She set the doll down carefully among the blouses, skirts, and two pairs of designer jeans she'd stuffed into the single piece of carry-on luggage. Her flight was less than an hour away. She had to hurry.

The sound of a car door closing startled her.

She ran to the window of her second-floor bedroom and looked below to the driveway and then to the street.

In the house directly across from hers, a man and a child bundled up in a snowsuit were exiting a large green van. The headlights lit up the front of the garage so that it looked like a cave of light in the wintry darkness.

She put a hand to her heart. Her pulse was racing, and she felt sticky and dizzy. She'd been afraid it was Stu Foster. At one time their plan to get big-league clients by blackmailing them seemed smart. As did having an affair with Brolan. He was a nice guy, and fun to be with, and there'd really been no reason not to... But Brolan had made the mistake (a mistake for both of them) of falling in love with her... And the other night Foster had killed a woman... Emma the strange, quiet, sad hooker they'd gotten to know through Charles Lane. After killing the woman, Foster had changed. She'd always sensed the violence in him, but then it surfaced completely. Violence had always been a part of their lovemaking but the other night... An image came to mind: his squeezing her breasts until they hurt, until she had to scratch his back bloody before he stopped. And then his laughing and staring at her, obviously aware that she'd seen him for the first time as he really was.

She couldn't go to the police. She was too much a part of all this. But neither could she trust Foster. She was the only other person who knew he'd killed Emma. Which meant he might well decide that now he must kill her, too...

Then she heard it.

A creaking on the stairs.

True, this old house made many plaintive moans and groans on freezing winter nights, but she knew that the sound hadn't been made by the house but rather by somebody creeping up the stairs.

Looking toward the partly opened door, she listened once more. Hard.

It was amazing how many things you heard when you really listened. The blower in the furnace. The creaking of the roof under the burden of a sheet of ice. The distant sound of a siren.

And footsteps.

Coming up the stairs.

Coming after her.

Kathleen laughed aloud. "My God," she said to herself. "My God, what a stupid, frightened little girl you are."

She went to the door and flung it back and walked out into the hallway and over to the head of the stairs.

Empty. Just as she'd expected.

She'd left the vestibule light on downstairs, so she could see, even from here, that the front door was snugly closed and the front part of the house empty.

She felt so relieved, she was practically light-headed, and that was when he grabbed her.

From behind. Wearing gloves.

He clamped one hand hard over her mouth so she couldn't scream. With the other hand he put the small butcher's knife to her throat.

She could hear him gasp and feel him sweat. He was pressed tight to her backside, and she could also feel the hardness of his erection.

"You fucking bitch," he said. "You were going to walk out on me, weren't you?"

He drew a little blood, then, from a spot right next to her jugular.

"You fucking bitch," he said.

By the time Brolan finished with Charles Lane, the motel owner was bleeding from his mouth, nose, and ear. Brolan hadn't shown much patience or sympathy.

In the car Brolan thought about the most astonishing part of Lane's confession... that Kathleen was working with Foster.

As he moved onto the Crosstown, heading toward Kathleen's place, he thought of all the elaborate ruses they'd used to convince him that they hated each other. He should have asked so many questions... How could they both go out and do what nobody else in Twin Cities advertising seemed capable of... steal some of the largest accounts in the area, in some cases, accounts that had even been held by New York and Los Angeles agencies.

So stupid... stupid.

He was almost afraid of seeing Kathleen. Afraid of what he might do when he saw her beautiful, lying face. He'd never struck a woman... and he did not want to start.

211

ED GORMAN

He gave the car more gas… and hurried.

Foster threw her on the bed, held her captive, and mesmerised her with the knife he held out in front of him.

She could see in his handsome features a different man… the crazed man who had been hiding inside Foster all these years.

He grabbed the large glass lamp with the rattan shade and hurled it into the corner. The noise it made smashing against the wall made Kathleen clamp her hands over her ears.

"You bitch," he said again, moving toward her.

"Stu, what's wrong with you? We're supposed to be working together." The closer he got, the more she scrabbled up the bed to huddle near the headboard.

"Yeah. And that's why you were packing your bag, huh?"

She tried to find her voice. Her whole body seemed to be collapsing in on itself. Her throat was dry; her bowels felt loose; her breathing came in ragged, painful bursts. "I just wanted to get out of here so I could take a little time off and –"

His first swipe with the knife came perilously close to tearing a gash open on her throat.

"Stu, please; please, listen –"

Without quite being aware of it, she'd begun sobbing, her words lost in her cries.

His second swipe cleaved the shoulder of her mauve silk blouse and cut a thin, hurting line along the flesh of her upper arm.

Blood bloomed immediately. She clamped a hand over the wound and rolled sideways on the bed just as he was plunging the knife downward toward her chest.

"Stu! Please! Don't!"

She rolled until she was off the bed, scrambling on her hands and knees across the hardwood floor.

She was trying to reach the door before –

This time the knife cut a long, curving arc across her back. She screamed. The odd thing was the delayed response of her flesh. She knew she'd been cut, but the pain did not come for long moments after.

His foot caught her in the stomach and rolled her back against the wall.

This time, when she started to crawl away, he was too quick for her, his foot against her chest pinning her against the edge of the door frame.

There was no more pleading on her part. Terror had overcome her ability to make any kind of protest. All she could do was huddle into herself and keep her eyes closed and wait for the final moments.

Brolan was driving too fast down the side streets. When he reached Kathleen's, he found that the car had gathered too much momentum to be stopped. He slid past, nearly ploughing into another car parked kerbside. The faint moonlight through the dead, black branches of winter trees did not lend much help. In a pocket of deep shadow, midpoint between the grounds of two large houses, he brought the car to a stop. Within a quarter minute he was on his feet and sliding along the ice-covered street. Foster's car was in Kathleen's driveway. The prospect of finally confronting Foster drove Brolan as nothing else could.

Then he heard the scream.

Raising his head, Brolan saw that the only light on in the house was in the rear – Kathleen's bedroom. It was not too difficult to imagine what Foster was doing to her; not when he thought of how lovingly Emma had been cut up.

Slipping on the stairs, having to grab hold of the black iron railing for purchase, Brolan went up the walk.

Just as he reached the front door, pushing his way in, he heard a second scream.

In the end Foster was about to cut her throat.

Hearing somebody pounding up the stairs – and suspecting it was Brolan – he found there was no time for real pleasure here. Just expediency.

He leaned down, grabbed her hair, put the knife to the centre of her throat, and started to slash but – She startled Foster by grabbing on to his leg. As he tried to run from the room, she clung to him like a weight that had been permanently affixed.

He hit her on top of the head, hoping to break her grip. But still she held to him. He had to drag her to the doorway as he tried to see who was pounding up the stairs.

"Foster! Foster!"

So, it was Brolan.

At Foster's feet, Kathleen now made a series of horrible gasps like that of somebody trying to vomit. He felt her grip loosen as she gave herself entirely up to her death.

Brolan was on the staircase.

Coming up fast.

Foster had to make a quick decision. There was a gable off one of her bedroom windows. He could smash through the glass and land on the gable and let himself down to the ground.

Or he could –

As Brolan reached the last step, panting, face sleek with sweat, rage turning his handsome features into a grotesque mask, Foster realised that he had no time to do anything except stand there and defend himself.

Brolan had decided to leap at him, even though Foster kept his bloody knife in full view.

He tackled Foster around the waist, trying to get in under the knife Foster wielded. He wasn't quick enough. The knife ripped a bloody trench in his back, running along the left side of his spine. He dropped to one knee just as Foster moved forward, ready to finish him.

Foster raised the knife over his head and brought it down with slashing fury.

Brolan hit him directly in the crotch. This time he acted quickly enough to inflict damage. Foster screamed and fell back half a step, just enough to make the arc of his downward slashing knife useless. He missed Brolan's shoulder by half a foot.

As Brolan jumped to his feet, he smashed Foster in the mouth with a quick punch and then grabbed Foster's hand, trying to pry the knife loose.

But as he moved in, Foster lunged forward. This time he cut Brolan right across the chest. Brolan fell against Foster, once again finding the man's wrist, and twisting it so he could shake the knife free.

Foster tried to raise the knife at such an angle that he could cut Brolan again, even though Brolan still had hold of his wrist.

He was just about to do this when Brolan surprised him, snapped Foster's wrist around so that the knife was now pointing to Foster's stomach.

"You son of a bitch," Brolan said. "I owe you this."

Brolan concentrated all his weight and motion into the knife handle so that when it tore into Foster, it went in deep, ripping through vital organs in its path.

Brolan watched blood bloom in Foster's mouth and nose. Foster's eyes got huge and ugly.

Brolan kept ramming the knife in.

"P – please," Foster said, blood so thick inside his mouth that his tongue could scarcely form words.

"Is that what Emma did, Foster? Begged you to live?"

Deeper, deeper the knife went, cutting, killing.

"P – please," Foster said again.

But it was too late. Blood had started coming from his ears now. His pants were filled with a horrible stench.

Brolan let him slip to the floor.

From Kathleen's bedroom door he could see a hand flung carelessly, like the limb of a doll that had been torn off and cast down.

Chest heaving, his wounds starting to hurt, Brolan stepped over the bloody form of Foster and made his way down the hall to Kathleen.

Death had robbed her of beauty. She lay in her own blood, staring up at the high ceiling. He tried not to notice how viciously her throat had been cut.

He staggered into her room. He dropped to the blood-soaked bed and picked up the phone. He would call the police, but first he'd call his friend Wagner and see what was going on.

A gruff male voice said, "Sergeant Peterson. Homicide."

"Homicide?" Brolan said. "What the hell's going on there?"

The voice grew kinder. "Why don't I let you talk to Mr

Wagner?"

Then Greg came on. Brolan could tell right away that the man was trying to keep from crying.

"Are you all right?" Brolan said, terrified of the news he was about to receive.

"I am," Wagner said. "But I'm afraid Denise isn't." Then it wasn't so easy for Wagner to hold his tears. Then it wasn't so easy at all.

35

SIX DAYS LATER the funeral was held on the downslope side of a small cemetery eighty miles outside St. Louis. The morning was sunny and brilliant because of the newly fallen snow. Two huge black stone archangels, both more than a hundred years old, sat on either side of the iron entrance gates observing the human drama below them.

In movies and books graveside attendees always wear black. But not there. This was farming country, and not prosperous farming country at that. So, clothes ran all colours in the morning light, from the worn red of a once-elegant dress coat on the back of a frayed farm woman to the lime-green of a blast jacket on the shoulders of a teenager who looked not only cold but bored. Even the minister, a hawkish-looking bald man, wore a blue trench coat over his ministerial garb.

Brolan stood next to Greg Wagner, who sat in his wheelchair, a blanket across his legs. The prayers had been said, and the minister was saying the last of his goodbyes. Off to the left two burly workers stood next to a tree, waiting to put the body into the wide, wintry hole they'd dug the day before. Their breath made silver plumes in the gold sunlight.

Somewhere a woman sobbed.

Brolan put his hand on Wagner's shoulder.

"Let us remember her as she was before she left us," the minister admonished. Then he glanced up at the brown

Oldsmobile that had brought her there. "Let us pray for her soul."

The minister, followed by the twenty or so other mourners, left. Only Brolan and Wagner stayed behind.

Wind came, scattering silver snow beads. Near the top of the hill a fawn stood watching the two men, graceful and supple against the white hills and the cloudless blue sky.

Wagner stared into the empty hole of the grave. "I'm never going to be the same, Brolan."

"I know."

"She was some goddamned kid."

"She sure was."

Wagner started crying. "I don't have anybody," he said. "And I'm going to miss the hell out of her."

Brolan put his hands on the wheelchair handles and started pushing Wagner through the snow to where Brolan's car sat on the winding gravel drive.

At the car, after Brolan had helped him inside and folded up the chair and made him comfortable on the front seat, Wagner said, "Think you'll ever come over and see me, Brolan?"

Brolan didn't answer. He closed Wagner's door and then went around the car and got in behind the wheel. The car had just had a tune-up. It started almost silently. He drove them out of the cemetery.

"I don't think I probably will come to see you," Brolan said as they reached the two-lane highway and started driving past farms huddling against distant hills. "You've got rotten taste in movies."

"What?" Wagner said, startled by Brolan's light tone.

"You like the early Charlie Chans. I like the ones that were done at Monogram."

"Monogram? You're crazy, Brolan. Did I ever tell you that?"

And just for a moment Brolan didn't answer. Wagner saw why. Something had caught in Brolan's throat, and he had a hard time swallowing, and something silver appeared in the corners of his eyes. Wagner had been wondering if Brolan was ever going to show that he, too, mourned Denise. Now Wagner had his answer.

217

"That's what I mean," Brolan said, clearing his throat at last. "Why the hell would I want to hang around with somebody who doesn't appreciate Monogram movies?"

Something like a laugh rumbled through Wagner's chest as he looked out on the vast white mid-western landscape and saw a ghost image of a pretty little girl doomed to run away to the city and die.

Brolan said no more then. They drove for many miles in silence, up and down the rolling white mid-western hills. Wagner thought of Denise. God, how he thought of Denise.

CT Publishing

If you have enjoyed this book, we are quietly
confident you will enjoy the following titles as well.

ED GORMAN
CAGE OF
NIGHT

TWENTY-ONE-YEAR-old Spence returns to his hometown after two years in the Army and falls in love with Cindy Brasher, Homecoming Queen and town goddess to a long line of jealous men. A string of robberies put Spence at odds with his obsessive love for Cindy. One by one Spence's rivals are implicated in horrific crimes. Spence wonders how much Cindy knows, and why she wants him, like her past boyfriends, to visit the old well in the woods...

"The book is full of Gorman's characteristic virtues as a writer: sympathy, humour, commitment to the craft of storytelling, and a headlong narrative drive. A real writer is at work here and there aren't many of those to go around."

–DARK ECHO.

"Cornell Woolrich would have enjoyed Cage Of Night."

–LOCUS.

"A book that combines romance, sex, violence, madness and an almost oppressive degree of grief, Cage Of Night is one of the most unique noirs ever written."

–PIRATE WRITINGS.

"Gorman is defining noir for the nineties."

–CEMETERY DANCE.

Price: £4.99 ISBN: 1-902002-03-2

Available from all good bookshops, or post free from: CT Publishing, PO Box 5880, Birmingham B16 8JF

email ct@crimetime.demon.co.uk

ED GORMAN

GWENDOLINE BUTLER

COFFIN IN OXFORD

"It was like a Chinese puzzle. In St Ebbe's was a flat, in the flat was a trunk, and in the trunk was a body. The body of a woman..."

Ted was brought round from the first attack, if you could call it an attack, with difficulty. He had been found shut up in a cupboard with a scarf tightened around his neck: his own scarf, to add insult to injury...

THIS IS THE FIRST TIME in paperback for this novel featuring Gwendoline Butler's popular sleuth, John Coffin. The fact that Gwendoline Butler is one of the most borrowed authors in Britain will come as no surprise to her many readers. She is also one of the most universally praised, and with good reason. Recently voted one of the world's Top 200 crime writers, If you haven't tried Gwendoline Butler, why not start now?

'Gwendoline Butler is excellent on the bizarre fantasies of other people's lives and on modern paranoia overlaying old secrets; and her plots have the rare ability to shock'
–ANDREW TAYLOR, THE INDEPENDENT

Price: £4.99 ISBN: 1-902002-00-8
Available from all good bookshops, or post free
from: CT Publishing, PO Box 5880,
Birmingham B16 8JF
email ct@crimetime.demon.co.uk

JENNIE MELVILLE
WINDSOR RED

CHARMIAN DANIELS, on a sabbatical from the police force takes rooms in Wellington Yard, Windsor near the pottery of Anny, a childhood friend. The rhythm of life in Wellington Yard is disturbed by the disappearance of Anny's daughter with her violent boyfriend. Dismembered limbs from an unidentified body are discovered in a rubbish sack. A child is snatched from its pram. Headless torsos are found outside Windsor.

Are these events connected? And what relationship do they have to the coterie of female criminals that Charmian is 'studying'...? All is resolved in a Grand Guignol climax that will leave the most hardened crime fiction fans gasping.

JENNIE MELVILLE is the pen name of bestselling crime fiction author Gwendoline Butler, one of the most borrowed authors in Britain under either name, and recently voted by *The Times* one of the world's top 200 crime writers. This is the first time in paperback for this novel featuring her popular Police Inspector, Charmian Daniels, one of the most universally praised of police procedural series, and the first to feature a female protagonist.

Price: £4.99 ISBN: 1-902002-01-6
**Available from all good bookshops, or post free
from: CT Publishing, PO Box 5880,
Birmingham B16 8JF**
email ct@crimetime.demon.co.uk